DESPERATELY SEEKING "NINA"

We met during the blackout at Randi Howell's non-wedding reception. You wore black with pearls. We sipped champagne and danced. You left without saying goodbye. I *must* see you again.

Call Alex at 555-6932.

Dear Reader,

Sometimes your life can change in a heartbeat. For the residents of Grand Springs, Colorado, a blackout has set off a string of events that will alter people's lives forever....

Welcome to Silhouette's exciting new series, 36 HOURS, where each month heroic characters face personal challenges—and find love against all odds. This month a sexy tycoon searches desperately to find a woman he has met only once. Alex Bennett thinks Nina Lindstrom might be the answer to his prayers—and he has a *very* interesting proposition for her!

In coming months you'll meet an industrious reporter who has one chance to save his high school sweetheart—and his unexpected daughter; a bride on the run who must depend on a sexy stranger for protection; and a single woman who marries a co-worker to gain custody of the baby she helped deliver. Join us each month as we bring you 36 hours that will change *your* life!

Sincerely,

The editors at Silhouette

CINDERELLA
STORY

ELIZABETH
AUGUST

Silhouette Books

Published by Silhouette Books

America's Publisher of Contemporary Romance

Special thanks and acknowledgment are given to Elizabeth August for her contribution to the 36 HOURS series.

SILHOUETTE BOOKS

CINDERELLA STORY

Copyright © 1997 by Harlequin Books S.A.

ISBN 0-373-65010-8

Elizabeth August

is the author of many bestselling novels,
including *Like Father, Like Son* and *The Seeker.*
Haunted Husband, the second book in her
Smytheshire series, won the National Readers'
Choice Award. She is also the recipient of the
Diamond Author of the Year Award. In addition to
traditional romances, she is published in both the
historical and suspense fields. Her books have been
translated into more than a dozen languages and
published worldwide, including China and Russia.
Born and raised in Missouri, she has lived in
New York, Ohio and Delaware, and currently
resides in North Carolina.

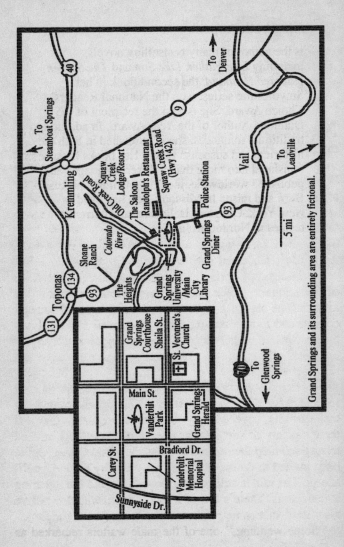

Grand Springs and its surrounding area are entirely fictional.

Prologue

Nina Lindstrom breathed a sigh of relief as she hung up the phone. Her children were safe and happily pretending they were camping out in their grandmother's living room. When she'd learned that the electricity was out all over town, they had been her number one concern. As usual, while she worked, Elizabeth, Pete and Tommy were being looked after by her mother-in-law, and Nina's rational mind had assured her that they were being well cared for. Still, the mother in her had insisted on calling.

"I'm collecting aprons," Susan Smith, one of the owners of the Squaw Creek Lodge, announced, entering the kitchen. She set the lantern she was carrying on the center counter and looked around at the assembled servers. Frustration showed on her face. "This evening seems to be just one disaster after another. First we lose our electricity, and now the backup generator is refusing to work. Officially, the reception is canceled. However, the food has been paid for and there's no place to store it. The bar is closed but the Howells have already bought the champagne and there's plenty of soft drinks. The guests have been invited to stay and help themselves to what's available. And you've been invited to do the same. If you want my advice, you'll accept. The rain is still coming down hard and the lightning is dangerous. There's lots of it and it's touching down. I've also heard that some roads are blocked by mud slides."

"Some wedding," one of the male waiters remarked as

Nina unfastened the frilly white apron she was wearing and handed it to Susan. "First the bride bolts just before the ceremony begins, and now the electricity is gone. I'll bet there are a few people here wishing they'd pulled the covers over their head and stayed in bed this morning."

"Me, for one," one of the bartenders grumbled. "I'd figured on enough tips from this crowd to pay this month's rent."

It did seem to be one of those days when plans went askew, Nina thought silently, leaving the kitchen. She'd been counting on the money from this moonlighting job to buy a few extras for her children. Now she'd only get pocket change for the time she'd been here setting up the buffet. She shrugged off her disappointment. Life had taught her never to count on anything happening the way she hoped it would. She was always happy when it did but had learned to roll with the punches when it didn't. And compared to some of the punches she'd sustained, a few lost work hours were nothing.

Glancing out the large plate-glass windows, she saw a flash of lightning come straight down. A loud pop followed. The lightning had struck a tree. Susan Smith was right. For the moment, it would be safer to remain here.

Ahead of her, she heard the mingling of numerous voices. The guest list for this wedding included all of the politically and socially elite of the town. Because it was to be a very dressy affair, the female waitresses had been asked to wear basic black so that, with the ruffled white aprons provided by the lodge, they would blend into the elegant atmosphere of the occasion.

A quirky smile tilted the corner of Nina's mouth. She was wearing her best black cocktail dress. Actually, it was her only cocktail dress. The candlelight illuminating the hall mirrored her image in the large plate-glass window.

With her best dress, her one set of good jewelry consisting of a pearl necklace and pearl earrings, and her hair in a chignon on top of her head, she looked as sophisticated as any of the other guests. *So why not go mingle with the blue noses?* It had been a long time since she'd been to a party, and never to one as high-class as this.

Alex Bennett stood leaning against the wall in a shadowed corner of the room watching the rest of the wedding guests as they milled around serving themselves. He noticed Melissa Howell, the mother of the bride, flitting from guest to guest, and he frowned. He'd already had one encounter with the woman tonight and didn't want another. His frown deepening, he told himself that he should be feeling more sympathetic toward the woman. Her daughter had left her in an embarrassing situation. But Melissa was a hard woman to feel sympathy for. She had an irritating way of trying to rule her children's lives, and when things went wrong, she placed the blame on everyone but herself.

His gaze shifted to the band. They were packing up, their amps and electric instruments being of no use. Judging by their response to being invited to join the guests for food and drink, he guessed they were planning to stay the night once their equipment was safely stored.

However, in spite of the warnings about the roads, he was contemplating leaving. Weddings generally brought out, more strongly than usual, the husband-hunting instincts in women, and he was in no mood to fend off a female with a ring on her mind. But then, there hadn't been a wedding. In place of tears, hugs, congratulations and predictions about the bride and groom's future, gossipy conversations, held in lowered voices and speculating about why Randi Howell had fled her wedding to Hal Stuart, reached his ears.

Alex refused to speculate. Women, he mused wryly,

were unpredictable creatures with hidden agendas. Trying
to figure out their motives for any action was a waste of
time. They could, however, turn an otherwise dull evening
into something memorable, he added, noticing the slender,
dark-haired female who had just entered and was making
her way to the buffet table. She had a graceful
walk…enticing, actually. Pretty, too, he noted as the large
candelabra on the table illuminated her face. Her cheek-
bones were high and her features finely cut. His gaze went
to her hands. No ring on her ring finger.

Thoughts of leaving faded. He followed her movements,
waiting to see if an escort joined her. When she finished
gathering her plateful of food and made her way, alone, to
a discreet corner, his interest peaked more. Leaving his
shadowy hideaway, he crossed the room, picking up two
glasses of champagne on the way.

"I thought you might like a beverage," he said as he
reached her.

Nina looked up at the tall, dark-haired, imposing man
who had halted in front of her. She recognized him from
other parties she'd worked at. He'd even come into the
diner once or twice. She didn't know his name, but she'd
heard a couple of women whispering about him once. *The
oil tycoon who'd built the summer place on the mountain*
was how they'd referred to him. They'd also mentioned that
he was a bachelor who was playing very hard to catch.
Strikingly handsome, he was the kind of man who could
take a woman's breath away, and a flush of pleasure that
he was paying attention to her brought a tint of pink to her
cheeks. "Thank you for your consideration. Now if I only
had a third hand," she replied.

"I'll hold your glass for you while you eat." He grinned.
"It's a good ploy, don't you think? Unless you want to go
thirsty, you have to put up with my company."

She regarded him with dry amusement. "I doubt very much that you need any ploy. It's my guess that very few women have told you to get lost."

Alex didn't deny her assessment. "I'm Alex. Alex Bennett."

"I'm Nina." She chose not to add her last name. She was allowing herself a momentary fantasy. No need to reveal she was not one of the guests.

"You're here alone?" He normally made it a rule never to browse in another man's store, but in this case he was seriously considering trying to take her away from her date if he'd been mistaken and she was here with someone.

"Yes." She wondered how she could sound so cool and in control. Since she'd been widowed nearly three years ago, she hadn't even dated. She thought she'd forgotten how to talk to a single man, much less how to flirt with one. Yet, she must be doing something right because Alex Bennett was still there.

"Interesting nonwedding." Watching her take a bite of a strawberry, Alex wondered how her lips would taste.

"Very." *Think of something to say!* she ordered herself, but small talk had never been her strong point. Smiling stiffly, she bit into a tiny finger sandwich.

You're boring her, Alex chided himself. "Rather a Gothic atmosphere, don't you think? The bride flees the wedding in the midst of a raging storm, and the mother of the groom doesn't even show up. Now the groom appears to be missing, and we, the guests, are left to fend for ourselves by candlelight."

"A night fraught with intrigue," Nina quipped.

"And music," Alex noted as the strains of a popular song filled the air. A glance over his shoulder told him that one of the guests had discovered the piano in the corner. The opportunity to test the feel of her in his arms was too strong to resist. "Would you care to dance?" Without giving her an opportunity to say no, he quickly set the glasses of champagne on a nearby table, then gently eased her plate from her hands and set it down with the glasses.

As he drew her into a loose embrace, the scent of his after-shave teased her senses, and she was acutely aware of his strength. How much she liked being in his arms shook her, and a curl of guilt wove through her. Tom Lindstrom had been her childhood sweetheart, and there had never been another man in her life other than him. *It's just a dance*, she admonished herself.

Alex didn't think any woman had ever felt so good in his arms. Nor had he ever been so sharply aware of another...her soft perfume, the cut of her jaw, the curve of her hips, the velvet look of her lips. *It's this strange night. The lightning is filling the air with electricity, causing my perceptions to be heightened*, he reasoned.

Nina felt herself wanting to move closer. For the first time since Tom's death, she found herself missing male companionship. Well, she was only human, and thirty-one was still young.

The song finished, and at the shouted request of one of the guests, the pianist began pounding out an old rock and roll tune. Still Alex held her and continued to move slowly, as if the strains of the other song still filled the air.

"I think we're out of sync with the rest of the room," she said, but did not fight his lead, choosing to remain in his arms and move with him.

"I prefer to think they are out of sync with us."

His breath played on the sensitized skin of her neck, and her blood began to heat. A crack of thunder shook the building. She trembled and he drew her closer. "I'll protect you," he said gruffly, and marveled at just how much he wanted to do that and a whole lot more.

Her senses reeling, Nina looked up, uncertain what to say. Until now she'd been too nervous to look into his eyes. Now she realized they were green...a warm, inviting green like the woods on a summer day. Her gaze locked with his, and she felt herself being drawn into their lush depths.

"You have the most kissable-looking lips I've ever seen," he said, his face moving closer to hers.

Suddenly panic flowed through her. Her resistance was dangerously too low. This was all happening much too fast! She was letting her fantasy get out of hand. In the cold light of dawn, when he discovered she was a poor widow with three children, he was bound to bolt.

"I just remembered something I have to do." She squirmed out of his arms and rushed from the room.

Alex followed her into the hall, but in the dimly lit passages, he lost her.

One

"The end is near," the lanky, white-haired, eighty-five-year-old man propped up by pillows in the large four-poster bed announced with conviction. "I can feel death breathing down on my neck."

Alex studied his grandfather's lined, weather-worn features with concern. He wasn't accustomed to seeing William Bennett pale and weak. "You should be in a hospital."

"I ain't goin' no place. When you've got as much money as I have, the doctors come to you." The frown on the old man's face deepened. "But there are things money can't buy. I'd hoped to bounce a great-grandchild on my knee before I went to those oil fields in the sky, but that doesn't seem likely now. However, I'd die a happy man if I knew you'd, at least, found yourself a wife. You're thirty-seven. A man should be putting down roots at that age."

"We Bennett men don't have much luck at finding women whose roots take hold," Alex reminded him.

The old man scowled. "Be that as it may. Your dad and I both tried. If we hadn't, you wouldn't be here today. You need an heir, boy. When I'm gone you'll be the last of our line."

Alex had been certain the old man was too ornery to die. At twelve, William had gone to work in the oil fields, learning the business from the bottom up. He was tough as leather and had the determination of a bull with a purpose.

It had been by sheer grit, willpower and the sweat of his brow that he'd held his fledgling drilling company together until they'd hit their first oil well some sixty years ago.

The muscles in Alex's throat constricted. William Bennett was the only real family he had. He'd raised Alex and taught him all he knew about the oil business. The day Alex turned twenty-one, William had made him a full partner. He loved the old man and hated to feel he'd let him down in any way. A small lie couldn't hurt, he reasoned. "I have found someone."

William Bennett's eyes, jade green like those of his grandson, flashed with pleasure. "You have?"

"She's got raven hair...so black it shines in candlelight. Her eyes are hazel with tiny gold flecks." Startled, Alex realized he was describing the woman he'd encountered more than three weeks earlier at Randi Howell's nonwedding. Grudgingly, he admitted she'd haunted his dreams that night. The next day, he'd thought he'd seen her on the street, but when he'd caught up with the woman he'd thought was her, he realized his mistake. He'd felt like an idiot. He'd made it a practice never to get too interested in any woman.

Still, after the incident on the street, he'd made an attempt to find her, but no one he asked knew a Nina who fitted her description. Then he'd had to leave Grand Springs on business and had only been back once, just long enough to attend Olivia Stuart's funeral. He'd thought he'd put the dark-haired Nina out of his mind. Apparently, he hadn't.

"Sounds very tempting," William said.

"She is," Alex admitted, recalling how much he'd wanted to taste her lips.

"I want to meet her."

"She doesn't live here in Denver. She lives in Grand Springs." Even as he said this, Alex had his doubts. His

inability to find anyone who knew her had caused him to
come very close to concluding that she had merely been in
town for the wedding...probably a school chum of the
bride. The only thing keeping him from being absolutely
certain of this was the nagging feeling that there had been
something familiar about her. As a part-time resident of
Grand Springs, he only attended a few social functions a
year there. It was possible he'd seen her across a room but
never spoken to her. Again her face haunted him. Had she
been with someone, and that was why he hadn't approached
her one of those other times he'd seen her? It occurred to
him that she might already be spoken for and had only been
alone the night of the wedding because the man in her life
couldn't attend or they'd had a lover's quarrel. An emotional attachment to another man would explain her sudden
flight. This thought caused a bitter taste in his mouth.

"Grand Springs. That's that town where your school
buddy, Noah...something or other..." William said, jerking Alex's attention back to his grandfather.

"Noah Howell," Alex said, filling in the blank and marveling at how completely his mysterious black-haired
woman could take over his mind.

"Noah Howell, the doctor. Right. That's where you built
that vacation place you run away to when you want to get
off by yourself. And you donated some money to a children's wing for their hospital there, didn't you?"

"That's the place."

William nodded, satisfied he knew the locale about
which they were speaking. "Have you two set a date?"

"Not yet," Alex hedged.

"I hope you don't plan to wait long. No sense in cooling
your heels. That ain't going to get you heirs."

"I'm sure we'll set the date soon." Alex didn't like the

way this lie was escalating, but he didn't see any way to stop it, short of disappointing the old man.

"I probably won't live to see the wedding, anyway." William sighed heavily and grasped Alex's hand. "Bring her here. I want to meet her before I meet my Maker."

Mentally Alex kicked himself. He should have known the old man would make this request. "I'm not too sure she can get away."

"Persuade her," William insisted. He tried to rise, then sank back. "Otherwise, I'm going to get to Grand Springs on a gurney if I have to. I want to meet my future grand-daughter-in-law."

Alex read the determination in his grandfather's eyes. There was no stopping William Bennett once he set his mind to something. "All right, I will," he promised.

William smiled triumphantly. "Well, get cracking," he ordered.

As Alex drove back to Grand Springs, the scowl on his face deepened with each mile. He didn't like lying to his grandfather. On the other hand, seeking this Nina out and enlisting her aid wasn't a bad idea. That he could close his eyes and actually feel her in his arms made him uneasy. No other woman had ever had such a lasting effect on him. He was certain it was merely a residual effect induced by the strangeness of that night. But she had disturbed his peace of mind. However, once he found her, she would no longer be a mystery woman and he'd no longer be haunted by her.

He'd offer to pay her to play his fiancée for a couple of days. A sudden worry that she wouldn't cooperate crossed his mind. A cynical smirk distorted his features. Any woman could be bought for the right price.

* * *

"What you did to Mr. Alex was unconscionable," Matilda Hastings scolded. Knowing the old man was up to something, she'd remained in a far corner of the room during his grandson's visit. William, she knew, had allowed her presence because her hovering over him had made him seem even more ill. Now, returning from seeing Alex off, she approached William Bennett's bed. Coming to a halt beside it, the fifty-seven-year-old, short, plump woman, her auburn hair dulled by strands of gray, stood, her arms akimbo, frowning reprovingly. "I helped you raise that boy, first as his nanny and then staying on as your housekeeper. I know how much he loves and admires you. He must have made me swear a dozen times that I'd let him know if there was any change in your condition, and I'm to see that the doctor comes both morning and night to check on you. He's heartsick thinking you're dying."

William shrugged. "We're all dying from the day we're born. It's the cycle of nature."

The frown on Matilda's face darkened even more. "But you are not currently in any danger of meeting your Maker. We both know you're going to live to be a hundred. You're just exhausted from staying day and night at that last drill site until oil was struck."

William drew in a robust breath and smiled broadly. "You don't understand the invigorating smell of fresh crude."

Matilda crinkled her nose. "You're right, I don't."

"As for my grandson, it's time he married and sired an heir or two."

"Has it ever occurred to you that he simply hasn't met the right woman?"

William suddenly frowned. "I'm not so sure that there is a 'right woman' for us Bennett men. Our luck in that area doesn't run too good. But he needs a wife at least long enough to give him a child." His frown turned to a speculative smile. "This should light a fire under his feet. And, if there is a female like the one he described, I'm going to enjoy meeting her."

"Or maybe he'll rush into something you'll both regret," Matilda warned. "There are mistakes and then there are *mistakes*. Remember the one his daddy made."

William's smile faded. "I hadn't thought of that. We'll have to keep a close eye on the boy."

Matilda issued a loud snort. "I'd find me another job and leave you to your own devices except that you'd never find anyone else who'd put up with you. Besides, someone has to stay and look out for Mr. Alex."

It was late into the night by the time Alex arrived at his home outside of Grand Springs. The two-story, sprawling log structure sat on a mountainside in the midst of several acres of wilderness. The back faced a vast lake. He'd had it built large enough to house guests comfortably, figuring it would be a good place to bring business associates he wanted to soften up or impress. But once it was finished, he'd kept it as a private retreat.

Glancing at the pile of newspapers Roberta Nyes, his cleaning lady, had left on the hall table, he frowned. According to the latest headline, the murderer of Olivia Stuart had not yet been found, nor did the police seem to have any definite suspects.

He recalled the funeral. Olivia had been mayor of Grand Springs. He'd met her at various fund-raisers Noah had dragged him to. After learning of all she'd done and was trying to do for the town, he'd grown to admire her. Out of respect, he'd made a special effort to attend the service. It had been a strained affair. Her daughter, Eve, and son,

Hal, had delivered eulogies. As she spoke, Eve's voice had broken and tears had trickled down her cheeks. Hal had seemed more in shock than in sorrow, but then everyone handled death in different ways. Besides, having one's mother murdered would shake anyone up. And to have been left standing at the altar on the same night as his mother's death had to have been a double whammy.

"Women. From the very beginning of time, they've been nothing but trouble," Alex muttered. A grudging grimace played across his face. Even as he'd tried to concentrate on the funeral rites, he'd found himself surveying the assembly, looking for the dark-haired, hazel-eyed woman from the night of the storm.

His jaw firmed. It was definitely time he sought out this Nina person and got her out of his system once and for all.

Nina Lindstrom sat on the side of her son Tommy's bed and smiled encouragingly down at his pale face. "We're going to meet Dr. Genkins at the hospital tomorrow. He's going to find out why you're feeling tired and dizzy lately and make it all better." Silently she said a prayer that this would be the case.

The towheaded, hazel-eyed six-year-old had always been an active child, constantly getting into things and squirming when made to sit too long. When he'd begun to slow down a couple of months ago, both she and her in-laws had attributed his behavior to the maturing process. But lately they'd begun to worry. When he'd started complaining about being dizzy, she'd called Dr. Genkins.

A preliminary examination had shown nothing serious, and the pediatrician had hypothesized that Tommy could be having some fluid build-up in the inner ear. He'd prescribed a mild antihistamine. But the dizzy spells had continued to grow worse. Now Tommy swayed when he walked, and she'd noticed he was dropping things more than usual. She kissed him lightly on the forehead. "Now, you go to sleep and get your rest."

His mouth tightened and his jaw tensed. She recognized his brave face, the one he used when he was scared but didn't want to admit it. "I'll be with you all of the time," she promised.

His jaw relaxed and she kissed his cheek. "Sleep tight," she said, rising.

Moving to the second bed in the room, she looked down at the sturdy little dark-haired, blue-eyed four-year-old boy there. "You get some sleep, too, Peter." Ruffling his hair, she kissed him good night.

"Tommy be well soon?" he asked worriedly.

"Yes, soon," she promised. She needed to hear herself say the words to bolster her own courage. She'd heard the concern in Dr. Genkins's voice when she'd called about Tommy's increasing symptoms.

Leaving the boys' room, she found her eight-year-old daughter huddled, clutching her favorite doll, in the recliner that had been Tom Lindstrom's favorite chair. Elizabeth, blond and blue-eyed like her father, looked anxiously up at her mother. "Is Tommy going to join Daddy?"

Nina's jaw firmed. She couldn't bear another loss. "No," she said with conviction. "Come on, it's time for you to be in bed, as well."

Elizabeth slipped out of the chair and, taking her mother's hand, accompanied her into the second bedroom of the small two-bedroom apartment. There Nina tucked her daughter into one of the two twin beds. But she was too tense to climb into the other and go to sleep.

She went into the tiny kitchen and made herself some warm milk, then went into the living room and sank down onto the couch. It seemed like lately if anything could go wrong it had. The storm had caused extensive damage to the Grand Springs Diner where she worked as a waitress. Because of that, the diner was closed, and there was no telling when it would reopen. Or even if it would. Ma and Pa Olsen, the owners, had put the place up for sale.

In the meantime, she hadn't been able to find a steady job. She'd been called a couple of times by the various catering services she normally moonlighted for, but those had been one-day jobs and the pay didn't come anywhere near meeting her monthly expenses. She'd have to dip into her meager savings to pay the rent and buy food. And now there would be doctor's bills.

Other than her children, she had no close family of her own. And she refused to ask Tom's parents for financial help. So that they could save enough to retire without having to worry about putting food on the table, his father worked fifty-to sixty-hour weeks as a mechanic and his mother had cleaned houses until arthritis in her shoulder and hip had forced her into retirement.

Besides, Helen Lindstrom was already helping enormously by baby-sitting Nina's children while she worked. Nina wanted to pay her but Helen refused, saying that watching her grandchildren was an act of love that helped ease the pain of having lost her son. Even more, both Helen and Ray treated Nina like a daughter and gave her emotional support for which she would be forever grateful. Nina wouldn't ask for more from them.

"I'll find a way to make ends meet," she vowed.

Closing her eyes, she leaned back and, searching for a moment of peace, tried to clear her mind of all thoughts. Instead of the blank slate she sought, a man's image appeared. In the past, the image had always been of her late husband...blond, blue-eyed Tom Lindstrom. But tonight the man who filled her mind was brown-haired and green-eyed.

Frowning, she opened her eyes. The cords in her neck had tensed and she massaged them. Ever since the night of the storm, the green-eyed man had haunted her, popping into her mind and her dreams, unexpected and uninvited.

"He and I come from two different worlds," she grumbled at herself. If the lights hadn't gone out and she'd waited on him as she had on other occasions, he would never have given her a second look. She would have been nothing more than the hired help, someone to ignore unless there was reason for complaint. He would have been so oblivious to her that if she'd passed him on the street the next day, he wouldn't have recognized her. She pushed Alex Bennett from her mind, returning her attention to her real concerns.

The thought of Tommy lying pale and afraid in his bed brought her own fear back to the surface. She recognized the bud of panic. Following Tom's death, she'd had several moments when anxieties about her ability to care for herself and her children had threatened to overwhelm her. But she'd overcome them. Her jaw tensed with resolve. She would not let fear rule her.

Tom's death had taught her a very valuable lesson. It had taught her to rely on herself. Following her parents' deaths, she'd turned to him for comfort and support, and he'd encased her in a protective blanket of love. Two months later, when she'd turned eighteen, she'd married him. She'd trusted him to be there always to take care of her and their offspring. Then came the day the drunk driver had forced him off the road and down a two-hundred-foot drop to his death. Suddenly, for the first time in her life, she was really on her own, and with three small children to care for. It was like learning to run before she'd even learned to stand. But she'd made it. They had a roof over their heads and food on the table.

But for how long? demanded the nagging voice of fear that would not completely disappear.

"For as long as I have the strength to work," she replied curtly.

Abruptly she recalled Jessica Hanson predicting that things would work out well for her, and there had been gossip that the woman could see into the future. *But how far?* Nina wondered dryly. Since the storm, her luck seemed to be going from bad to worse and was showing no signs of changing. "People make their own luck." She repeated aloud a phrase that had been one of her grandmother's favorites.

She picked up the newspaper, intending to go directly to the Help Wanted section. Instead, her attention was caught by the article about the murder of Olivia Stuart. The police, it reported, still had no solid suspect. She hadn't really known the woman, but she was aware that Mrs. Stuart had done a great deal of good for their town, and she hoped they caught the culprit soon.

Her gaze shifted to an artist's rendering of a young girl's face. The story accompanying it was an update regarding the abandoned baby who had been born the night of the storm. The face belonged to the mother.

"Well, at least she went to the hospital to give birth so the baby had a chance for survival," Nina noted, her heart going out to the infant.

The story again recounted how the teenager had come into the delivery room in labor, given birth, then fled soon after. She'd given the hospital staff a false name and address, and the authorities hadn't been able to locate her as yet. The baby, the article stated, was doing well, and the doctors didn't expect any complications. They'd named the child Christopher.

How could someone abandon a child? she wondered. Was the mother so callous she was indifferent to her baby, or had she run away because she was terrified of the responsibility of taking care of a new life?

Nina thought of her own three children. It was her love for them and theirs for her that had kept her going during those dark months following Tom's death. Because of them, she'd overcome her anxiety and found the strength to go on. She couldn't imagine her life without them.

Again Tommy's small, trusting face filled her mind and her chin trembled.

"Everything is going to be all right," she stated firmly, and turned to the Help Wanted section.

Two

Alex entered Vanderbilt Memorial Hospital and made his way to Noah Howell's office. He'd called to see if Noah had time for lunch, but Noah's receptionist had informed him that his friend had a full schedule. Not being a man who liked to be put off when he had a purpose, Alex had been insistent, and she'd penciled him in for a few minutes between morning appointments. Because he knew Noah had so much on his mind following his sister's disappearance from her wedding, Alex hadn't mentioned Nina to him earlier. Now, with no one else acknowledging knowing her, he hoped that Noah could lead him to the woman.

"He's expecting you," the receptionist said, lingering annoyance at Alex's insistence in her voice.

"Thanks." He gave her a quick, quirky smile to say he knew he'd irritated her and was sorry.

A slight upward tilting of one corner of her mouth let him know he was forgiven.

He entered Noah's office and eased himself into one of the leather chairs facing Noah's desk. He wanted to inquire immediately about Nina, but instead, after waiting until his friend had finished jotting down something on a patient's chart, he felt obligated to ask, "Have you heard anything more from Randi?"

"Only that one phone call, which didn't really offer much." The lines of worry on Noah's face deepened. "A part of me wants to strangle her for not letting us know where she is. Another part just wants her back safely.''

"Maybe she's staying away because she's embarrassed to face her wedding guests, or maybe she's afraid to face your mother. Melissa seemed to want that marriage pretty badly.''

"My mother can be insistent at times," Noah conceded. "Too insistent.''

"Well at least you have Amanda to help you through this.'' Alex felt a slight nudge of envy toward his friend. Immediately he dismissed it with a mental shrug. If other men wanted to risk the betrayal and hurt that could come with falling in love, then they were welcome to take the gamble. As for himself, he'd rather be safe than sorry.

Noah nodded. "I'm a lucky man in that respect." He leveled his gaze on his friend. "My receptionist says you steamrollered your way in here. I appreciate your concern regarding Randi, but I have the feeling that my sister's situation isn't the real reason you're here.''

Wondering how to broach the subject of Nina, Alex decided that bluntness was the best way. "You're right. I'm looking for a woman.''

Amusement sparked in Noah's eyes. "I've never thought of you as a man who would have trouble finding one.''

"Not just any woman. She was a guest at Randi's wedding. She left before I could get her phone number or her last name.''

The amusement left Noah's eyes, and he studied his friend speculatively. "If a woman has stayed on your mind this long, it must be serious. Are you considering giving up your bachelor status?''

"No. We Bennett men don't have much luck in choosing the right woman. Like I've told you before, I've decided not to even try. When I get ready to have a family, I'll find someone with all the right attributes…looks, brains…and cut a business deal with her to sire me a couple of heirs."

"Not all women can be bought," Noah cautioned.

Alex regarded him dryly. "They all have their price. Love. Money. Power. Security. It's different for each one. But if what you're willing to pay doesn't meet their expectations, they're gone, searching for greener pastures."

"You're a cynic."

"I prefer to think of myself as a realist. Now, how about helping me find this woman. She's in her late twenties or maybe early thirties, long black hair, hazel eyes, around five feet, nine inches tall, slender, pretty. Her name's Nina."

Noah frowned and leaned back in his chair. "And just why are you looking for this particular woman?"

Alex read the protective glint in his friend's eyes. "You know her, don't you?"

"I know someone who matches that description."

"I have no intention of misusing her," Alex assured him. "I simply want to make her a business proposition."

"To sire you a couple of heirs?"

"No." Alex knew the only way he was going to get Noah's cooperation was to tell him the whole story. "My grandfather's dying. He wants me married, so I invented a fiancée. Turns out I found myself describing this Nina. I want to hire her to pose as my fiancée to make Grandfather's last days happy."

Noah's expression remained serious. "I do know of a Nina who matches that description, and she could have been at the lodge that night."

Alex was aware of his friend's hesitation. Normally he respected Noah's opinion and would have asked why Noah seemed less than enthusiastic about him meeting this Nina. But like a predator on the scent of his prey, he refused to be deterred. "My grandfather is the only family I have. I'll pay the woman well and behave like a gentleman at all times. You have my word on that. Just tell me where I can find her."

"She's not your usual type."

Impatience brought Alex to his feet. "This is important."

"You've always been a man of your word." Noah hesitated for a moment longer, then said, "Her name is Nina Lindstrom. She was in the MRI waiting room a few minutes ago."

A jolt of concern shot through Alex. "She's having a magnetic resonance imaging? What's wrong with her?"

"Nothing that I know of. It's her son."

"Her son? She wasn't wearing a wedding ring." A reason for his friend's hesitation occurred to him. "Is there a jealous ex-husband in the shadows?"

"No. She's widowed."

"Thanks." Alex was already on his way to the door.

"Don't thank me yet," Noah called after him.

Ignoring the doubt in his friend's voice, Alex strode down the hall and punched the button for the elevator. Then, too impatient to wait for it, he headed for the stairs.

Emerging on the second floor, he made his way to the MRI waiting room. Through the windowed wall, he saw her. She was dressed in a faded blue cotton blouse, much-worn jeans and sneakers...all of which he guessed had come off the racks at the local discount store. Her thick black hair was pulled back and worked into a French braid that hung to the middle of her back. She wore only a hint of lipstick for makeup. The strain she was under was evident in her features. Her eyes were closed, and her hands were clasped in her lap, giving the impression she was praying.

This was not the Nina he'd expected to find, nor the

place he'd expected to find her. He'd thought she was either one of the idle rich or a successful businesswoman. Clearly she was neither.

He'd pictured himself meeting her at one of the finer restaurants in town. She'd arrive wearing something chic, in red, perhaps, that showed off her figure. Her delicate features would be softly defined by just the right amount of makeup. Her thick black hair would hang loose and flowing around her shoulders. Every man's head would turn as she crossed the room.

Instead, they were in a hospital, and she looked tired and drained. His plan to ask her to help him fool his grandfather seemed suddenly frivolous. He told himself to leave, find an actress to play the part and forget about Nina Lindstrom. But she looked so close to desperation, he couldn't make himself walk away. He'd bullied a friend in order to find her. He should at least speak to her.

Hearing someone enter the room, Nina stiffened and prepared herself to hear the worst. Opening her eyes, she thought for a moment she was seeing things. She closed her eyes, then opened them again. She wasn't seeing things. Alex Bennett was still standing in front of her. Today he was dressed in slacks and a pullover shirt. She guessed his Italian loafers cost more than her entire shoe wardrobe...probably more than her entire wardrobe. She also noticed that even in casual attire, he had an authoritative demeanor that left no doubt in her mind that he never allowed himself to lose command of whatever situation he found himself in.

"It appears our paths have crossed again," he said.

"Yes." Recovering from her initial surprise at seeing him, sympathy spread over her features. "I hope the test goes well for whomever you're here with."

"I'm not here with anyone." Unwilling to admit he'd

been trying to track her down, he added, "I stopped by the hospital to visit Noah Howell. He's on staff here, and I saw you. You looked as if you could use a friend."

Drawing a shaky breath, she glanced through the plate-glass windows in the direction of the testing rooms. "It's my son Tommy. He's been ill. Dr. Genkins ordered a brain scan." The knot of fear in her stomach tightened.

Lucky kid, Alex thought. His mother honestly cared whether he lived or died. In the next instant, he was reminding himself that he'd survived just fine without a mother's love. "Your son's in good hands," he said, recalling Dr. Jim Genkins from one of the charity functions organized to raise money for the hospital. He'd been impressed by the tall, slender, white-haired physician's dedication. He'd also heard several people, including Noah, praise the man's ability.

"I know, but that doesn't make the waiting any easier." He made her nervous, awakening stirrings that had been dormant since her husband's death…stirrings she had no energy to deal with at the moment. Her gaze dropped to her hands, and she waited for him to make some final encouraging remark, then leave.

The urge to sit down beside her and put his arm around her shoulders was strong. Instead, recalling the way she'd bolted the night of the storm, Alex seated himself across from her.

Surprised that he appeared to intend to remain, she looked up to meet his gaze. "I'm sure you have more important things to do than baby-sit an anxious woman."

Alex didn't think he'd ever seen a pair of softer, sadder eyes. "A knight would never desert a damsel in distress. And I've always wanted to play the part of a knight in shining armor," he quipped, amazed by how much he wanted to remain and offer comfort.

Nina had to admit he appeared to be a man a woman could lean on. But she wasn't in the market for a temporary hero who, in a moment of pity, was offering aid he would shortly bore of giving and regret. "I really will be just fine," she assured him.

He saw the proud determination in her eyes. *Tough lady.* Still, he didn't feel comfortable leaving her alone. "I'll just stick around for a while. See how the test comes out."

"That's really unnecessary."

Alex knew when he was being told to get lost. He ignored the unspoken request. "I've got nothing pressing to do, and no one should face something like this alone."

Nina tried to think only of Tommy. Her attempt didn't work. She was acutely aware of Alex's continued presence and knew that behind his polite facade he was studying her. She also knew he could tell by her clothing that she wasn't one of the town's aristocrats. *He's probably wondering how I ended up at a reception with the town's elite,* she concluded, her nerves growing brittle. "I didn't crash the wedding," she blurted. "I was supposed to wait tables, but when the lights went out we were all told the reception had been canceled but we were invited to share the food and drink. In fact, we were encouraged to stay."

"But you didn't stay," he reminded her.

"I had pressing responsibilities." Again she glanced toward the testing rooms.

Definitely the nurturing type, he mused. He'd always figured that was one of the primary qualities he'd look for if he ever changed his plans and decided to actually marry in order to produce an heir. However, at the moment, he wasn't in the market for a wife. He was in the market for an accomplice. "What does Dr. Genkins think might be wrong with your son?"

"A brain tumor." Every time she said those words a

tremor of fear ran through her. She lowered her gaze to her hands clasped in her lap. "He's only six. He's too young. It's not fair."

The pain he heard in her voice tore at him. "He'll be all right." *Who did he think he was, giving her that assurance?* Alex chided himself. But he hadn't been able to remain silent. The urge to soothe her had been too strong.

Her embarrassment about the wedding reception forgotten, Nina smiled gratefully. "I know you can't know that for sure, but thanks for saying it. I needed to hear it from someone besides myself. I keep thinking that if I say it enough, it'll prove to be true." Unable to sit any longer, she rose and began to pace. "Of course that's foolish. A person can't will bad news to go away."

"No," he agreed, surprised by how pleased he was by her small show of gratitude. "But it can't do any harm to hope for the best."

Nina nodded and continued to pace. "My grandmother had a framed needlepoint on her wall. It was a proverb she'd heard or read somewhere, and it impressed her so much, she stitched it. She gave it to me when I married. It read *Were it not for hope, the heart would break.*" She told herself to shut up, but she'd been holding too much inside, and the strain had worn her down. Stopping in front of the plate-glass window of the room that faced the door through which they'd taken Tommy, she fought back tears of frustration and pain. "But hoping hasn't done me much good. For two days I did nothing but pray and hope my husband would survive his injuries. But he didn't."

The anguish he heard in her voice made it obvious she'd loved her husband. *Just another example of how painful falling in love can be,* Alex mused. "I'm sorry," he said solicitously.

Her mind returning to the days following Tom's death,

rage flared in Nina's eyes and she swung around to face Alex. "Do you know that the drunk driver who caused the accident didn't even get a scratch? He was tried for manslaughter and found guilty, but that was two years ago. I'll bet he's out on the roads again and will kill some other father or mother or child, or maybe a whole family this time."

"Most likely," Alex agreed.

Nina drew a terse breath. It would do no good to dwell on Tom or his killer. Right now she needed to focus her attention on Tommy. His pale, trusting face filled her mind. A tear trickled down her cheek. Nina quickly turned her back to Alex and brushed it away. She hated for anyone to see her cry, especially a stranger. Her jaw tensed with resolve. "I've got to believe that this time my prayers will be answered."

Alex watched her standing rigidly. To lose both a husband and a child wasn't fair, he thought grimly. But then, fate rarely was. That's why he relied only on himself. Hearing a sharp intake of breath, he saw her stiffen. Looking beyond her, he saw Dr. Genkins coming out of one of the rooms and approaching.

"Tommy is still groggy from the sedation," Dr. Genkins said, smiling encouragingly at Nina as he entered. "I told the nurse to stay with him for a few more minutes so I could speak to you alone."

Nina had known the doctor all of her life. He'd been her pediatrician and now he was her children's physician. Through the years, she'd learned to read him well. That he'd arranged to be at the hospital during Tommy's examination had told her how worried he was about her son's condition. Now, looking beyond his smile, she saw the results in his eyes. "It's bad news." The words came out shakily around the lump of fear in her throat.

Alex was on his feet. Nina Lindstrom had turned ashen, and he was afraid she was going to faint.

"Maybe we should sit down," Dr. Genkins said. Although delivered in a fatherly tone, this was an order rather than a suggestion. Slipping a hand under Nina's arm, he guided her to a nearby chair.

Alex remained in the background. Obviously the doctor had the situation under control. Nina Lindstrom's wait was over, and he was free to go. But he didn't like leaving her on her own, not with the news he was certain the doctor was about to deliver. Besides, he wasn't busy. He might as well stay, he decided, and eased himself back into his chair.

"Tommy does have a tumor," Jim Genkins told her gently.

"Is it malignant?" Just asking caused a rush of terror.

"We won't know until the tumor is removed and the lab can examine it." He smiled encouragingly. "But there is good news. I had Dr. Zycros, a very capable neurologist, come in and take a look at the scan with me, and both he and I believe it's operable."

Nina saw the slight tic in his left jaw. It was a sure sign he was holding back, not telling her everything. "You're not being entirely honest with me. I need to know the whole truth."

He took her hands in his. "The operation will be tricky, but Dr. Zycros feels there is no other choice."

"None?" She looked at him pleadingly.

"The rapid increase in symptoms suggests the tumor is fast growing. It needs to be removed before it can do any damage."

Tears of fear welled in Nina's eyes. "Damage?"

"I know how you feel. It's terrifying when any child is in danger, and hundreds of times more so when it's your child. But I can assure you that I will do everything I can for Tommy.''

Nina's throat was so constricted she could barely speak. She did manage to choke out an, ''I know you'll do your best.''

''I'm going to have my receptionist set up an appointment for you tomorrow. That will give me time to take another look at the MRI and consult with some of my colleagues. I doubt very much that their diagnosis will be any different, but I want to be certain we don't have any alternatives.'' He gave Nina's hands a final reassuring squeeze. ''Now, shall we go get Tommy?''

As he started to rise, Nina laid a hand on his arm, keeping him seated. ''I don't have much money right now. I've been out of work since the storm,'' she said stiffly. ''But I want Tommy to have the best of care. I'll pay whatever it costs. It just may take a little time.''

Dr. Genkins patted her hand. ''Don't worry about the cost for now. We'll work out something. You just think about your son.''

Nina nodded and forced her legs to hold her as she rose. ''I want to go to him. He's probably wondering where I am.''

''He was asking for you,'' Dr. Genkins confirmed, holding the door open.

Alex watched Nina cross the hall with the doctor and enter one of the rooms. Again he told himself to leave. Again he stayed. He wasn't certain why. Curiosity, he decided. A few minutes later Nina emerged with a young towheaded boy. *Must take after his father,* he thought. Grudgingly, he admitted that he wouldn't mind having a son of his own. He just wasn't interested in having a wife.

The boy stumbled, and Nina scooped him up in her arms.

Alex frowned. She didn't look much steadier than the child. In the next instant he was on his feet heading toward them.

"You've had a pretty bad shock. How about if I carry your son," he said, starting to reach for the boy.

Nina's hold on Tommy tightened. She knew it wasn't rational, but as long as he was in her arms she felt as if she could keep him safe. "I can carry him."

Alex read the fierce protectiveness on her face. "Then, I'll walk along and open doors for you."

By the time they reached Nina's run-down Ford, Tommy was asleep, his head limp on her shoulder. She shifted his weight to a hip so she could hold him with one arm. Standing slightly tilted, she dug in her pocket for her keys.

Some women carry independence too far, Alex mused. Without asking, he lifted the boy into his own arms. "I'm not trying to steal him," he assured her in hushed tones. "I just didn't want you to drop him or pull a muscle."

Nina drew a shaky breath and ordered herself to calm down. "Thanks."

Tommy woke and lifted his head. Seeing Alex, fear spread over his face. "Mommy," he called, attempting to squirm out of Alex's grasp.

"You're all right, son." Alex tightened his hold on the boy to prevent him from falling.

"Just one second," Nina said, turning the key in the lock.

Tommy looked over his shoulder. Seeing his mother, he stopped his struggle. Still, he studied Alex skeptically, as if not quite certain the man was safe to be with.

Alex had dealt with many tough, single-minded businessmen during his lifetime. He, himself, was considered one of the toughest and most single-minded, but the child's stare had an intensity that unnerved him. "I'm Alex Bennett," he introduced himself, feeling the need to say something.

Tommy's eyes seemed to glaze over, and Alex realized the child had lost the fight to remain completely alert. Tommy was in a state of dazed exhaustion caused by the residual effects of fear and the drug the doctor had administered to calm him. He gave the child an encouraging smile and a wink.

Tommy continued to frown, clearly not yet convinced Alex was a friend, but having neither the strength nor the coordination to struggle.

"I'll take my son now," Nina said.

"I'll set him in the car," Alex insisted, seeing her own exhaustion etched deeply into her features.

Nina stepped aside and let him put Tommy on the seat and buckle the boy in. "Thank you again," she said when he straightened and closed the door.

"You're welcome." *Time to get back to his own problems,* Alex told himself.

Nina noticed that his smile didn't reach his eyes. They remained cool and distant, as if he found her an interesting specimen but wasn't interested in getting too close. *A mother with a child with a brain tumor wasn't every man's dream woman,* she mused dryly, rounding the car and climbing in behind the wheel. And even if she'd been childless, she was certain she wouldn't have been Alex Bennett's choice for a companion. He traveled in a much more elite crowd.

Driving away, she glanced in her rearview mirror to see him heading back into the hospital. Again she wondered why he'd bothered to give her any of his time. "We must have been Mr. Bennett's good deed for the day," she said to Tommy.

When he made no response, she glanced toward him to see that he was again asleep.

Brain surgery! The thought terrified her. "We'll get through this," she said aloud, using the sound of her voice to give her courage.

Alex Bennett ordered himself to start thinking about finding someone else to play the part of his fiancée. Instead, Nina and Tommy Lindstrom's faces haunted him. The mother had looked desperate. The child was clearly scared.

He had his own problems! he reminded himself. His grandfather was on the brink of death and expecting him to produce a wife-to-be.

The frown on his face deepened. Approaching the desk, he asked the nurse to page Dr. Genkins.

Three

Nina sat cross-legged on the floor of her living room. It was late afternoon. The sandwich Helen had insisted on packing for her when Nina had picked up the children was lying uneaten on a plate on the coffee table. Tommy had made a small attempt to eat his, but he'd only managed a couple of bites. Helen had been supportive, and at any other time Nina would have stayed with her during the afternoon, gaining strength from their combined hopefulness. But today she'd felt the need for some time alone with her children. She'd also sensed that Helen needed a little time on her own. Her mother-in-law had been as shaken as she had. So, leaving Helen to break the news to Ray, she'd left and come home.

Beside her, Pete was building with his Legos. Elizabeth had set out her toy tea service on the near end of the coffee table and was hostessing a tea party. She'd set places for Pete, her mother, Tommy, herself and her dolls, Sarah Jane and Mary Beth. Nina had provided juice in place of the tea, and there were homemade cookies provided by Helen Lindstrom for all.

Pete, who had already eaten his cookie, periodically stopped his building to take a bite out of Sarah Jane's. Elizabeth, having finished hers, was nibbling on Mary Beth's.

Tommy, still looking drained and pale from the trauma of the MRI scan, was lying on the couch watching television. He was only nibbling at his cookie, and Nina was certain his bouts of dizziness were getting worse.

A knock on the door brought a mental groan. She was not in the mood for visitors. All of her energy was being expended in not letting the children guess how terrified she was for Tommy.

A second knock brought her to her feet. Its firmness let her know that whoever was there was not going to leave.

As she headed to the door, it occurred to her that it was probably Ray and Helen coming to check on her and the children. And their company would be welcome. The children loved their grandparents, and both Helen and Ray were good at putting on cheerful faces for them in times of adversity. As for herself, having Helen and Ray here might help keep her mind from the more morbid paths it kept trying to follow.

In case she was wrong about who was on the other side, she opened the door only partially. A gasp of surprise escaped. Standing there, looking totally out of place in this low-rent district, was Alex Bennett.

"I thought I'd stop by and see how Tommy is doing," he said, thinking she looked even more drawn and vulnerable than she had this morning. Clearly the strain of worrying about her son was wearing her down. That could be to his advantage, and hers as well.

"He's fine. He's watching television." Embarrassed by how shabby she knew her apartment would appear to him, she continued to keep the door mostly closed.

It was obvious she didn't want to invite him in, but Alex refused to be deterred from the purpose that had brought him here. "I was wondering if I could speak to you."

Nina had to admit she was curious about why he was taking such an interest in her and her son. His manner wasn't that of a man pursuing a woman he found attractive.

He was polite but cool, almost formal. Her place, she told herself, was clean, and although the furnishings were not quality, they were functional. Still, she remained uncomfortable about inviting him in and continued to block his entrance. "What is it you want to speak to me about?"

"You mentioned to Dr. Genkins that you'd been out of work since the storm."

Hope that he might have a job for her bloomed. "I worked at the Grand Springs Diner. It had extensive damage done to it during the storm and has been closed," she confirmed.

Alex's gaze narrowed in recognition. "Yes. That's where I've seen you before. I knew your face was vaguely familiar."

Mentally she patted herself on the back. She'd been right in assuming he'd never have given her a second glance if she'd simply waited on him the night of the canceled reception.

"I have a business proposition for you." Alex glanced up and down the public hallway and frowned. "However, I prefer to keep my business private."

Her hopes grew stronger. Maybe he needed a maid or a housekeeper. Either would suit her. Stepping aside, she allowed him to enter.

Alex passed her, then stopped short. "Are all of these children yours?"

Nina had been closing the door. Now she turned to find him surveying her brood with a stunned expression. Her shoulders stiffened defensively, and motherly pride glistened in her eyes. "Yes."

Alex frowned at himself. "I'm sorry. That didn't come out right. I was just surprised. I thought you only had the one child." *Try to be more diplomatic in the future,* he chided himself. He wanted her cooperation. Making her angry wasn't going to achieve that.

"You said you had a job for me?" Nina reminded him sharply. "Or has my having three children caused you to change your mind?"

For a moment he hesitated. Three children would be a shock to his grandfather. However, William had no need to know about the other two. "No. No, it hasn't," he replied. He looked toward the children and saw recognition in Tommy's eyes. The other two were watching him as if fearful of trouble. Their mother's curt manner was causing them to be apprehensive. He smiled at them encouragingly, but they continued to remain guarded. *Great first impression you've made,* he told himself dryly. Glancing back at Tommy, he saw the boy push himself further into the pillow, the anxiousness of his siblings registering on his face, as well.

"I've had a very long day, Mr. Bennett. If you would just tell me about the job..." Nina left off the "and leave," but it was in her voice. She knew she should be grateful for any work, but she was tired, and his reaction to the discovery that she had three children was still grating on her nerves. His momentary hesitation hadn't been lost on her, either.

Recalling that children were not good at keeping secrets, he asked, "Could we speak in private?" He read the refusal in her eyes. "Children sometimes repeat what they hear and this is a very personal matter. It involves my grandfather. He's very ill, and I've come to ask you for a favor...a favor I'm willing to pay for."

Nina had to admit the affection she heard in his voice when he spoke of his grandfather was genuine. That he had referred to what he'd come to ask of her as a favor intrigued her. She could think of no favor a person in her position could do for one in Alex Bennett's position. *It can't do any harm to listen to what he has to say,* she reasoned. "The kitchen is as private as you and I are going to get." She looked to her daughter. "Elizabeth, keep an eye on your brothers."

Elizabeth nodded.

Noticing the young girl's shoulders straighten, and her manner become instantly adult, Alex experienced a sense of kinship. Like him, this child had been forced to grow up more quickly than others, accepting responsibilities beyond her years.

Pete was on his feet, moving toward his mother. Squatting to his level, Nina kissed him lightly on the tip of his nose. "Go back and build something really special for me. I'll bring you another cookie."

Remaining by his mother, the boy stared up at Alex anxiously.

"I just want to talk to your mother," Alex assured him.

"Go on and play." Nina turned Pete around and gave him a light nudge back toward his toys.

"Come on, Pete. I'll help you build something," Elizabeth coaxed, seating herself in the place her mother had previously occupied.

Pete cast a backward look at Nina.

"Run along," she said, this time sternly.

Still looking unhappy, he obeyed.

Following Nina, Alex glanced back over his shoulder to see Elizabeth and Pete sitting on the floor together, but neither was building. Both were watching him suspiciously. Tommy was studying him, as well, the worried expression on his face causing the circles under his eyes to seem even deeper. Alex gave them an encouraging smile, but the three pairs of eyes continued to cause a prickling sensation on the back of his neck as he entered the kitchen.

Inside the small room, Nina wished she'd had an alternative. It was barely large enough for two people to move around in, and Alex Bennett seemed to dominate what space there was. "Now, what is this favor you want to hire me for?"

"I need a fiancée for a short while."

Nina stared in disbelief. "A fiancée? Me?" Anger replaced her disbelief. "Look, Mr. Bennett, I'm having a rough time right now. I'm not interested in playing any game or being the brunt of some joke one of your high-society friends has cooked up. What is it? Some kind of scavenger hunt...find the most unsuitable match?"

The woman has fire. Alex blocked her attempt to exit. "This is not a scavenger hunt. I told you, it involves my grandfather. He's dying. I want him to leave this world in peace, and he says the only way he can do that is to know I've found a wife."

Nina continued to regard him skeptically. "Why me?" she asked again. "I'm sure you have plenty of sophisticated women friends who would gladly pose as your fiancée."

"You come fairly close to matching the description I gave him." Alex refused to admit he'd described her. That could give her ideas, and he wasn't seeking to get involved with her. Admittedly, if she'd been the type to have an affair he might have considered pursuing a short liaison— he still didn't think he'd ever seen a more kissable pair of lips. But she didn't strike him as a woman who would be interested in casual sex. If she was, she wouldn't have fled the night of the storm. No, Mrs. Lindstrom was more the "wedding ring first" type. "And I figured we'd both be doing each other a favor. You pretend to be my fiancée and I'll pay for your son to have the very best medical care money can buy, plus living expenses until you find a permanent job."

"You want me to help you fool a dying man?"

Alex scowled at the disapproval in her voice. "Better I find a fake fiancée than marry on his whim and end up with an expensive divorce and a lot of bitter feelings."

"You have a point," she conceded.

"I spoke to Dr. Genkins after you left. He wouldn't discuss Tommy's case specifically, but we talked theoretically. There's a gifted neurosurgeon in Denver. He's one of the best in the world."

"Denver?" Nina paled. "I thought someone here..."

Time for the hard sell, Alex decided. "There is a surgeon here who can perform the operation, and if you don't accept my offer, you can stay here and he'll probably do an adequate job. But I'm sure you want the best for your son. You want him to have every chance of a full recovery. I'm offering you that opportunity." Alex knew, even as he attempted using her son to blackmail her into agreeing to his scheme, that no matter what she said, he would pay for the boy to go to Denver. But life would be a lot easier if she would play along. Otherwise, he'd have to find someone else who matched her description.

In her mind's eye, Nina saw her son lying on the couch. He trusted her to take care of him. Besides, what harm could playing along with Alex Bennett's scheme cause? "All right. You've got yourself a fiancée."

Triumph flowed through Alex. "Shake on it?"

As his hand closed around hers, heat traveled up Nina's arm. It had a curiously sensual feel to it and wove through her until it reached her toes. Inside her shoes, they curled with pleasure. Immediately, Tom's image popped into her mind and she experienced a rush of guilt.

Tom's gone, a little voice reminded her. She recalled her ringless finger. A year ago she'd removed her wedding band because she'd decided it was time she started getting on with her life. Still, her body tensed. She wasn't entirely ready to tie Tom's memory up with pink ribbons and store it away. Besides, even if she was, Alex Bennett wasn't an option. He would never consider her a real possibility for a wife, and she wouldn't settle for anything less.

Alex was a little surprised by the strength of her hand. He was used to women whose grasp was delicate, as if they were too fragile to participate in a real handshake. In the past, he'd considered that light touch seductive. Now it seemed insipid. The firm contact spread through him, reminding him of how good she'd felt in his arms. He had to fight the urge to pull her to him. Reminding himself that he'd already determined that she was the marrying kind, he released her. "I'll go with you to see Dr. Genkins tomorrow, and we can begin making the arrangements to take Tommy to Denver."

Nina nodded.

"We'll need to make arrangements for your other children as well."

"They can stay here with their grandparents."

Alex breathed an inner sigh of relief that the problem was solved so easily. "That's probably for the best. Three instant great-grandchildren might be a little too much for my grandfather to take at one time. In fact, it might be best if he was led to believe you only have the one child."

Nina scowled at him. "I will not deny my children."

"I'm not asking you to deny having them. I'm merely saying that if the subject doesn't come up, we don't have to bring it up."

They were playing this charade to ease his grandfather's mind, she reminded herself. "You have a point," she agreed stiffly. "He could think you were taking on too much paternal responsibility."

Alex caught the cynical edge in her voice, suggesting he

wasn't capable of carrying so great a load. He chose to ignore it. "And what will you tell your parents about us?"

"My parents are dead. It's Tom's parents, and I'll tell them the truth. I don't like the idea of lying to them. They're good people and I trust them."

Alex wasn't happy about too many people knowing of his ploy, but he could tell she had her mind set on this. "What about your children? What will you tell them?"

"I'll tell them that you're a friend who's going to help me see that Tommy gets well."

"Since they'll have no contact with my grandfather, that should work just fine. What time is our appointment with the doctor tomorrow?"

"One o'clock," Nina replied, already feeling uneasy about the bargain she'd made.

Alex read her nervousness. "We're both doing the right thing."

Again she thought of Tommy. "I suppose."

Exiting the kitchen, Alex intended to leave, call one of the available women he knew, then have a quiet dinner and an intimate evening. But as he entered the living room to find himself the focus of three worried gazes, he heard himself saying, "How about if I treat you to some pizzas and soda for dinner?"

"That really isn't necessary," Nina said quickly, wanting some time on her own to get used to the idea of the arrangement she'd agreed to.

Alex had noticed a gleam of excitement in the children's eyes at the mention of pizza. Now he saw them look to their mother with a plea on their faces.

Her uneasiness about the arrangement was replaced by embarrassment. Takeout pizza and soda was a treat she couldn't afford very often. And from her children's reaction, she knew Alex Bennett had guessed that. Her shoulders straightened with pride.

Watching her, Alex realized that Nina Lindstrom didn't like accepting anything she considered charity. "All of us should spend some time together," he said before she could refuse his offer. "My grandfather will expect me to know some details about you and Tommy." That he found himself honestly wanting to stay and spend the evening in the company of three children, rather than having a romantic tryst, surprised him. He told himself that he was doing this for William and to test his own feelings about fatherhood.

"Mom?" Elizabeth said hopefully.

He was right, Nina conceded. Besides, she was going to have to get used to having him around. "All right. Sure."

Alex had to admit to feeling insulted by her less-than-enthusiastic acceptance of his company. Generally women enjoyed his presence. As before, he found himself thinking that when he came back to Grand Springs in search of Nina, this was not the woman he'd expected to find or anything even remotely resembling the situation he'd expected to find himself in.

Elizabeth was studying him with interest now, her mouth pursed into a thoughtful pout. "Tommy said he thinks he saw you at the hospital, but he's not sure. He says it could have been a dream. Are you a doctor?"

"No, I'm not a doctor. But I was at the hospital."

A haunted look came over Tommy's features. "That machine was scary. They put me way up inside." His voice trembled. "It was loud, too."

He'd barely spoken since she'd brought him home. Now Nina realized he'd been so afraid, it had taken this long for him to be able to voice his trauma. "But the machine didn't hurt you," she said soothingly, hurrying to him and drawing him into her arms. "In fact, it helped the doctors. Now they know how to make you feel better."

"I don't want to do it again," he pleaded, crying quietly into her shoulder.

Nina was tempted to lie but knew that would shake his faith in her. "I can't promise you that."

"If you do have to do it again, it'll be easier the next time," Alex said confidently. "You'll know what to expect."

Tommy stopped crying and lifted his head from his mother's shoulder to look at the man. "It was really loud."

"But the noise can't hurt you," Alex replied.

Tommy drew in a long breath, then asked, "Can I have pepperoni on my pizza?"

"Sure," Alex said, startled by the child's sudden change in subject. Then he recalled some proud parent he'd been cornered by at a party talking about how a child's mind could jump from one thing to another. Clearly the boy had decided to forget the machine and concentrate on a more pleasant subject.

"Pete likes plain cheese," Elizabeth spoke up.

"And what do you like?" Alex asked, looking her way. She shrugged. "I don't know. Hamburger, I guess."

Alex turned to Nina with a questioning look. "What about you?"

"Anything but onions and green peppers," she replied, amazed by how calm his words had made Tommy. She was certain that if she'd said the same thing, her son would still be sobbing on her shoulder. She frowned. It had to be one of those male bonding kind of things...if a man says it, then it must be true.

"I'll be back soon," Alex promised, heading for the door.

Watching him stride out, Nina wondered if he was having second thoughts. That he'd chosen to go get the pizzas, instead of having them delivered, suggested he wanted to escape. Her children had behaved well. Both Elizabeth and Pete seemed to sense Tommy's trauma acutely and were more subdued than usual. But they had stared, and a crying child usually made most men nervous. She half expected him to send the pizzas back with a messenger and a note saying some important business concern had come up. However, in the event that he did return, she needed to make the atmosphere a little more comfortable. "Mr. Bennett is a friend. He's going to be around a lot for a while, so I don't want you staring at him as if he has an eye in the middle of his forehead."

"Is he a boyfriend?" Elizabeth asked.

Nina bit back an emphatic no. "He's a *friend*," she said firmly, hating to lie to the children. She doubted that she and Alex Bennett would ever be anything other than passing acquaintances. But she'd agreed to this charade for Tommy's sake, and for him, she'd see it through. Wanting to end this discussion, she headed into the kitchen to get the plates.

Alex used his car phone to call his favorite Italian restaurant and order an assortment of pizzas. He added some ravioli and pasta to the order, as well. Seeing a bakery ahead, he stopped and bought a cake. At a quick-stop shop he purchased sodas.

He had expected to feel relieved to be out of that apartment with its bevy of children. Instead, he was anxious to return with his gathered goodies. *Must be that Good Samaritan syndrome or maybe some primitive instinct that being the male, it makes me feel good to be bringing dinner home to someone,* he mused sarcastically.

A little later, when Nina opened the door for him, her

eyes rounded in surprise. "You got takeout from Fredrico's?"

Her amazement pleased him. Carrying the boxes of hot food inside, he paused only long enough to put them on the table, then headed back to the door. "There's a few more things in the car," he said over his shoulder.

Nina began to frown as she opened the containers. He'd bought enough for days, and knowing the prices Fredrico's charged, she guessed he'd spent nearly as much on this one meal as she budgeted for food for a month.

When he entered carrying the bakery box and a case of sodas, her pride again bubbled to the surface. She followed him into the kitchen, closing the door behind her. "We're not a charity case," she said in lowered tones so that her children would not hear. "You don't have to feel you have to feed us as if we haven't eaten in days. I have managed to keep food on the table."

Alex scowled. "That wasn't why I bought all of this. I thought you deserved a treat. You've obviously been through a rough time lately. And to be honest, I have no idea how much children eat." He thought of the woman he'd met the night of the storm. That she had disappeared so completely bothered him. "I was hoping to make you smile. As I recall, you have a very nice smile."

Nina drew a harsh breath. She'd overreacted. She should consider him Tommy's guardian angel; instead, she seemed to be trying to find fault in everything he did. "I'm sorry. My pride can get a little out of hand at times." She smiled a crooked, embarrassed smile. "Thank you. This was very kind."

Alex glimpsed the woman from the night of the storm and smiled back, hoping to encourage her to emerge further. "You're welcome."

Nina's smile stiffened. She knew now why she'd been

so guarded with Alex Bennett. She was afraid of him. When he turned on his charm, he stirred emotions within her she didn't want to feel toward him. They would only lead to trouble.

Seeing the woman from the storm disappearing again behind shuttered eyes, Alex frowned. "I get the feeling you're fighting very hard not to like me."

"I don't dislike you. I just don't see us remaining friends after this arrangement is over. You'll go back to being a guest at parties, and I'll go back to being one of the serving people. I figure it's best if we both remember our places and stay in them."

Alex had never thought of himself as a snob, and he didn't like the picture she painted of him as one. "You're overly class conscious."

"I'm realistic. Just wait and see."

What he saw was that her resolve was firm. He'd already determined that keeping a distance between them was the right thing to do, he reminded himself. "Have it your way," he said without further argument.

"Mom, when can we eat?" Elizabeth called from the other side of the door.

"Right now," Nina replied, exiting the kitchen. She waved the children toward the table. "You can all sit down, and Mr. Bennett can help you get what you want while I get the drinks."

"Alex," he corrected her. Then, in lowered tones for her ears only, he added, "My grandfather is never going to believe you're my fiancée if you keep addressing me as Mr. Bennett."

"Alex," she conceded, fighting to ignore the erotic effect his warm breath on her neck was having on her senses.

Ordering himself to forget how much he'd wanted to nip her earlobe, Alex joined the children at the table. Pete was reaching for a slice of pizza, and he quickly helped the child get it onto his plate. Immediately the boy began to eat, ignoring all the others.

"My mother says you're a friend," Elizabeth said, regarding him speculatively as he dished her up a slice of pizza and some ravioli.

"That's right," he acknowledged, marveling at how much more intense a child's gaze could be than an adult's.

"Are you going to ask her on a date?" Elizabeth persisted.

"As a matter of fact, I consider this our first one," he replied, wondering if the girl was going to object.

Elizabeth smiled with satisfaction. "Grandma will be happy to know Mommy is dating. Our dad's been in heaven a long time. Pete doesn't even remember him. He was only one. I don't remember him real well, but Grandma says I take after him. He had blue eyes and blond hair, too."

Alex realized she didn't expect any response, as she abruptly stopped talking and turned her full attention to her food. *Children,* he mused. *They simply say what's on their minds, then move on to other topics. No small talk for them.* Turning his attention to Tommy, he saw the boy sitting, his chin propped in his hands. "How about a piece of pepperoni pizza," he offered, putting one on the boy's plate.

Tommy forced a tired smile but continued to remain leaning into his hands. Concern for the boy flowed through Alex. "You need to eat," he said.

"In a minute," Tommy replied.

Nina brought in the drinks, and Alex saw the worried look on her face when she saw her eldest son staring lethargically at the food he'd been looking forward to having. "Try to eat a little," she encouraged.

Tommy picked up the slice and began to nibble at it.

Concern for the boy foremost on his mind, Alex joined

her in coaxing Tommy to eat. By the time the meal was over, he thought he'd never had so exhausting an experience.

After a couple of bites, Tommy had turned pale and looked as if he was going to be sick. Nina had carried him to the couch and laid him down. Alex's worry that the boy was in much more immediate danger than the doctor had led them to believe increased.

Pete, clearly having inherited his mother's bold independence, wanted to serve himself. The others had all tried to keep an eye on him, so that when he suddenly stood in his chair and made an attempt to reach something outside of his grasp, they were there to help. But none had been quick enough when he made a grab for another slice of pizza and spilled his soda.

Although Elizabeth was polite and ladylike at all times, Alex felt her watching him. He'd been sized-up by some very powerful men in his time and many a calculating female. None of those inspections unnerved him the way the little blonde's did.

Helping Nina clear the table, he wondered how she'd had the energy to care for three children and hold down a job. It was a heavy load for such a delicate set of shoulders, he thought admiringly. He'd considered leaving soon after the meal. But the tiredness and the strain on her face brought out a protectiveness in him. He would stay awhile longer and help with the children, he decided.

Putting the leftovers in the refrigerator, Nina was sure Alex Bennett had had enough of her and her children. He'd never relaxed, but remained tensely alert in order to aid Pete, especially after the spilled soda episode. And Elizabeth hadn't been able to keep her eyes off of the man. Knowing that a child's nearly constant stare would make anyone uneasy, Nina had cast her daughter several reproving glances and Elizabeth had tried to behave herself. But, Nina had to admit, Alex Bennett was the kind of man any female would be drawn to study. She, herself, had found her gaze wandering to him several times, but she quickly jerked it away. Then there had been Tommy's bout of threatened nausea.

Nina was used to active mealtimes and her children watching her, especially when they were anxious. But she was certain Alex was accustomed to a more sedate dining atmosphere with much more comfortable companions. Returning to the living room, she found him on the floor helping Pete build while Elizabeth introduced him to her dolls. She expected him to rise, make a polite excuse about business he needed to take care of and leave. Instead, he ruffled Pete's hair playfully and added another block to the tower they were constructing.

Her jaw firmed. Even if he wasn't tired of them, his presence was wearing her down. She needed some time alone with her children to absorb the impact of the events of the day. But politeness kept her from ordering him out. After all, he had provided dinner. She'd give him another fifteen minutes. If he wasn't ready to leave by then, she'd politely but firmly send him packing. Seating herself in a nearby chair, she gave in to fatigue, leaned her head back and closed her eyes.

It seemed only moments had passed when a strong hand, gently shaking her shoulder, woke her.

Alex hated disturbing her sleep. She'd looked so peaceful. But he knew the children wouldn't allow him to tuck them in, and he was ready for them to go to bed. Their company had been interesting but tiring. Both Elizabeth and Pete had vied for his attention, and he'd tried to give it equally. Tommy had continued to study him warily, and he'd sensed that all three were trying to decide if it was all right to like him. The effect put a strain on his nerves different from any he'd experienced in a long time. It was, he thought dryly, a lot like his first day in school when he wasn't certain where he would fit in or if he would fit in at all. "Elizabeth tells me that it's Pete's bedtime," he said when she opened her eyes.

Nina glanced at the clock. She'd been asleep for nearly two hours. "I'm so sorry," she apologized, her cheeks reddening with embarrassment.

She was cute when she was flustered, Alex noted. "You obviously needed the rest."

She saw a softness in his eyes that sent a curl of warmth through her. *He's way out of your league,* she chided herself, and jerked her gaze to her children. "Time for baths," she announced, rising and picking up Pete.

For the next hour, she washed backs, read stories and tucked all three kids into bed. Returning to the living room, she found Alex reading the newspaper. "I would have thought that you'd had enough of me and my family for one day," she said, as surprised to find him there as she was by how at home he looked in her living room.

He laid aside the paper. While she'd been away, he'd had a stern talk with himself. He couldn't deny he was physically attracted to her, but he vowed to keep the attraction under control. Having spent the evening in her home, not only was he more certain than ever that she would want more of a commitment than he wanted to give, but he wasn't ready to take on the role of father to three children he hadn't even sired. Not that they weren't nice kids, he just wasn't in the market for a ready-made family. Ignoring the curve of her hips, he kept his mind on business. "We don't have much time to get to know each other."

She noted that the warmth she'd seen earlier in his eyes

was gone, and his cool, calculating tone let her know there was nothing personal in his inquiry. *A few second thoughts about the reality of getting physically or emotionally involved with a woman with three children have obviously dampened any ardor he was experiencing,* she thought cynically. *It was just as well,* she added. She would never be a wealthy man's playmate, and that was all he would ever offer her. "What do you want to know?"

"Elizabeth filled me in on her age and those of her brothers. From that I figured out you've been widowed approximately three years."

"Yes," she replied when he paused, clearly expecting a response.

"You mentioned that your parents are deceased."

Realizing that this twenty-questions game could go on forever unless she began to elaborate, Nina said, "My father had a small one-man, one-plane charter service. When I was sixteen, he and my mother were flying to Las Vegas for a short vacation. The plane got caught in a storm and crashed. My father's mother was widowed and lived here. I didn't want to leave Grand Springs, so she took me in. She died five years ago. My only close living relatives are my maternal grandparents. They live in a retirement community in Florida. We write but rarely see one another. Tom was my high school sweetheart. After my parents' deaths we became even closer. As soon as I graduated from high school, we married. He worked with his father as a mechanic at a local garage. A drunk driver caused the accident that killed him."

Tom's image came strongly into her mind. Too tired to keep her emotions under control, tears welled in her eyes. "I thought he'd always be here. I let myself rely on him too much."

She's still in love with him, Alex noted. That explained

why she'd fled when he'd started to kiss her. *And another very good reason not to get involved with her,* he added. Only a fool would compete with a ghost. "What kind of music do you like?"

She pushed Tom from her mind and ordered herself to concentrate on the business at hand. "All kinds. Country and western, mostly."

"Movies?"

"I haven't seen any in years. I don't know." Her nerves wearing thin, she frowned at him. "Do you really think your grandfather is going to grill you so closely about me?"

Alex had to admit he'd only continued to question her out of curiosity. He already knew enough to satisfy his grandfather. *And curiosity did kill the cat.* "You're right. I know all I need to know."

Her tiredness suddenly lessened as she realized that it was her turn to ask questions. "What about you? I'll need to know something."

"My father died before I was born. My mother preferred the jet-setting life to motherhood. As soon as I was born, she left me in my grandfather's care and took off to lead her own life. She married several times. I lost track. About five years ago she drowned in the Mediterranean. I didn't know her. I was raised by my grandfather and Matilda Hastings. Matilda was hired as my nanny and has remained as my grandfather's housekeeper."

Nina found herself picturing him as a lonely child. "I'm sorry about your parents."

Alex shrugged. "My grandfather gave me all the attention any child could want. And Matilda was as protective as a mother hen. I figure I didn't miss much." But even as he made this declaration, a deep-rooted anger stirred within, and he scowled. He didn't normally allow his mother's desertion to awaken emotion. Long ago, he'd vowed to remain as indifferent to her as she had been to him. He glanced at his watch. "I think we both need to get some rest," he said, rising. "I'll come by and pick you up in time for your appointment tomorrow."

"I need to drop the children off at their grandparents' house. I'll meet you at the doctor's office," she countered, then gave him directions.

He nodded and, bidding her good night, left.

As the door closed behind him, Nina frowned thoughtfully. If Alex Bennett had been truthful, and she had no reason to doubt him, he'd been loved and well cared for. But she'd seen the flash of anger in his eyes and knew his mother's desertion had bothered him. "At least I know one subject to avoid," she muttered, and headed into the bathroom to take a long, hot shower.

Alex's knuckles whitened around the receiver of the phone as he fought to keep his temper in check. Soon after arriving back at his mountain retreat, he'd called his grandfather's house to tell Matilda to expect him, Nina and Tommy. He'd also told her about the boy's need for surgery. He would decide after he saw what condition his grandfather was in if it was necessary to tell the old man about the seriousness of the boy's condition. "No need in causing him any grief in his last days," he'd said.

"Sounds like you've bitten off an awful lot to chew," Matilda had remarked with concern.

"Don't worry about me. I can take care of myself," he'd replied.

Now, half an hour later, he was again speaking to Matilda. When he'd first answered the phone and heard her voice, he'd been certain it was bad news about his grandfather. His stomach had twisted into a knot, and he'd barely been able to speak around the lump in his throat. Now anger had replaced his panic. "My grandfather is not dying?" he demanded in clipped tones, repeating what she'd just told him.

"Now, don't go getting too upset with him. He only wants what's best for you," Matilda soothed. "But I got to worrying that to please him you might go and do something rash. I'm sure this Nina person is very nice, and if you love her, then I wish you both well. But I wouldn't want you marrying her just to please your grandfather."

"I appreciate you telling me this." His voice took on the tone of command. "I want your word that you won't tell him that you told me the truth about his condition."

"What are you going to do?" she asked anxiously.

"I don't know. But he should be taught a lesson about trying to manipulate other people's lives."

"I suppose he should," Matilda conceded.

"I want your word," Alex demanded again.

Her voice firmed. "He really did go too far this time. You have my word I won't tell. Shall I cancel the plans for Mrs. Lindstrom and her son's arrival?"

"No. The boy needs surgery and I intend to see that he has the best care available." Alex thanked her again for telling him the truth, then hung up. Slouching in his favorite chair, he contemplated his options.

He could call off the charade entirely. In which case, he would still insist on paying for Tommy's medical care. The problem with that plan was that Nina Lindstrom was a proud woman, maybe too proud for her own good. She, he was certain, would insist on paying him back.

Besides, he liked his second option better. "Tit for tat, as Matilda would say," he muttered.

Four

Alex waited for Nina to join him at the door of the red-brick building housing Dr. Genkins's office. Her stride was firm and her shoulders were squared as she left her car and made her way across the parking lot. When she drew nearer, he could see the dark circles under her eyes and the hard set of her jaw. She reminded him of someone prepared to face the worst without letting it break her.

Seeing him ahead of her, Nina admitted she was glad she wasn't facing this alone. Ray had volunteered to come with her or stay at home with the children so that Helen could accompany her. But she'd assured both of them that she could handle this on her own. However, with each step nearer the building, fear was threatening her control. *I must be feeling really desperate to consider someone who's nearly a total stranger as a supportive companion,* she thought. Especially someone she'd half expected not to come. "I wasn't certain you'd be here," she said when she reached him, her nervousness causing her to say bluntly what she'd been thinking. "I thought an evening with three children might have made you decide to choose a less encumbered fiancée."

"Three children can be intimidating, but I found the evening interesting."

Interesting? He made it sound as if she and her children were some sort of curious life forms he'd enjoyed observing, like a spectator at the zoo. "A change of pace from your real life? I suppose when it's only a game you know won't last long, anything, even putting up with three small children, is palatable." Immediately, she berated herself. She was being much too sarcastic and even unfair. "I'm sorry," she apologized quickly. "I didn't get much sleep last night."

Another good reason for not taking a wife, Alex noted. Women had their moments when they could be unreasonably difficult, and marriage required a husband to learn to deal with them. In an affair, the woman generally attempted to control her moods, and if she didn't, he could simply walk away. Of course, this situation was different from either of those. Nina had good reason to be on edge, and he was willing to overlook her outburst because he needed her help. "Apology accepted." Then, because he disliked seeing her in so much pain, he added reassuringly, "Try not to worry so much. You and I are going to make certain Tommy has the very best of care."

She nodded and stepped into the elevator. For a long moment she remained silent. Then, fear overwhelming her, she said, "I let the children have chocolate cake for breakfast. I've never done that before." Her chin trembled. "It just suddenly dawned on me how short life can be." Her chin tightened. "Still, it was a stupid thing to do. They'll probably have stomachaches all morning."

"I was under the impression that children had cast-iron stomachs," he said, trying to offer comfort.

Tears welled in her eyes. "Tommy was always my tough little guy. Now he's so..." The elevator stopped, and her jaw tensed in her fight to maintain control.

"He's going to be all right."

Nina looked up at Alex Bennett. His authoritative bearing made her believe that if anyone could make that so, he could. Even though she'd promised herself that she would never rely on a man again, she was grateful for the support he was providing at this moment.

A few minutes later, sitting in the doctor's office looking at the diagrams of the human brain Dr. Genkins was showing her, Nina was no longer fighting to keep her emotions under control. She didn't have to. She'd reached a state of numbness.

"The tumor is on the cerebellum," Dr. Genkins explained, pointing to a circular mass he'd drawn on the diagram. "It's easily accessible and does not look as if it has sprouted any tentacles. Provided he is operated on quickly, there is every hope that Tommy will experience a full recovery."

"Thank you, Doctor," Nina managed to say.

Dr. Genkins glanced from Alex to Nina. "I've contacted Dr. Wayne O'Conner in Denver. He's an extraordinarily talented neurosurgeon and comes highly recommended by his colleagues. He wants to see Tommy as soon as you can get him there."

"If you will give me the information, I'll make the arrangements immediately," Alex replied.

Jim Genkins jotted down Dr. O'Conner's name and phone number and handed it to him. Turning back to Nina, he said encouragingly, "Tommy is going to be in very capable hands."

Nina nodded mutely.

"You look pale," Alex noted as they left the doctor's office a couple of minutes later.

"I've never been so scared." Her mind took an abrupt turn down a path she did not normally allow it to travel. "Well, maybe that's not entirely true. The day of Tom's funeral, when I was standing by his grave and realized that I had the responsibility for three children now fully on my shoulders...that was pretty terrifying."

"But you handled that well, and you'll make it through this," he assured her.

"Yes," she returned firmly, embarrassed she'd been so open with him. "Yes, I will."

Studying her strained countenance, Alex decided he should give her some time to get over the shock of what the doctor had told her before making the new request he had of her. "It's lunchtime and you look as if you need something to eat." He took her by the elbow and began to guide her to his car.

Nina's stomach churned at the thought of food. "What I need is to get back to my children." The anxious expression on her face deepened. "I'll have to be away from Elizabeth and Pete for several days. I've never been away from them before. I want to spend as much time as possible with them while I can."

She'd offered him an opening and Alex took it. "I want to talk to you about that." He maintained his hold on her elbow. "I want them to come along with us. Perhaps you could invite your mother-in-law, as well. Although I have a home in Denver, I've arranged for us to stay at my grandfather's house so that he can get to know his new family. But I don't want to overburden Matilda. Your mother-in-law would be a great help to her in watching over Elizabeth and Pete while you and I are at the hospital with Tommy. And I'm sure having their grandmother with them will ease the children's minds."

Startled by this sudden change in plan, Nina frowned up at him in confusion. "I thought you wanted to avoid telling your grandfather about my other two children. Now, suddenly, you want to inundate him with family? I don't understand."

"My grandfather is not as ill as I thought. Last night I

discovered that his deathbed wish was simply a way to manipulate me into doing something he wanted me to do.''

Pride caused Nina's shoulders to stiffen. ''Then, there is no need for us to continue this charade. I'll get Tommy to Denver on my own. There is no reason for you to concern yourself with us.''

''I'm not a coldhearted man,'' he growled. ''Whether the charade goes on or not, I intend to see you and Tommy through this.''

''I will pay you back.''

''I don't want you to pay me back. I want you to continue with the charade.''

An ugly suspicion replaced her confusion. ''Why?''

''To teach the old man a lesson. I want him to believe that I'm marrying you to make him happy. I'm not only providing him with the granddaughter-in-law he wants, but with instant great-grandchildren.''

Anger flared. ''You want my other children there so that he can see firsthand what a horrible mistake marrying me would be? Well, my children are well-behaved and good kids. Anyone with any heart should be happy to be related to them!''

Alex had guessed she'd be difficult about this, but he had his argument well thought out. ''I didn't mean any of this as an insult. You have to admit that marrying a woman with three children is a serious step and one that shouldn't be entered into lightly. The two people should be deeply in love, and for the marriage to be a success, the step-spouse should have a good relationship with the children. We aren't in love, and I'll make it clear that I barely know your children. My grandfather does care for me. He'll see the pitfalls.''

Nina didn't like involving her children in Alex's scheme. But the images of Tommy's brain, with that ugly lump attached, tormented her. And it wasn't only his future she had to think of, it was her other children's, as well. If she didn't continue with the charade, she could face financial ruin. Still... "I can't allow my children to be subjected to an environment in which they're made to feel uncomfortable or unwanted."

"My grandfather can be manipulative, but he's got a good heart. Your children will not be made to feel uncomfortable or unwelcome. And if at any time you feel they are, I'll move them to my home."

And if he didn't keep his word on this, she could pack them up and move them to a hotel, she reasoned. Aloud, she said, "I've never believed in people meddling in other people's lives. I guess your grandfather should be taught a lesson, and I would like to have my other children with me. Besides, it would take me years to repay you, otherwise."

Alex smiled triumphantly. "Then, it's settled. Shall we go get some lunch?"

Nina shook her head. "I don't think I can eat."

His business with her was accomplished. He didn't need to stick around. But instead of leaving, Alex heard himself saying, "You have to keep up your strength." Then, placing an arm around her waist, he again guided her toward his car.

It had been a long time since a man had taken care of her. Nina reminded herself that she'd vowed to stand on her own two feet, but the sturdy feel of him and her own sapped strength overpowered her will for independence. It couldn't hurt to let someone else take command for a short while, she argued.

Sinking into the plush bucket seat of his Porsche, she felt enveloped in luxury. *Don't get used to it,* she warned herself.

She looked totally drained, Alex thought. "Don't worry. We'll see this through together," he said. Shifting the car into gear, he admitted he liked taking care of her. *Guess I have a stronger "Knight in shining armor" complex than I thought*, he mused dryly. "Chinese or Italian?" he asked, pulling out of the lot.

"Whichever you prefer," she replied.

"Chinese, then. We had Italian last night."

Nina nodded, then turned her gaze to the view beyond the window. None of this seemed real...Alex Bennett, handsome, rich bachelor coming to her rescue. Of course, his actions were self-serving. *And don't ever forget that*, she cautioned herself. She was merely a pawn in the game he was playing with his grandfather.

She stiffened and frowned as they passed the Grand Springs Diner. The For Sale sign was still in the window, and the place looked totally vacant. "I can understand why the Olsens want to sell. They're getting on in age and the diner took a lot of energy to run, not to mention the cost of having it repaired. The check the insurance company gave them wasn't nearly enough. They would've had to dip into their retirement money. But the place did a good business. I know that for a fact, because they'd begun to let me manage it when they went on vacation."

Surprise showed on Alex's face. "You managed the diner?"

She gave him a dirty look. "I'm not a bimbo with a brood of kids." The thought that he'd been picturing her as an uneducated child bride who'd ended up in her present predicament because she'd been naive or stupid or both grated on her nerves. "I didn't get married because I had to. I got married because I wanted to. And I didn't get pregnant by accident. Tom and I wanted a family. We just never thought he'd die and I'd end up on my own."

Alex was beginning to feel very irritated with Tom Lindstrom. "When he took on the responsibility of fatherhood, he should have bought insurance. No one can predict the future."

Nina's anger flared. "Don't you dare criticize him! He did his best. We were living on a shoestring, saving money so he could buy his own garage. There wasn't any money for insurance."

Kicking himself for having said anything, Alex tried to think of a way to apologize that wouldn't sound condescending.

Nina glared at him, his silence adding fuel to her fury. It wasn't fair for him to blame Tom for the situation she found herself in. "We didn't have the children right away. When we first got married we both worked and saved so that we could buy a house. And we did buy one. A really nice one. After that, Tom got to thinking about buying his own garage and wanted to wait to start a family until we'd saved more money. But I didn't want to wait any longer to have children." Her chin threatened to tremble. She stiffened it. "I suppose you think I was foolish. Well, I wouldn't trade my children for all the gold in the world."

"What I think is that I should have kept my mouth shut," Alex said.

Nina's glare turned to a flush of embarrassment. Maybe she was being too hard on him. "I'm sorry." Leaning back, she closed her eyes. "The truth is, I was venting my own doubts and fears," she heard herself confessing. "Sometimes I feel guilty for having brought my children into the world. I want a better life for them than the one I can provide." Her embarrassment returned. She'd never told anyone about these feelings before. They'd been her private demons that came to haunt her in the small hours of the morning.

Alex thought of his own mother, and a bitter taste filled his mouth. "You love them, and that means a lot."

Nina told herself to remain silent. Instead, the demons had surfaced and refused to be ignored. "It won't put food on the table or provide the money for them to go to college."

"If they have half your pride and independence, they'll do just fine."

Nina nodded. "You're right. My grandmother used to say that wallowing in self-doubt never got anyone anywhere. I'm just so worried about Tommy. It's making me a little weak right now."

"Everyone has their moments of self-doubt. You and your children are going to do just fine." Silently he vowed that he'd make certain they did. He owed her extra for going along with his ploy, and he always paid his debts.

Nina felt the return of her belief that the future would be better. Startled that Alex could have such a reassuring effect on her, she studied him covertly. It was the hard set of his jaw, she decided. He looked like a man who could carry the world on his shoulders. Again she reminded herself that she wasn't looking for a man to lean on. And he wasn't looking for a woman to lean on him. Still, for the moment, she remained grateful to have him at her side. *Just don't get used to it,* she cautioned herself.

Definitely don't get used to it, she repeated the next morning as the limousine his grandfather had sent to Grand Springs to drive them to Denver wove its way up the long, tree-lined drive to the huge manor house of William Bennett's estate. Alex Bennett and his family were way out of her league.

"Nice little place your grandfather has here," Helen Lindstrom remarked.

Nina glanced toward her mother-in-law. The woman's hand had gone up to her once blond, now mostly white hair to nervously pat it into place. From there it traveled to smooth the skirt of her inexpensive dress, while a pink flush of anxiousness gave added color to her softly rounded cheeks.

"I want you to feel at home here," Alex said firmly. "Matilda knows everything, and she's looking forward to your stay. As for my grandfather, he's a manipulator who needs to be taught a lesson, but he's got a good heart. He'll treat you well."

"Yes, sure," Helen muttered, the uneasiness in her eyes growing by the moment.

"Think of it as a once-in-a-lifetime adventure," Nina suggested, speaking aloud the ploy she'd been using to keep her courage up.

Helen nodded, but didn't look convinced.

As the limousine came to a stop in front of the house—a huge stone structure, three stories in the center with two-story wings on either side—Nina experienced the urge to call the whole thing off. Then she looked at Tommy, and her back stiffened with resolve. William Bennett had more money than she did, but that didn't make him any better than her or her family.

The front door opened as the chauffeur, who had been introduced merely as John, came around and opened the door for his passengers. A tall, slender man in a black suit came out of the house and descended the wide marble steps. He looked to be in his late fifties or early sixties, and his expression was staid.

Reaching the group exiting the limousine, he said with deference, his English accent adding even more stiff formality to his words, "Good morning, Mr. Alex." Then, turning his attention to the others, he added, "Mr. William extends his greetings and apologizes for not being able to welcome you in person.''

Nina noticed Helen's uneasiness growing stronger. She, herself, didn't think she'd ever heard a greeting issued with such lack of emotion.

"Nina, Mrs. Lindstrom, children, this is Charles, my grandfather's butler.'' Alex knew he should have warned them about Charles. But he hadn't wanted to give Nina or her mother-in-law any reason to change their minds about coming. Besides, he was counting on Matilda to counter any adverse effects Charles was having on them.

If this was what Alex Bennett thought being made welcome was supposed to feel like, he had very peculiar notions, Nina thought acidly. Experiencing the sensation of being watched, she looked upward and saw an elderly man standing at one of the windows in the west wing. Immediately, he stepped back into the shadows, giving the impression he hadn't wanted to be seen. *The manipulative grandfather,* she mused. Well, if the rest of the household was anything like Charles, Alex Bennett was going to have to find another way to teach the old gentleman a lesson.

"Mr. Alex.'' A woman's voice called out a greeting, drawing Nina's attention back to the others.

She looked past the formidable butler to see a short, plump woman in a flowery dress descending the steps.

Alex stepped aside so that the woman could have a full view of the arrivals. ''And this is Matilda, my grandfather's housekeeper. If you should require anything, just ask her.''

Matilda smiled as she joined them. ''Welcome.''

The honest warmth on the housekeeper's face eased Nina's uneasiness some. ''Thank you,'' she said, while the children continued to stare dubiously at Charles.

Matilda scowled at the butler. ''I've told you a dozen times not to scare our guests. It's acceptable to smile once in a while. You're going to get cross-eyed staring down your nose like that."

The man turned his gaze on her. "When I was hired, I was told that Mr. William wanted a proper English butler. My family has butlered in titled households throughout England and Europe, and I can assure you that any display of emotions is not proper behavior."

Matilda's frowned darkened. "You can help John with the luggage. I'll show our guests to their rooms."

"Yes, madam," he said sharply, and moved with elegant dignity to where the chauffeur was unloading the suitcases from the trunk.

"I don't understand why your grandfather hired that man," Matilda snapped.

Alex grinned. "Because he wanted someone here who irritated you more than he did."

"Well, he certainly got that."

"It's been a long morning," Alex said, interrupting any further complaining the housekeeper was considering. "And Nina will want to satisfy herself that her mother-in-law, Elizabeth and Pete are properly settled in before she and I leave for the hospital with Tommy." He glanced at his watch. "We're due there at three."

Matilda jerked her attention back to Nina and the others. "I shouldn't have let myself get distracted." Her gaze shifted past Nina's shoulder to where the butler and chauffeur stood with the luggage in hand. "But that man has been here five years now. You'd think he'd learn to relax a little," she added, loud enough for Charles to hear.

Nina glanced back to see that the butler continued to show no reaction.

"Maybe he is relaxed. Now, shall we go inside?" Alex said more forcefully.

"I just didn't want him scaring the children or making

the two Mrs. Lindstroms feel unwelcome," Matilda grumbled, leading the way.

As they started up the steps, Tommy swayed, and Nina's hold on his hand tightened. She intended to pick him up once he was steadied, but Alex scooped him up instead. Reading the protest in Nina's eyes, he said in lowered tones, "You've got your hands full with Pete and your mother-in-law."

Nina noticed that while Elizabeth had fallen into step behind Matilda, Helen was standing immobile, staring up at the house. "Come along," Nina coaxed, lifting Pete into her arms. Giving her mother-in-law a nudge, she added in hushed tones, "Think of all you'll have to tell your friends back home."

"Matilda seems friendly enough," Helen conceded, following Nina's lead and continuing into the house.

The interior was as grand as the exterior, Nina noted as they passed through the huge entrance hall on their way to the stairs leading to the second floor. At the second-floor landing, they took a turn to the right and headed down a corridor into the right wing of the house. Matilda stopped at the third door on their left. "Mr. Alex said he thought everyone would be more comfortable if the children were near their grandmother. So I thought she and Elizabeth could sleep in here. There are twin beds." She'd entered the room as she spoke. Crossing to a door to her right, she motioned toward the interior of the room it opened into.

Nina saw a second, smaller bedroom. A personal maid's room for one of their more elite guests, she assumed.

"Pete can sleep in here," Matilda was saying. With a wave of her arm, she indicated a door on the opposite wall. "That's the bathroom."

"It's lovely," Helen said, slightly breathless, her gaze traveling over the expensive furnishings.

Matilda smiled with satisfaction. "I'm glad you like it." Her attention turned to Nina. "If you will follow me, your room is across the hall."

While Helen and the children surveyed their rooms, Nina accompanied Matilda and Alex back into the hall. Away from the others, Matilda turned to Alex. "I prepared your old room for you, as well. I assume your plan remains to stay here with Mrs. Lindstrom and her family rather than spend the nights at your residence."

Her tone had become pointed, and Nina realized that as friendly as Matilda was behaving, the housekeeper was not prepared to deal with all of them and the grandfather on her own.

"Of course I'll be staying here," Alex assured her.

Matilda nodded her approval, then returned her attention to Nina. "This is your room," she said, opening a nearby door. "As soon as you and your family have told Charles and John where to put your suitcases, and have had a moment to freshen up, we'll go down to the dining room. I was not certain as to your tastes, so I had a variety of dishes prepared for luncheon. I hope you will find it agreeable."

"I'm sure we will." Nina again wondered what in the world she was doing here. She'd worked in homes like this on special occasions, but never in her wildest dreams had she ever imagined being a guest in one.

"Nina and I will call on my grandfather before joining the rest of you in the dining room," Alex said. Noticing Charles and John waiting with the luggage a discreet distance away, he leveled his gaze on Charles. "You may set the luggage in the hall. John will see it is placed in the correct rooms. Until it's time for Nina, Tommy and I to leave for the hospital, I am placing Tommy under your care. You will treat him as if he is a crown prince whose safety lies solely in your hands."

Charles snapped to attention like a soldier being given an order. "Yes, sir."

Nina's protest died on her lips. The man reminded her of a palace guard ready to die for his king. Knowing Helen would be busy with the other two and not wanting to take Tommy in to see William Bennett, she realized that Alex's solution was a good one.

To Matilda, Alex said, "I am taking Tommy to the playroom. When you and the others are ready to dine, you can let Charles know."

Nina half expected Tommy to protest being separated from her. Instead, he continued to rest his head on Alex's shoulder and watch Charles out of one eye. She wasn't certain if he was really that comfortable with and trusting of Alex or if he was just too ill to care. Again fear for her son threatened to overwhelm her. The knowledge that he would be getting the very best of care was all that kept her from giving in to panic.

Alex glanced back at Nina. "As soon as I have Tommy settled, I'll return and we can go say a quick hello to my grandfather."

Nina wasn't ready to face William Bennett. But that was part of the bargain she'd struck. "Yes, of course."

"Shall we wait luncheon for you and Mrs. Lindstrom?" Matilda asked.

"No." Alex strode down the hall with Charles following.

For the next few moments there was a shuffling of luggage. "I'll be back in fifteen minutes to show you to the dining room, Mrs. Lindstrom," Matilda informed Helen as John left. Without waiting for a response, she too headed down the stairs.

"I don't know if I can get used to this. I'm used to waiting on myself. On the other hand, I might get too used to it and not want to leave," Helen muttered, then was given no more time to fret when Pete announced he needed to use the bathroom.

Elizabeth had already returned to the bedroom and was walking slowly around the room, making a visual inspection of its contents. "Don't touch anything that looks breakable," Nina ordered her.

"I am just looking," Elizabeth replied primly, insulted that her mother had felt the admonishment was necessary.

Nina breathed a tired sigh. Her eight-year-old daughter was more responsible than some adults. Guilt that Elizabeth had had to grow up faster than many children swept through her. It was followed by motherly pride that Elizabeth was so mature. Entering the room, she gave the girl a hug.

Returning the hug, Elizabeth patted Nina on the back. "Everything's going to be all right, Mother. I'll help Grandma with Pete, and the doctor will make Tommy well. You'll see."

"Yes. Everything is going to be all right." Nina repeated this phrase for the umpteenth time, hoping that if she said it enough, it would prove to be true.

"You'd better freshen up if you're going to," Helen said, coming out of the bathroom with Pete.

Remembering that she was to meet William Bennett, Nina quickly straightened and hurried across the hall to her room and into its adjoining bath. After using the facilities, she stood staring at herself in the mirror. Her eyes looked sunken from lack of sleep, and her features were drawn. "I don't want to scare Alex's grandfather," she murmured, applying a touch of makeup to lighten the lines of strain. It did very little good. The objective was for him to realize that she wasn't the right mate for his grandson, she reminded herself, and guessed that would not be difficult.

Leaving her room, she found Alex waiting for her in the hall. They returned to the main part of the house, then turned into the other wing. At a pair of intricately carved double wooden doors, Alex stopped and knocked.

A barked "Enter" sounded from the other side.

Alex opened the door, then stepped back to allow Nina to go in ahead of him.

She'd expected a dark, dungeonlike room cloaked in shadow. Instead, sunlight streamed in through the windows. A television set, tuned to the business channel, was on mute, its ticker-tape of the New York Stock Exchange and NASDAQ buys and sells streaming across the bottom of the screen. On the bed were the latest editions of several financial publications.

"It appears you're feeling much better," Alex said as he and Nina approached the bed.

William Bennett scowled. "You can't expect me to lie here and wait for death. Dwelling on the inevitable never did any good. It only drives people crazy. I intend to go with all my faculties intact." His gaze shifted to Nina. "You're as pretty as my grandson said. A little too skinny at the moment, but worrying about your son would do that. Matilda will see that you put some meat on those bones." His gaze narrowed on her. "Are you marrying my grandson for his money?"

For someone trying to marry off his grandson, he wasn't very diplomatic, Nina noted. "No, I'm not."

"Grandfather." Alex's voice held a sharp warning.

"Just thought I'd get that out of the way," William replied, nonplussed. His features relaxed and he smiled at Nina. "Common stock and no stranger to hard work. I like that. I'm from common stock. Started out dirt poor. Been better off if I'd married a woman from my own class. Fell in love with a debutante, instead. Figured I was one lucky man. I'd get me a wife I adored and some social standing at the same time. But she got tired of my country ways, and I got tired of her highfalutin friends. We were a real oil-and-water mix.''

Nina felt as if she should make some sort of response. ''I'm sorry your marriage didn't work out like you'd planned.''

''I just went shopping in the wrong cow pasture.'' William's smile vanished and again his gaze narrowed on her as if trying to read into her soul. ''My daddy and mama were hardworking folk. They were a team, inseparable. I'm not saying they didn't have their spats, but they loved each other. My marriage was a bad match. Alex's dad's was even worse. I made the mistake of letting his mother raise him. He got roped in by a fancy piece of goods with an impressive family lineage...claimed they came over on the Mayflower. Problem was they'd gone through all their money. She married him because she was looking for fresh cash. I'm hoping you're going to change the Bennett men's luck with wives.''

''You have an interesting way of welcoming a person into the family,'' Nina commented, finding his history of the Bennett wives interesting and his frankness startling.

''I believe in laying my cards on the table.''

''We need to eat.'' Alex slipped an arm around Nina's waist and began guiding her to the door. ''I'll speak to you again later, Grandfather,'' he added over his shoulder.

Outside the room, Nina gave him a wry look. ''If I were you, and I found a woman I really wanted to marry, I'd exchange my vows before I brought her here to meet Grandfather.''

Alex shrugged. ''It's nice to know that although he wants to see me married, he's still concerned about my making the right choice.''

"In which case, your plan to teach him a lesson should work out well."

Alex nodded. "Matilda will mention to him tonight that I've asked her a couple of times if she thinks he'll be pleased with his new granddaughter-in-law and step-great-grandchildren. Then she'll voice the worry that I might be rushing into this marriage simply to see that all of his wishes are met."

Nina stopped and faced him. "I've already warned you, but I'll say it again...I won't stand for my children being made to feel unwelcome."

"I promise you, Matilda will guard over them like a mother hen. And although my grandfather can be a difficult man, he is not a cruel one. Your children will be treated well here."

"And if Helen or I feel that they aren't, you'll move them to your place," she said, repeating his promise.

"I'll move them." She looked so worried, Alex couldn't resist pulling her into his arms. "You just concern yourself with Tommy. That's enough for you to handle right now. Leave all the rest to me, Helen and Matilda."

Nina told herself to push free. Instead, she leaned her forehead into his chest. "That's the most tempting offer I've had in a long time," she admitted, marveling at how safe she felt in his embrace.

"You obviously don't get out much," he quipped, trying not to think about how very well she fit in his arms. She was in a vulnerable state, and he'd never been the kind of man to take advantage of a woman.

"Not much." Again Nina ordered herself to push free from his embrace. This time her body obeyed. "But I can't accept your offer. My children are my responsibility."

"We're business partners, and your children are a valuable asset to our business. That makes them, for the moment at least, my responsibility, as well.''

His reminder that she was allowing her children to be pawns in his game brought a sharp pang of guilt. ''You're right about one thing. They are very valuable.'' She glanced back in the direction from which she'd come. ''And I'm not so sure I should have agreed to bring them. It was selfish of me. I know they would have been surrounded by love back in Grand Springs.''

Alex cupped her face in his hands. ''I swear to you that they will be made to feel like a little prince and princess while they're here. And you have Helen to tell you if they aren't. I've watched her with the children. She's a devoted grandmother. And I'm also certain that if Elizabeth and Pete knew they were helping their brother, as well, they would be even more pleased to be here.''

His words soothed her guilt. ''You're right.''

Not for the first time, he found himself thinking that no woman had ever looked so kissable. The urge to show her that a live man was preferable to a ghost was strong. His lips moved toward hers.

Nina knew he was going to kiss her. Panic swept through her. She wasn't ready for this. Besides, once Tommy's operation was over, they would be parting company. All Alex Bennett would ever offer her was a romantic tryst. This thought was supposed to chill her. Instead, deep inside she was tempted, and that frightened her even more.

Alex saw the panic in her eyes. *What the devil was he thinking?* If he scared her off, his plan would fail. Changing direction, he kissed the tip of her nose. ''Now, let's go get some lunch. We've got a long afternoon ahead of us.''

His brotherly manner should have been a relief. Instead, Nina experienced a twinge of disappointment. *Just think about Tommy. And remember who you are.* To give substance to this last command, she pictured herself waitressing at a fund-raiser. Alex came in with a wealthy socialite on his arm. She approached with her tray. He accepted a glass of champagne with the barest nod of recognition, then continued across the room to visit with friends. *And that's just how it will be,* she told herself. They would each go back to their own worlds and pretend their paths had never crossed.

Five

Nina sat beside her son's hospital bed, holding his hand while he slept. Just checking in had been traumatic for the six-year-old.

Standing on the other side of the bed, Alex looked down at the boy's pale face. "I wish there had been some way I could have eased his fear when they took the sample of his blood."

Nina had noticed Alex's discomfort but had thought he simply didn't like needles. Now she realized that he was honestly concerned about Tommy.

"No matter how much we want to, we can't protect children from all of life's pains," she said, repeating what she told herself every time one of her kids suffered from a cut or bruise or an unkind comment from a playmate.

Alex shrugged. "Maybe it's just as well. It's the struggles that make us strong."

"And discover who we are," she added, more to herself than to him.

Alex studied her with interest. "You sound as if you only recently made that discovery."

Nina leaned back in her chair and met his gaze. "I didn't realize it until after Tom's death. Before that, I was like a shadow of a person. Growing up, I was my father's little girl. Both my mother and I allowed him to make our decisions for us...we made little ones, but he always made the important ones. After he died, I turned to Tom and let him take care of me." She frowned introspectively. "I'm not being critical of my father or Tom. The truth is, I liked being taken care of. But it kept me from maturing. Then suddenly, overnight, I had to become an adult, responsible for three other lives."

"I'd say you've done a very good job."

Her gaze returned to Tommy and her chin trembled. "Sometimes I get really scared that I will fail them."

"As long as you do your best, you can't fault yourself."

"That's easier said than done." The tears she'd been holding back welled in her eyes. "I see him lying here like this and wonder if I couldn't have gotten him help sooner. I took him to the doctor, but maybe I should have insisted he run more tests."

Alex disliked seeing her suffer. "From what I gather both you and the doctor acted prudently."

"I know." Nina sighed shakily. "But self-doubt can be an insidious thing. I wish I could be more rocklike. Tommy needs me to be strong."

A surge of protectiveness washed through Alex. "Sometimes even a rock needs a friend to lean on."

Nina's gaze rested on his broad shoulders. "Is that an offer?"

"Yes."

She was tempted. But she reminded herself that as soon as their arrangement was completed, he would be gone like a sand castle at high tide. "I don't think that's such a good idea."

He scowled with impatience at her stubborn independence. "I'm only offering friendship. I'm not trying to take your late husband's place."

She scowled back with equal impatience. "I didn't think you were. But friends are people who, even if you don't see them for years, are always at the back of your mind.

They're people you think about and wonder how they're doing. You can pick up the phone and call them just to chat and they're happy to hear your voice. That doesn't describe our arrangement. You hired me to do a job. When it's done we'll go our separate ways. I doubt you'll be popping in for dinner or be pleased to have an evening interrupted by a call from me. So I figure it wouldn't be smart for me to begin to think of you as a friend.''

"You have a point," he conceded.

Nina again leaned back and closed her eyes.

Alex frowned at the exhaustion etched into her features. "This is a private room. I had them wheel in a spare bed so that you could rest comfortably. Why don't you lie down for a while. I'll keep an eye on Tommy."

Surprised that he intended to remain, she opened her eyes and looked up at him. "I don't expect you to baby-sit me and my son."

Alex hadn't intended to do that, either. He'd planned to get them settled, then go back to his grandfather's home and make a few business calls. Instead, he was reluctant to leave them on their own. "My grandfather would expect me to remain with you and Tommy."

The whirlwind of packing for this trip, in addition to nights of restless sleep, were taking their toll. The bed, like an oasis in the desert, was beckoning to Nina. But as her gaze returned to her son, she shoved the temptation from her mind. "Tommy is my responsibility." Easing her chair even closer to his bed, she took his hand in hers, then again sat back and closed her eyes.

"I've never encountered a more stubborn human being either male or female," Alex muttered. Nina Lindstrom was as opposite from his own mother as any woman could get. The hint of a cynical smile played at one corner of his mouth. But she could still be bought.

Going into the hall so as not to wake Tommy, he placed a business call he'd put off until now. When he hung up a few minutes later, he returned to the room and found Nina sleeping also. Rounding the bed, he began to ease her out of the chair.

"No," she protested groggily.

"You're going to lie down. You're not going to be any good to Tommy if you're exhausted and have a stiff neck to boot."

Nina was too tired to fight him. When he raised her to her feet, she leaned heavily against him like a limp rag doll, her mind in the world between wakefulness and sleep, unable to guide her movements with rational thought. As Alex lifted her into his arms, she snuggled her face into his neck. "You smell good," she murmured, inhaling the light scent of his after-shave.

Her soft breath and the feel of her body against his were arousing Alex. *This is not the right place, time or woman,* he admonished himself. Quickly, he lay her on the bed.

Nina, now more asleep than awake, felt suddenly deserted. In this dreamlike state, her mind returned to Tom's grave site. "You weren't supposed to leave me." Tears began to run down her cheeks. "I shouldn't have to be facing this alone."

Alex gently brushed a tear from her cheek. "You're not alone," he said gruffly.

"Tom?" Nina's hand captured his and pulled it to her lips. Opening her eyes, she looked up, hoping against hope that Tom was standing there and the past three years had been nothing more than a horrible nightmare.

A sharp jab of displeasure pierced Alex. *Male ego,* he told himself. No man liked being mistaken for another man. "No, it's Alex Bennett."

Meeting his cool green gaze, she abruptly released him. 'I'm sorry. I was dreaming.''

"It's all right." He stepped back, the arousal she'd wakened in him completely gone. The woman was devoted to a ghost. He pitied any man who got emotionally involved with her. No living male could compete against an idolized memory. "Now, get some sleep. As I said before, you won't do Tommy any good if you're so exhausted you can't stay awake when he really needs you."

A flush reddened her cheeks. "I sounded like a whiny wimp. It won't happen again."

"You sounded like a woman who has worried herself into a state of exhaustion," he replied. "Now, sleep."

This time she didn't argue.

Returning to his chair, Alex sat staring at Nina and her son for a long moment, then, reaching for the phone, he placed two short calls.

Nina awoke to the sound of her son's voice.

"Wow," he was saying with an enthusiasm she hadn't heard in a long time.

As she shifted into a sitting position and faced him with her legs over the side of the bed, she rubbed the sleep out of her eyes. When she could focus, she saw her son, his bed in a partial upright position, surrounded by toy versions of his favorite cartoon characters.

Alex Bennett was leaning on one of the metal guard rails on the side of Tommy's bed, grinning down at him. A pretty blond nurse stood beside him, smiling also. Nina looked out the window and saw it had grown dark outside. She glanced at the clock and realized she'd slept several hours.

A thick strand of hair that had escaped from her French braid fell forward and tickled her cheek. Tucking it behind

her ear, she slipped off the bed and joined the others a
Tommy's bedside. She bit back an admonition that Ale:
shouldn't have been so extravagant. She'd speak to hin
later. Right now, she couldn't make herself do anything tha
would take the delight out of her son's eyes.

"This is Bernadette," Alex said, introducing the young
woman in white. "I've hired a private nursing service sc
that Tommy will have around-the-clock care. Bernadette
will be on the night shift tonight."

"You have a charming son." Bernadette winked a
Tommy, and Nina saw him flush with pleasure. Clearly
he'd made a new friend.

Alex started around the bed. "And now you and I are
going to get some dinner and leave Tommy to teach Ber
nadette all about these super heroes."

"I don't think I should leave," she said, ignoring th
gnawing hunger in her stomach.

Alex had reached her. "You have to keep up your en
ergy."

"Run along, Mrs. Lindstrom. I assure you I won't leav
Tommy's side," Bernadette encouraged. She grinned at th
boy. "We're buddies. Right, Tommy?"

"I'll be okay, Mom," Tommy assured her, then quickl
began explaining to Bernadette about the figure he wa
holding.

Nina's gaze shifted to the telephone. "I should ca
Helen and find out how Elizabeth and Pete are doing."

With the expression of a man who knew he'd be fightin
a losing battle if he refused, Alex picked up the phone an
dialed his grandfather's number.

Hanging up a few minutes later, Nina regarded him wit
a frown. She definitely needed to have a talk in private wit
Mr. Alex Bennett. Leaning over the rail of Tommy's bec

she kissed her son lightly. "I'll be back very soon," she promised.

He nodded, then continued to relate the history of the figure he was holding to Bernadette.

Realizing he was happy to have a fresh audience, Nina kissed his cheek once more and then preceded Alex out of the room.

"You're angry with me," he said as they headed down the hall.

"You're spoiling my children. Helen said Matilda got a call from you. The next thing she knew, she and the children were being driven in the limousine to a huge toy store and the children were given orders to choose some toys for themselves and some for Tommy. She said she tried to keep their purchases to a minimum, but John said his orders were that they choose several items each and he insisted that they do just that."

"I'm simply playing my part." Silently, Alex confessed that he'd enjoyed hearing how much fun the children had had at the toy store. He'd felt a little like Santa Claus. Aloud, he continued in coolly impersonal tones, "My grandfather would expect me to spoil them as a way of making you and them happy. Besides, Tommy has a long day of tests ahead of him tomorrow. I figured it wouldn't hurt to take his mind off of them for a while. And Pete and Elizabeth needed a few things to keep them occupied. There aren't any children's toys in my grandfather's house."

"They brought a few things with them," Nina reminded him curtly.

"It won't harm them to have a few things more. Busy hands don't get into things they should stay out of."

Nina regarded him dryly. "You don't know much about children do you? Bribery only lasts a short time, and even the most well-behaved children have a curiosity that will get them into trouble at one time or another. At least, that has been my experience."

"I'm sure Matilda and Helen can deal with any problems that arise. In the meanwhile, my conscience is clear. I've done what I could to help."

Nina shook her head and continued to the cafeteria in silence. Nerves had caused her to eat very little today, and the smell of food reminded her stomach of how long it had been since it had received anything substantial. Hunger taking control, she concentrated on fulfilling this need.

But halfway through her entrée, she found herself covertly studying Alex Bennett. Why did his grandfather feel the need to resort to trickery to get his grandson down the aisle? She told herself that his life was none of her business. Still, her curiosity was too strong to control. "In a way, I can understand your grandfather's concern about you getting married and producing children. If you don't, what good is your wealth? You'll be comfortable during your lifetime, but why worry about increasing it? You won't have anyone you care about to leave it to."

Alex paused with a bite of dessert halfway to his mouth. "Oh, I fully intend to have heirs."

The thought that he looked like a very healthy specimen for mating crossed her mind. In the next instant, she was visualizing him in the nude and a heat kindled within her. Quickly she lowered her gaze to her plate. Having lascivious thoughts wasn't like her. She recalled that he'd had a similar effect on her before. After Tom had died, she'd thought that she'd never be attracted to another man. Obviously her hormones were becoming active again. *Bad timing. Wrong man*, she chided herself. "Your grandfather will be relieved."

"Maybe."

Nina looked at him questioningly.

"He probably won't approve of my method. In spite of both his and my father's failures at marriage, he still believes in the old-fashioned family concept."

"And you don't?"

"It revolves around love, and that is a very iffy emotion where a man and a woman are concerned. A couple meets. If the chemistry is right, primal urges are aroused. They call it romantic love, but it's nothing more than a primitive hormonal attraction. After a while, the passion dies down. If the couple is actually well suited to each other and they meet each other's needs, they may have learned to care for each other enough to overlook their mate's faults. In which case you have a successful marriage. Or they might stay together because of financial reasons, religious reasons or their children. In which case you have two unhappy people caught in a trap of their own making. Marriage is a shot in the dark, a crapshoot, a wager on a long shot. I'm not willing to take that chance."

"That's a very dour outlook on love and marriage."

"But realistic."

She shrugged, uncertain of what to say. As cynical as his description of marriage was, there was a lot of truth in it. "So if you don't believe in love and marriage, how do you plan to get your heirs?"

"I'll hire a wife for a period of time. She'll produce my heirs, then leave me to raise them. I'll see that she's well-compensated for her time."

He planned to purchase his children! Nina tried to hide her shock. "An interesting solution," she said levelly.

He raised an eyebrow. "You don't approve."

"In spite of the risks, I still think children need two loving parents."

"Your children seem to be doing quite well with only you," he countered.

"It's not easy to be both a mother and father to them." She frowned at him. "Besides, what makes you think you can find a woman who'll be willing to bear a child and then walk away?"

He gave her a dry look. "And what makes you think that would be so hard? Not all mothers are as nurturing as you. There's that preemie back in the hospital at Grand Springs, if you need an example of the other side of the coin."

"Maybe the mother realized she couldn't take care of him or was scared by the prospect of being a single mother," she argued. "It might have been difficult for her to leave her child. You can't know for certain."

He shook his head at her naiveté. "Do you always give people the benefit of the doubt?"

"I try."

"You're an innocent."

"And you're a cynic."

He shrugged. "So I've been told."

That he thought he could buy whatever he wanted caused a bitter taste in her mouth. Making it worse, she was forced to acknowledge that she was added proof that he could. Her reasons had been selfless. She'd done it for Tommy's sake. Still, she'd allowed him to buy her cooperation. "I should be getting back to Tommy," she said stiffly.

The disapproval he read in her eyes irritated him. "I'm not an ogre. I don't use or coerce people against their will. I hire them for a job, and I give them a fair price for their time."

"I know," she conceded. "I'm angry with myself for proving that you're right...that people can be bought."

Without giving him a chance to respond, she rose, picked up her tray and headed to the door.

By midafternoon the next day, Nina was totally drained. She hadn't left the hospital since Tommy's arrival there. During the night, she'd slept restlessly, woken several times by unfamiliar noises. Today she'd used all of her energy to reassure Tommy as he was being put through a battery of tests.

Now he was sleeping. The day nurse, Claudia, like Bernadette, was young. In her early twenties, Nina guessed. She had brown hair and eyes and a lively personality. She'd even managed to get Tommy to laugh a couple of times.

Nina heard the door open and saw the feminine appreciation on Claudia's face. Without even looking, she knew that Alex had arrived. He'd called several times during the morning to check on her and Tommy, but she hadn't expected him to actually stop by the hospital.

"I've come to take Mrs. Lindstrom home," he informed Claudia.

Nina remained firmly seated. "I can't leave. If Tommy wakes up, he'll expect me to be here."

Alex had approached her chair. Now he leaned forward, his hands on the arms. "Claudia will reassure him. That's her job. You need to take some time for yourself. Freshen up. Shower. Change clothes."

"I suppose I should before I begin to smell rank," Nina admitted reluctantly.

"And you need to say hello to your other children so they won't think they've been forgotten," he added.

The nagging worry about Elizabeth and Pete that had persisted at the back of her mind all morning came to the forefront. Helen had sworn that all was going well; still, Nina wanted to see for herself. "You're right." She turned to Claudia. "If he wakes and wants me, you will call the house immediately?"

"Immediately," the nurse promised. "Now, you run along and don't worry."

Nina nodded and left the room with Alex.

"I spoke to the doctor," he said as they continued down the hall. "He's made a preliminary examination of the tests. This afternoon, he'll take another, closer look. For now, he's scheduled the surgery for seven tomorrow morning."

Nina's legs threatened to weaken. "How long will it last?"

"Eight to sixteen hours, maybe more if there are complications." Alex saw her pale and slipped his arm around her waist. "He needs to proceed slowly so that he doesn't do any damage."

All she could do was nod her understanding.

During the ride back to his grandfather's estate, Alex asked her about the tests that had been conducted on Tommy. From a couple of comments he let slip, she was fairly certain he'd already covered all this material with the doctor and that he was merely making conversation to keep her from dwelling on what tomorrow would bring. But she didn't care about his motives. Talking helped, and by the time they reached the mansion, she felt in control once again.

Elizabeth and Pete came running to greet her as she entered. Kneeling on the floor, she hugged them tightly.

"Alex says that Tommy can't come home for a while, but that he's going to be just fine," Elizabeth said as her mother released her. Her intonation made this a question.

"He does have to stay at the hospital for a while, but he is going to be just fine," she replied, determined to only think positive thoughts.

"You look exhausted," Helen commented worriedly as

Nina straightened and rose. Giving her daughter-in-law a hug, she asked in hushed tones, "How is Tommy, really?"

"He's doing well," Nina assured her. "Alex has hired private nurses to watch him around the clock. He couldn't have better care."

Helen smiled gratefully at Alex. "Thank you."

Recalling the conversation in the hospital cafeteria the day before, Nina was tempted to remind her mother-on-law that he was merely living up to his part of the bargain, but now wasn't the time or place.

"Come see." Pete grabbed her hand and began pulling her down the hall.

"He's learning to build an oil rig," Elizabeth explained, falling into step beside her mother. "He and Alex spent the entire morning constructing it."

Surprised, Nina glanced over her shoulder. "I thought you'd gone into your office."

"As long as I have access to a computer and a telephone, I can run my business from wherever I choose. Right now, your family comes first."

He sounded so genuine, she would have believed he really meant that if she hadn't known he was only saying that for the servants' ears.

"Look!" Pete demanded as they entered a room with a huge wide-screen television at one end and a pool table at the other. Down at the end where the television was housed, in front of the couch and chair grouping, were a variety of toys. To one side was an authentic looking oil rig, nearly as tall as Pete.

"My grandfather had miniature replicas created of all the equipment he used in the field for drilling and pumping oil so that he could teach me how to build them. He believes in a person knowing their business from top to bottom,"

Alex explained. "This is a drilling rig. We're going to work on one of the pumps next."

Pete beamed as he pointed to the replica. "Drill oil."

"Looks like my grandson is already teaching your son how to be an oil man," an elderly male voice said from behind them.

Nina turned to discover William Bennett. He was in his pajamas and robe and leaning heavily on a cane.

"Grandfather. I thought you weren't supposed to be out of bed," Alex admonished, continuing to play the part of the grandson concerned his grandfather would die at any moment.

"Matilda told me about the young'un building on the rig and I had to see for myself. Nothing like having a bit of youthful blood in the house to give the place life. Must've rubbed off on me. I'm feeling a lot better."

"So it appears," Alex noted, fighting to keep a dry edge out of his voice.

"'Course, I ain't saying I'm ready to be doin' cart-wheels," William added hurriedly. He made his way to a chair and sat down. "But I ain't in no mood to lie up there waitin' for Death to come knocking on my door."

Fear spread over both Elizabeth and Pete's faces, and Nina realized they'd taken the elderly man's words literally.

"Death is coming here?" Elizabeth asked in horror.

"No. No, he's not," Nina said firmly.

She'd expected the children to accept her word. Instead, both Elizabeth and Pete looked to Alex for confirmation. How much they'd learned to trust the man shook her, and she hoped they weren't getting too attached to him.

"No, he's not," Alex assured them. "You're safe here."

Both children visibly relaxed but kept their distance from the old man, as if not totally sure he wasn't a friend of Death's and hadn't invited the specter for a visit.

"Can you show me how the rig works?" William asked Pete, clearly trying to take the children's minds off of the fright he'd given them.

Making a wide circle to avoid getting too near William, the four-year-old went to the structure and sat down in front of it. He looked up at Alex and, after getting a nod of approval, began to turn one of the gears.

William laughed. "Right smart little fellow."

Pride spread over Pete's face and he grinned happily.

Nina saw Elizabeth look at Alex, the hurt expression of one who felt left out on her face. She was about to place a comforting arm around the girl's shoulders when Alex turned to the child.

"I believe I heard Charles instructing you on the proper etiquette for serving tea earlier today," he said.

A smile spread over Elizabeth's face. "Yes. He told me that he thought every young lady should know how to serve a proper tea."

Alex gave her a comradely wink, then turned to Matilda who had just entered the room. "Would you see that a tea tray is prepared? While Nina freshens up, Elizabeth will practice what Charles has taught her and preside over an afternoon tea."

"Really? Could I really?" Elizabeth asked.

"I'll see what pastries Rosemary has in the kitchen and have her start some water brewing," Matilda said, already on her way to the door.

Elizabeth looked excitedly at Nina. "Will you hurry so you can join us?"

"Yes, of course," Nina replied.

As she left the room, Helen accompanied her, asking questions about Tommy. Once satisfied that her grandson was getting the best of care, Helen said, "Alex Bennett really surprised me today. He played with Pete for quite a while this morning and actually seemed to be enjoying himself. And just now when he saw Elizabeth looking left out, he made her feel important. He's good father material. Who would have thought?''

"Yes, who would have thought?" Nina muttered, not convinced that Alex's behavior wasn't all an act.

"I'd better get back," Helen said. "Alex seems to be able to control the children well, but I like to keep an eye on them, as well."

Continuing into her bedroom, Nina frowned. Tom used to play with the kids just like Alex was doing now. But Alex Bennett wasn't anything like her Tom. Alex Bennett was a cynic. "And he's only putting on a good show for his grandfather," she told herself as she shed her clothes and climbed into the shower.

Six

Nina never thought time could pass so slowly. She'd again spent the night at the hospital with Tommy. Both she and the surgeon had agreed that it would be best not to give the boy any specifics regarding the operation. All he knew was that the doctor was going to fix him and make him better. Still, he was scared, so she'd stayed to ease his mind and because she was as afraid as he was and couldn't bear to leave his side. Alex had stayed late, as well, and had arrived at the hospital early enough to see Tommy before the boy went into the operating room.

Now she sat by her son's empty bed. Trying not to dwell on what was happening to him, she studied Alex Bennett. Earlier, he'd been working at his computer. At the moment, he was standing at the window. She recalled the light, brotherly kiss he'd placed on her nose following her first meeting with William Bennett, then frowned at herself when the memory caused a curl of warmth to spread through her. He did not fit her requirements for a man she could learn to care deeply for. He scorned love and marriage. To her those were basic values that went to her core.

Alex looked at his watch. "Four hours. Only four or eight or more to go."

The phone rang, causing both of them to jump. Alex grabbed it up. He listened for a couple of moments, said "Thanks," and hung up. "That was the operating room. The nurse called to tell us that everything is going well."

"Do you think she was telling the truth?" Nina asked, fighting a rush of terror.

"Yes."

He sounded so positive, her fear subsided to a manage able level. "I should call Helen and tell her everything i going well."

Alex punched in the number and handed the receiver t her. Reassuring her mother-in-law when she wasn't at a certain of the outcome was difficult, but she forced her ton to remain positive.

"It's taking a very long time," Helen said, voicin Nina's concern.

"You wouldn't want them to rush," she replied, repea ing Alex's argument.

"You're right about that," Helen conceded. "Alex grandfather has been very generous. He's offered to arrang for the children and me to go to a fireworks display, but thought it would be best if we stayed here. I know there a cellular phone in the limousine, but I don't feel like bein out in a crowd. So he's sent John out for a few sparkle and we're going to have our own Fourth of July celebratio here."

"That sounds nice." Nina had forgotten all about th holiday. The mention of sparklers brought a flood of mem ories to the forefront of her mind. She took a couple c minutes longer to ask about Elizabeth and Pete, then ran off.

Alex watched her hang up, then stare vacantly towar the window. "What sounds nice?" he asked, wonderin what Helen had said that had triggered that faraway look

"Your grandfather has arranged for a small Fourth c July celebration at his estate." She forced her mind bac to the hospital room. "I didn't even realize it was th Fourth of July." Again the memories took control. "Whe

Tom was alive, we always went to the park for a picnic and afterward watched the fireworks.''

Alex suffered a jab of frustration. Her deceased husband seemed to be always on her mind. That she hadn't buried Tom Lindstrom and moved forward with her life was her problem, not his, he told himself. Not in the mood to listen to reminiscences about her and her former spouse, he merely nodded and returned to his computer.

Nina frowned at herself. Alex Bennett wasn't interested in her mundane life. As she had done so many times during the past three years, she sought refuge in her memories.

Normally Alex had no trouble concentrating on his work. But Nina Lindstrom was a hard woman to ignore. He saw the distant look return to her eyes and his irritation with her returned. The woman needed to bury her dead and get on with her life. *It's her choice,* he told himself curtly. Still, the urge to force her mind off of her deceased husband was too strong to resist. "Working with those toy models yesterday reminded me of a design I'd once considered but never had any time to pursue."

Jerking her mind back to the present, Nina looked at him questioningly. She'd expected him to ignore her. That he hadn't, surprised her.

You've got her attention. What now? Alex mocked himself. "Pete's very clever with his hands."

A glow of pride gave color to her cheeks. "Yes, he is." But instead of picturing her son at play with his building blocks, her gaze shifted to Alex's hands. The remembered feel of them against her skin brought back a memory that was so vivid, it was as if he was actually touching her. Startled by how strong an impression they'd left on her, she quickly jerked her attention to the computer screen.

Seeing the flicker of uneasiness cross her face, Alex wondered what had caused it. "I was surprised a child so young could actually be of so much assistance in putting the models together," he persisted.

Alex Bennett is not a man to let get under your skin, she cautioned herself. She pulled Tom's image from the back of her mind. He was the kind of man she should look for if she ever decided she wanted another man in her life. "Pete inherited his father's knack for mechanics."

Tom, again, Alex grumbled silently. Would any man ever break the bond the deceased man held over Nina? Alex doubted it but the urge to try worked its way through him. Unfortunately, he reminded himself, she'd want an emotional commitment, the kind he was determined never to feel toward any woman. Burying the urge, he returned to his computer and allowed a silence to fall between them once again.

Ten hours! Nina fought to keep the hot tears in her eyes from flooding down her cheeks. This had to be one of the longest days of her life. "What can they be doing?"

"Their best," Alex replied.

She glared at him. "It's easy for you to be patient. That isn't your child on the operating table."

His expression darkened. "This waiting isn't any easier on me than it is on you. Do you honestly think I'm so cold-blooded I don't care what happens to the small boy in there?"

The intensity of his anger startled her. "I'm sorry. It was unfair of me to lash out at you like that."

Silently Alex admonished himself. He knew she was under stress. What he hadn't realized was how strongly he'd become attached to Tommy. The image of the frail, hollow-faced six-year-old looking up at him for courage had been haunting him for the past several hours. "It's all right. We're both stressed out."

Nina's hands balled into fists. "I feel so frustrated. I want to do something to help, and there is nothing I can do."

"Just keep reminding yourself that he's getting the best care possible."

Nina nodded.

The opening of the door caused them both to jerk to attention.

"Everything is looking good," the nurse who entered said. "They're finished with the operation and are closing now. He'll be in recovery for about six hours. After that he'll be transferred to intensive care. You can see him then."

"Was the operation a success?" Nina demanded around the lump in her throat.

The nurse continued to smile reassuringly. "The doctor will be in to fill you in on the details. But don't worry. Dr. O'Conner is the best."

As the woman made a quick exit, Nina looked to Alex with panic in her eyes. "She's not telling us the truth."

That same fear was spreading through him, but he refused to give in to it. "Yes, she is." His hands closed around Nina's upper arms and his gaze locked on hers. "It's not her duty to give us the details. All she can do is relay messages from the doctor. She said everything looks good, and that's what we're going to believe until someone tells us differently."

Strength seemed to flow from his touch into her. "I needed to hear that," she said. "Thank you."

He grinned and kissed the tip of her nose. Straightening away from her, he returned to the window. That he'd been able to help her caused a rush of pleasure. Then Tommy's small, trusting face came back to haunt him and the pleasure faded. "I never realized waiting could be so difficult," he said, breaking the silence between them.

"Helen says that waiting is the hardest part of being a parent. You wait for them to be born. Then you wait for them to roll over for the first time so that you know they're getting stronger. Then there's the first step and the first tooth. Every time they reach another milestone, you feel more secure. Then there's that first day at school and you spend it worrying that they'll have trouble adjusting. They do just fine, but you've started getting white hairs. Then they learn to drive and you worry when they're late getting home."

"You don't paint a very happy picture of parenthood."

Nina's expression softened to one of motherly love. "Oh, it has its rewards. There is nothing that can compare to the thrill of seeing them take their first step or say their first word."

Alex abruptly frowned. "Not all women feel that way."

"Then, they shouldn't have children. Parenthood isn't for everyone."

"No, it's not," he agreed curtly.

The bitter edge in his voice made her certain he was thinking of his own mother. She wanted to say something soothing, but there was nothing to say. Besides, he'd made it very clear that this was not a subject he wanted to talk about.

Angry with himself for exhibiting emotion, Alex turned away from the sympathy he read in Nina's eyes. He had a good life. There was no reason for him to allow his mother's lack of the nurturing instinct to bother him.

However, he admitted grudgingly, knowing you were wanted by your mother would be nice for a child. This admission was followed by the thought that if he were looking for a woman who would be a real mother to his children, Nina Lindstrom would fit the bill. *Forget it!* he ordered himself. In the first place, he doubted she'd want any more children, and in the second, she wouldn't want any by any man other than her dear, departed husband.

The door opened, and thoughts of her grim-faced companion vanished from Nina's mind as she turned to see the doctor entering.

"Tommy came through the operation well," he said. "And I believe I got all of the tumor."

"Do you think it was malignant?" Nina asked, her mouth suddenly so dry she could barely get the words out.

"My guess is that it wasn't. But I can't say for certain until the lab has a look," Dr. O'Conner answered.

"Do you expect him to suffer any damage?" Alex asked bluntly.

"It's impossible to say for a certainty, but I'm very hopeful for a full recovery. However, the brain has sustained a trauma. As I told you before, there are no guarantees. He'll be in recovery for about six hours. After that he'll be moved to intensive care. At that time you can see him." His gaze rested on Nina. "In the meanwhile, I want you to get out of this room. Take a walk in the fresh air. Get something to eat."

"I can't leave. What if a problem arises and you need me?" she protested.

The doctor turned to Alex. "Get her out of here. I don't want her making herself sick."

"You have my cell phone number?" Alex asked. Even knowing the doctor was right, he too was finding it difficult to consider leaving.

The doctor nodded. "Go. My nurse tells me that it's a lovely evening outside."

"I can't leave," Nina protested again after the doctor was gone.

Alex saw the strain on her face and knew he had to

follow the doctor's orders. He tapped his pocket. "We'll only be a phone call away."

She could see that he was not going to give her any choice. "We should call Helen first. You talk to her. Tell her everything is going well. I'm afraid she'll hear the worry in my voice."

Alex nodded and made a quick call to his grandfather's house. Then, capturing her by the arm, he pulled her gently but firmly out of her chair and walked her out of the room and out of the hospital. They crossed the street and entered a small park. As she breathed in the fragrant summer air, her spirits lifted. "I've always loved this time of year," she said quietly.

"You look better. Some of your color is coming back," he noted with approval.

Again she felt herself drawing strength from his presence. "Thanks for being here."

"You're welcome," he said, then allowed a companionable silence to fall between them as they continued slowly through the park. How much her gratitude meant to him made him a little uneasy. *It's that "knight in shining armor" syndrome again*, he mocked himself.

Several hours later, Nina sat beside her son's bed in the intensive care unit. He was still on a respirator and heavily sedated.

"Tommy!" Dr. O'Conner was shouting loud enough to raise the dead. "Lift two fingers!"

Nina watched, her breath locked in her lungs. Nothing.

"Tommy! Lift two of your fingers!" the doctor shouted again.

Alex moved closer to the bed, staring at the boy's hand, willing it to obey.

"Tommy!" the doctor shouted again.

This time the child responded, trying to lift his whole hand.

The doctor nodded with approval, then smiled apologetically at Nina. "He's so heavily sedated, I have to speak loudly."

"Does this mean he's going to be all right?" she asked.

"It's a very good sign. Also, the tumor was not malignant and the lab tells me that we had a clean field."

"A clean field?" she demanded, suddenly worried that he was concerned about infection.

"That means I got all of the tumor. There should be no danger of it growing back."

Nina breathed a relieved sigh. "Thank you, Doctor," she said, then returned her attention to her son.

Dr. O'Conner laid a hand on her shoulder. "Children are very resilient and they heal amazingly well." Then with a farewell nod toward Alex, he left.

Alex followed Dr. O'Conner into the hall. He had some questions he wanted answered but not in front of Nina. "Does the fact that he lifted his whole hand instead of just two fingers signal the possibility of some damage?" he asked as soon as he felt they were safely where Nina could not overhear.

"Not necessarily," the doctor replied. "Any time the brain is traumatized, there can be residual effects. That he was able to respond to any extent is a good sign."

Alex thanked him and went back inside. Looking down at Tommy, he wished he could will his strength into the boy. Then his gaze turned to Nina. Worry and fear were etched deeply into her features. Feeling the need to comfort her, he said, "The worst is over."

"I hope so," she replied, knowing that she would not really believe that until she saw her son up and walking and talking.

Seven

Nina sat cross-legged on the floor of the recreation room in William Bennett's mansion watching Pete playing with one of the oil derricks he and Alex had constructed. Elizabeth was sitting on the couch, watching a video of Snow White on the huge projection-screen television.

It had been two days since the operation. Tommy was still heavily sedated and in the intensive care unit, but the doctor had assured Nina that his recovery was going well. Both the regular nurses and the private nurses Alex had hired were continuing to monitor him closely. However, she'd noticed that the hospital staff all seemed more relaxed. This, she was determined to believe, was a sign that they honestly thought her son was healing. At the moment, Helen was at the hospital with him. Nina had remained at the estate to spend time with her other children so that they would know they were also important to her.

"Tommy is going to come home, isn't he?" Elizabeth asked suddenly.

"Yes, of course he is," Nina said with conviction. She refused to think otherwise.

Elizabeth didn't look convinced. "Daddy didn't."

"That was different. Tommy is going to be just fine."

"Alex told me that, too." Relief showed on her face, signaling that her mother's confirmation of what she'd already been told was enough to satisfy her. "When will he come home?"

"Not for a while. He'll have to be in the hospital here for several more days. When it's safe to transport him, we'll take him back to the hospital in Grand Springs and he'll have to remain there for a while." Nina thought of the monstrous hospital bills Alex would be paying and wondered if he thought the price was worth what he'd purchased.

"'Morning, children. Nina."

Nina looked up to see William Bennett enter. Continuing to dress in a robe and pajamas, he was using a cane and leaning heavily on Charles's arm. Watching his slow approach, Nina wondered if he wasn't more ill than Matilda had led Alex to believe. "Should you be up?" she asked worriedly, rising to help if Charles should need it.

"Your children are an amazing source of strength," he replied, easing into a nearby wing chair, then shooing Charles away with a wave of his arm.

"William plays the banjo," Elizabeth said with enthusiasm, smiling at the elderly man.

"*Mr. Bennett* plays the banjo," Nina corrected her.

"I asked them to call me William. Makes me feel younger," William interjected.

Reminding herself that she was supposed to be blending in as if expecting to become a member of this family, Nina bit back a protest. "If that's what you prefer."

"I do." His gaze went to Pete, who was now disassembling the derrick. "Be interesting to see if the boy can put it back together," he mused. Then he turned to Elizabeth. "I was looking forward to a morning snack of some of Rosemary's famous gingerbread and milk. Shall we ring for Matilda?"

Elizabeth's eyes gleamed.

Nina noticed that William's did, as well, and in that moment, she knew without a doubt that Alex's grandfather was faking his illness. She'd seen that same look on her children's faces when they were playing at being sick to avoid doing something she wanted them to do.

"If you don't mind staying with the children, I'll go find Matilda," she said, getting to her feet. "I need to stretch my legs."

She found the housekeeper in the kitchen. After Matilda had arranged for a maid to take gingerbread and milk to the recreation room, she asked to speak to the housekeeper in private. "Alex's ploy doesn't seem to be working," she said when they were alone.

"You're right," Matilda agreed. "And I don't understand why. I know Mr. William cares very deeply for Mr. Alex. But when I tell him I'm convinced Mr. Alex is only marrying to please him, my words seem to fall on deaf ears."

A very likely reason for this had occurred to Nina. "From what I've seen of Alex, he's a man who travels his own paths. Maybe his grandfather refuses to believe that Alex would marry simply to please him."

"If that's the case, then Mr. William has his head stuck in the sand." Matilda frowned darkly. "Where anyone else is concerned, Mr. Alex cannot be induced to do something he does not want to do. But he would do anything for his grandfather, and Mr. William knows that." The frown on her face deepened. "If it were not for Mr. William, Mr. Alex would never have been born."

An uneasy curl wove through Nina. "What exactly do you mean?"

Matilda hesitated for a moment, then said, "His father died while his mother was pregnant with him. She'd only gotten pregnant to ensure her place in the family. With his father gone, she inherited his wealth. She didn't want a child, and certainly not one who would share in any inheritance. She told Mr. William as much and informed him she intended to have an abortion. Mr. William paid her to go through with the pregnancy and turn the child over to him.''

''And Alex knows this?'' Nina couldn't believe anyone would be so cruel as to tell him.

''We never wanted him to find out the details, but he did. When he was sixteen, he found out where she was and ran off to find her. She was furious. His sudden appearance caused her some embarrassment and destroyed her chances of snagging a wealthy count she was after. She'd had the man convinced she had strong maternal instincts. Anyway, in a rage she told Mr. Alex that one of the promises his grandfather had made her when she'd agreed to go through with the pregnancy was that she would never have to set eyes on her son. She also told him that she now wished she'd gone through with the abortion.''

''That explains a lot about Alex's views of marriage and motherhood,'' Nina said quietly.

Matilda nodded. ''He came home and confronted Mr. William in the library. I was there. He didn't ask me to leave. I don't think he even noticed my presence, he was so upset. So I stayed, hoping I could be of some help. It broke my heart to hear the pain in his voice when he repeated what his mother had said. Then he demanded to know if she'd told him the truth. Mr. William knew there was no way to soften the blow. He produced the papers she'd signed. I could see Mr. Alex's expression harden as he read them.

''Mr. William tried to reassure him. 'You were wanted, boy,' he said. 'Your dad wanted you and I wanted you. You've got family that loves you and that's all that matters.'

''There was a kind of deadness in Mr. Alex's eyes when

he looked up at his grandfather. It chilled me. 'Your grand-father's telling the truth,' I said. 'You're loved and wanted here. What that woman says is unimportant.'

"'You're right' he replied, then strode out of the room. The subject never came up again. But after that, I sensed a hardness about him, as if he'd closed a part of himself off." Matilda fell silent, her grim expression letting Nina know how difficult this memory was for her to relive.

"That's a terrible truth for a sixteen-year-old to face. Even an adult would have trouble facing it," Nina said.

"Yes." Matilda drew a terse breath. "His devotion to his grandfather had always been strong. Afterward, they grew even closer. That's why I don't understand why Mr. William isn't at least a little concerned about this proposed marriage. I would have sworn on a stack of Bibles that he cares more about Mr. Alex than he does about himself." She suddenly flushed. "I don't mean any insult to you or your children. They're very nice, well behaved, and if you're half as good a person as Helen has described, you would make an excellent wife for someone."

"But not for Alex," Nina finished.

"He needs a wife who loves him and not someone who sees him as a way to make her children's lives better."

So the housekeeper was worried that she would turn out to be a gold digger, after all, Nina realized. In all fairness, she couldn't blame her for this suspicion. "I have no in-tention of taking advantage of Alex."

"I'm relieved to hear that."

The motherly protectiveness Nina read on the woman's face told her that Matilda would not stand idly by and watch anyone misuse him. "I'd better get back before my children get restless and begin to cause Mr. William trou-ble."

"Maybe we should let them," Matilda suggested. "That old coot is being entirely unreasonable."

Returning to the recreation room, Nina found her daughter nibbling on gingerbread and watching her movie while Pete ignored the food and concentrated on his building. But it was the expression on William Bennett's face that caught her attention.

"You look like a man with something serious on your mind," she said, again seating herself on the floor near Pete. "Did my children misbehave while I was gone?"

Both Elizabeth and Pete looked up at her with self-righteous indignation. "We did not," Elizabeth said.

"They were the most pleasant of companions," William verified.

Both gave her an "I told you so" look and returned to their previous occupations.

William, however, continued to study Nina. "My grandson never mentioned you until very recently. I was wondering how long you've known each other."

So he wasn't as blindingly accepting of her as he wanted everyone to think, she mused. "We'd seen each other several times during the past couple of years at various functions but never really spoken." This was the truth. She didn't consider Alex thanking her for serving him to be a private conversation. It was merely a politeness, like when you bumped into a stranger on the street and said a quick apology as both of you hurried on. "Our first real encounter was early last month on the night of a storm."

"Tell me about it," William urged.

"We were both at a wedding reception. Not only did the bride not show up, but a storm had knocked out the electricity and the roads had become hazardous. There were mud slides reported and a warning issued that there could be more. The reception was officially canceled, but the food

was already paid for, so the guests were asked to remain
where it was safe and enjoy themselves. I had just gotten
a plate of food when your grandson approached and introduced himself.''

"And there was an instant attraction?''

Nina recalled looking up to see Alex standing in front
of her with two glasses of champagne. "He's a very impressive man.'' The memory continued. She remembered
the feel of Alex's arms around her when they'd danced
and how, when he'd been about to kiss her, she'd fled in
fear and confusion and found a safe, quiet corner in which
to hide until it was safe to go home. "Yes,'' she admitted,
"There was an instant attraction.'' *But it was only physical,*
she added to herself, *and there was no future in that.*

William's expression relaxed and he smiled. "Very romantic.''

Only if you believe in fairy tales, Nina corrected him
mentally. And she'd learned the hard way that fairy tale
"happily ever after'' endings were not to be counted on.

"I've never believed in long engagements. When are you
and Alex going to tie the knot?''

Clearly Alex's plan wasn't working at all, Nina noted.
Maybe she should have thrown in a few "in awe'' comments about Alex's wealth. But she hadn't been asked to
play the role of a gold digger, and she certainly didn't want
to give that impression in front of her children. "We
haven't set a date, and we won't until Tommy is better.''

Elizabeth looked at her in shock. "You and Alex are
going to get married?''

Nina experienced a rush of guilt. She hated lying to her
children. But she'd cut a bargain with Alex and she felt
honor bound to go through with it. Feeling trapped between
a rock and a hard place she said, "We were going to wait
and tell you, Pete and Tommy after Tommy was better. We

thought that him being in the hospital was enough for you to handle at the moment.''

Elizabeth smiled a very adultlike, indulgent smile. ''It's all right, Mom. Both Pete and I like Alex. Grandma does, too.''

Nina saw Pete nodding. Her guilt increased. How hurt would they be when Alex disappeared from their lives? She could handle it, she told herself. She'd seen them through the loss of their father. This charade would be over soon and Alex Bennett would be nothing more than a momentary blip in their lives. *Everything will work out just fine.*

''Will we call him Alex or Daddy after the wedding?'' Elizabeth asked. ''Peggy has a stepfather and she calls him Daddy. But Jeremy calls his stepfather by his name.''

''We can work all of that out later,'' Nina replied, her stomach knotting tighter with each deception. Hoping to stop Elizabeth's questions, she nodded toward the television screen. ''You're missing the best part of your movie.''

Immediately Elizabeth's attention returned to the screen. Pete had already gone back to concentrating on the derrick, and to Nina's relief, William seemed content to drop the subject of her and Alex and their wedding. After a final thoughtful glance in her direction, he picked up a magazine and began to page through it.

What was his grandfather up to now? Alex wondered. It was midafternoon. William had returned to his room following lunch and summoned Alex to his bedside. Matilda's presence had been requested, as well.

''I've called you both here,'' William said, ''because I want to talk to Alex about Nina and because I know you—'' he turned to Matilda ''—are as close to a mother as my grandson has ever had. You know as much or more than I do about his comings and goings, and I've never questioned the notion that you have always had his be: interests at heart.''

"I hope this means you're going to release him from an demands you've made on him recently," Matilda spoke u curtly.

Ignoring her, William returned his attention to his granc son. "I've had a man investigate your Mrs. Lindstrom, an she is exactly what she appears to be…a hardworkin widow, devoted to her children and trying to make en meet as best she can."

Alex was not surprised that his grandfather had had Nin investigated. What did surprise him was the indignation h experienced on her behalf. He didn't want Nina returnin to an environment where her neighbors whispered abor her behind her back because suspicions about her behavic had been raised by his grandfather's prying. "You had n right to invade her privacy."

"I refused to have you flimflammed like your father. Willam held up a hand to hold back any further protest "Don't worry, I gave strict instructions that the inquiry wa to be discreet. The investigator posed as a distant cousi who was passing through town and decided to look h up."

The ploy sounded okay, Alex admitted. Still, his expre: sion remained grim.

"He discovered from a particularly nosy, talkative neigł bor that you didn't appear on Nina's doorstep until just few days ago," William continued. "And this morning, sł confirmed that the two of you met only recently."

Had his grandfather finally decided to question his m(tives? Alex wondered. Was his plan working? "It's tru that I've only known her a short time."

"Matilda seems to think that your decision to marry h(was made to please me and that you're not in love wit her. And I must confess that several remarks you've made to me about her children being perfect instant great-grandchildren for me have caused me to think you might be seeking to fulfill all my wishes as quickly as possible."

"I'm very fond of Nina and her children," Alex replied, letting the absence of the word *love* speak volumes.

William grinned broadly. "I'm glad to hear that."

Alex frowned. That wasn't the response he'd expected. He'd expected his grandfather to caution him to proceed slowly and apologize for having nearly rushed him into a marriage with a woman he didn't love.

"From fondness, love can develop," William said. "In fact, it's probably a much better way to start a relationship. Lust can get in the way of reason and make a man do foolish things."

"You can't possibly want him to marry a woman he doesn't love just to please you!" Matilda snapped.

"Who's to say he isn't in love with her? We both know how cautious he is about his feelings where women are concerned," William countered. His gaze returned to Alex. "And even if you aren't, you could learn to be." His expression became stern. "I've given this a great deal of thought. Nina Lindstrom is a good woman and I like her children. Pete will make a fine oil man."

"I can't believe my ears," Matilda grumbled. "I thought you loved your grandson."

"I do." William's gaze again leveled on Alex. "I'm not asking you to continue with your plans for marriage without taking a close look at your real motives and feelings. That'd be like turning a blind man loose in a cow pasture. No telling what he'd step into. What I'm asking is that you give this union some serious thought, not for my sake, because I've decided not to die just yet, but for yours. You could do a lot worse."

"You have been looking a lot spryer than the last time I was here," Alex observed sarcastically.

"Children have a rejuvenating effect on a person," William replied. "So what are you going to do about Nina?"

Alex admitted that he was finding himself reluctant to part company with the dark-haired woman. He had no intention of ever being foolish enough to fall in love with her or any other woman. However, he'd been honest when he said he was fond of her and her children. Also, she would make a good mother to any offspring they might produce together. That would save him from having to search out a nanny. "I'll take your suggestion under advisement."

William's smile returned. "Good."

"Good for whom?" Matilda demanded.

"Good for Alex and Nina," William retorted. "He needs a wife and she needs someone who can provide some security for her and her children."

Matilda issued a disgruntled "Humph!"

"Grandfather makes a lot of sense," Alex said thoughtfully. "Successful marriages are those where the needs of each party are being met."

"You make it sound so cold, like a business merger," the housekeeper noted curtly.

"I've admitted that I'm very fond of Nina and I like her kids," he returned.

"What are you going to tell her?" she demanded.

"Women like romance," William interjected before Alex could respond. "He'll keep telling her that he's in love with her."

Ignoring him, Matilda's gaze remained locked on Alex. "I was asking you."

"I'll be honest with her."

Matilda nodded her approval. "Good. I warned her this morning I wouldn't stand by and see you taken advantage of, and the same goes for her. I know you well enough to know you can charm the fuzz off a peach when you want to."

William snorted. "You're both being fools. What harm could it do for Alex to let her continue to think he's completely smitten by her?"

"It'd be a lie," Matilda snapped back, adding pointedly, "And lies always have a way of surfacing." She cocked an eyebrow in Alex's direction.

"Matilda's right," he said. "You might as well know the whole truth. Nina Lindstrom does not believe I'm smitten by her. I met her a few weeks ago at a wedding reception. It was a short encounter, and I thought I'd put her out of my mind until you pulled your deathbed act on me."

William scowled at Matilda. "You told him."

Her shoulders squared with righteousness. "I didn't want him doing anything rash just to please you."

"Anyway," Alex continued sharply, "I found myself describing her. I went back to Grand Springs, found her and bribed her into playing my fiancée."

"Bribed her?" Disappointment spread over William's face. "I thought she was different, but I suppose all women have their price."

Although he'd cynically noted to himself that Nina could be bought just like any other woman, Alex found himself coming to her defense. "She didn't do it for herself. She did it for her children. I offered to pay for her son's medical bills and help her get solvent again. She's been out of a job since the storm."

William's smile returned. "You can't fault a mother for looking after her brood."

Matilda scowled at him. "This was all an act to teach you a lesson." Her gaze shifted to Alex. "You barely know this woman, you can't seriously be considering marryin her."

William chuckled at Alex. "Tossing my own game bac at me. Would have worked, too, if you hadn't chosen s well."

Alex rewarded this observation with a grimace, the turned to Matilda. "I do know her. You can't go throug the kind of stress she's gone through and not show you true colors."

Matilda shook her head. "Men!"

"We're just being practical," Alex said. "Grandfath and my father both approached marriage from an emotion standpoint, and look where it got them."

Matilda again shook her head. "I've got work to do, she snapped, and left.

Eight

The next evening, Nina frowned as Alex turned into an unfamiliar driveway. "Where are we going?"

"My place." He pressed a button on a remote control and the iron gates blocking their way swung open. "You've been spending the majority of your time at the hospital. When you're at my father's home, you occupy yourself with Elizabeth, Pete and Helen. I decided you and I needed some private time together."

She'd been staring at the two-story brick residence ahead of them. Gardens and a manicured lawn gave it an elegant air. The driveway ended in a circle with a fountain in the center. Now she turned to him and nervousness spread through her. "You and me? Alone?"

The reluctance he heard in her voice irritated him. He was used to women being more pleased with the thought of his company. But then, Nina Lindstrom wasn't his usual type, he reminded himself, recalling Noah's words. "Don't worry, I'm not going to turn into the big bad wolf."

Nina flushed. Of course he wasn't. In his mind, they weren't a man and a woman, they were cohorts in a scheme to teach his grandfather a lesson. Still, she felt herself stiffening. "I didn't mean to sound as if I was afraid you would. It's just been a long time since I've been alone with a man at his place. A very long time."

Alex berated himself. He didn't want her tense. "We won't be entirely alone. Unlike my grandfather, I don't keep a large staff on a daily basis, but I do have a couple, the Jensons, who live here and look after the place. Jed oversees the lawns and gardens and general maintenance. Ann functions as my housekeeper and cook.''

Relax, Nina ordered herself. She didn't want him getting the impression that she thought of him as anything other than a partner in a business arrangement. Because she didn't! Still, she discovered her hand going to her hair to work a loose strand back behind her ear.

Alex noticed the movement. Maybe she wasn't as immune to him as she wanted him to think. A smile played at the corners of his mouth as he parked and escorted her into the house.

''Good evening, Mr. Bennett.'' A slender woman with chestnut hair who looked to be in her early thirties greeted Alex. ''I have set out the drinks cart in the living room. Dinner will be on the table at seven-thirty, as requested,'' she informed him with deference, then left.

Nina noticed the woman covertly give her a quick once-over and wondered if Mrs. Jenson knew the reason she was here or if the housekeeper was wondering where in the world Alex had found his dinner companion. She suspected that most of his dates were glamorous-looking women wearing designer clothes. Having spent the morning playing with her children and the afternoon sitting beside her son's hospital bed, Nina knew she looked drawn and haggard, her discount store slacks and blouse were wrinkled, and her hair and makeup could both have used some touching up. But then, she wasn't a date.

Alex guided her into the living room. ''Make yourself comfortable,'' he said, motioning toward a plush sofa in front of a fireplace.

Sinking down into the cushions, Nina didn't think she'd

ever sat on a piece of furniture that felt so good or so luxurious.

"I thought we'd have some champagne." Alex lifted the bottle of Dom Perignon from the ice bucket and began taking off the wrappings covering the cork.

"Are we celebrating?" she asked, wondering if his grandfather had capitulated and their charade would now be ended. She told herself that if this was the case, she would be pleased. Instead, her tenseness increased. *I'm only concerned about how my children will react to Alex's quick exit from our lives,* she reasoned.

"Yes." Alex popped the cork and poured two glasses. He handed her a glass, then clicked his glass to hers. "First to Tommy's continued recovery."

Nina took a sip. *I'll definitely be glad to learn our charade is over,* she again assured herself. She didn't belong here in this fancy house, making a champagne toast with Alex Bennett. They were from two different worlds with views of life that were miles apart.

Alex clicked their glasses again. "And secondly, to the shedding of lies."

The joyous relief she wanted to feel refused to surface. Nina took a second sip and forced a smile. "Can I assume that means that your plan has worked and your grandfather has promised not to meddle in your life again?"

"He has made no promises. That would be expecting too much." Easing himself into a chair, Alex studied her reaction. Her smile, he noted, didn't reach her eyes, but then, she could be too tired for any depth of emotion. Still, it gave him hope that she wasn't as glad to have their fake engagement end as he'd thought she might be.

"Does he know the whole truth?" she asked, reasoning that she was feeling no joy because she was worried about her children and Helen being made to feel unwelcome in William's house.

"Yes."

She forced herself to her feet. "Shouldn't we move my children and Helen out of his house?"

Alex rose, gently clasped her upper arms and forced her back onto the couch. "No. He likes having them there."

Nina wasn't convinced. "Are you certain?"

"Yes." He knew her well enough to know that the best way to deal with her was to be blunt. "He thinks I could do a lot worse than marry you. And he could be right."

For a long moment, she stared at him in mute silence as the full impact of his words sunk in, then said, "You and me? Married?"

The incredulous expression on her face caused his irritation to return. "It's a thought. I've been told that most women would consider me a reasonably good catch." *That certainly sounded egotistical,* he mocked himself.

"I didn't mean to insult you," she said hurriedly. "I'm sure they would. It's just me. I'm not so sure I would ever fit in here." She made a waving motion with her arm. "We come from two very different worlds."

He read the insecurity in her eyes. "A person makes their own niche in life. You can belong here as well as anywhere else."

She had to admit that the luxury of the life he could offer was tempting. And she couldn't deny she found him attractive. But she wasn't ready to sell her soul for gold. "We don't have the same values. You don't even really believe in marriage, not the forever kind that I believe in."

Alex wanted Nina Lindstrom. He'd never felt this possessive about a woman before. It was good solid business sense that was guiding him, he reasoned. The time had come for him to have a family, and she was an excellent, practical choice to be the mother of his children...much better than his plan to hire a woman to breed for him. Her strong nurturing instincts would assure that any offspring they produced would have a mother and father who loved them. "My mind could be changed. You're a good mother, and I can see advantages to maintaining a long-term arrangement, especially where children are involved."

An alarm went off in Nina's brain. "Your children or Tom's children?" she challenged curtly.

"I would consider Elizabeth, Tommy and Pete as much mine as any children you and I might have together."

Her gaze narrowed on him. "You're honestly proposing marriage to me."

Alex shrugged. "I've always relied on my instincts, and they're telling me that my grandfather is right. We would make a good pair." Outwardly, he remained cool, businesslike. Inwardly, he felt like a teenager asking a girl out for his very first date. "We would both benefit. I'd have heirs and you'd have security for yourself and your children. Also, if you like, we can live in Grand Springs. The company owns a helicopter I can use to commute when my presence is required here."

Nina found herself fantasizing about joining him in his bed. Embers of desire began to glow with heat, and a part of her was tempted. Abruptly she reminded herself that she had three other lives for which she was responsible. From what she'd seen of Alex Bennett, he was fair, kind and trustworthy. But she'd only known him for a short while. "This is all moving too quickly for me."

A suspicion that had been nagging at the back of Alex's mind brought a scowl to his face. "I suppose you'd think you were cheating on Tom if you let yourself be touched by another man."

Her late husband's image came strongly into her mind.

"Maybe," she admitted. "I don't know. I haven't had any reason to think about that until now. Not really. Hypothetically, maybe. But that's a lot different from being faced with the real decision."

Alex refused to lose to a dead man. "You're still a young woman with a lot of years ahead of you. It's time you buried him and got on with your life."

Even Helen had suggested that, Nina recalled. There just hadn't been any time. Or, until now, any man who'd awakened the sleeping passion within her. "Yes, I suppose I should consider getting on with my life." Again she thought of her children. "But I'm not prepared to make any hasty moves. I'm more pedestrian than you. I'd known Tom all my life before we married. I knew what to expect from him. I don't really know you."

Alex mentally kicked himself for not approaching this more slowly. He knew she wasn't the kind of woman who behaved on a whim. The impatience he'd exhibited in proposing so quickly wasn't like him. Even with business deals he knew were solid, he took the time to think them out thoroughly and approach them in a manner he knew would make him the winner. "Then, we'll take some time and get to know each other." He lifted his glass to her. "To discovery."

Excitement wove through her as Nina lifted her glass in return. *Proceed with caution!* her inner voice warned, and she took heed.

A bell sounded from beyond the room.

"Dinner is being served." Alex rose and offered her his hand.

Accepting, heat trailed up her arm, and the embers that had begun to ignite earlier glowed once again. The physical attraction was definitely strong. Was she being a fool not to jump at his offer?

Alex guided her outside onto the back patio where a table had been set for a romantic dinner.

As the food was placed before them, Nina was again aware of being covertly scrutinized and wondered what Mrs. Jenson would think if she knew Nina served tables for a living, as well. Or maybe she already knew. When she left, Nina asked bluntly, "Does your housekeeper know my history?"

"All she knows is that you're someone I want to impress," Alex replied.

She looked across at his strong, handsome face. "I doubt very much that you have any trouble impressing whomever you wish."

He caught the glint of feminine admiration in her eyes and smiled. "I hope that means you're impressed."

Her gaze traveled from the table with its expensive linen tablecloth, fine china and silver candlesticks to the swimming pool that fronted the patio and the gardens that lined both, then back to her handsome, very virile dinner companion. "Yes, I'm impressed."

"This could all be your domain," he coaxed.

"You have no idea how tempting your offer is."

"Tom, again?" Alex asked, hiding a surge of angry impatience behind a cool facade.

"In a way." She again recalled her abrupt ascent into self-reliance. "After his death, I promised myself I would never rely on anyone else again."

"That's an admirable vow, but not entirely practical," Alex argued. "You have three children you're responsible for." A part of him felt like a heel again, using her children to try to influence her to do what he wished. But he was a businessman and was used to using any leverage to cut a deal.

Again the thought of being in his arms brought a warm

curl of excitement to Nina. She must be an idiot to turn down not only him but all of this opulence, she chided herself. Then, recalling a past conversation, her chin stiffened with pride. "You're right. But I hate the thought of proving to you that you can buy whatever you want, including me."

"I would never think of you as a purchase. I'd think of us as having made a business compact that was beneficial to both."

"My practical side tells me that you're making a lot of sense. But the romantic side of me refuses to believe that a marriage based on practicality alone can work. Or maybe I just don't want to believe it. I've always thought of love as being the binding glue of a family."

"Friendship can work just as well. Maybe better," Alex countered. Reaching across the table, he took her hand in his. "And I think you and I could become very good friends."

Nina was glad she was sitting. The seductive look in his eyes caused her legs to weaken, until she was certain they would not have supported her weight. "That is a possibility," she heard herself admitting. Suddenly afraid that she might let her hormones do her thinking for her, she freed her hand. "But for right now, I'd like to concentrate on eating."

Alex was certain he'd sensed her weakening, but this time he would not move too fast. "No friend would deprive another of sustenance," he said, and turned his attention to his food.

The thought that if he would learn to love her, marriage to him could prove very satisfying, crossed her mind. *But that's never going to happen,* she cautioned herself. He was too much of a cynic to let himself fall in love. And she

HOW TO VALIDATE
YOUR
EDITOR'S FREE GIFT
"THANK YOU"

1. Peel off gift seal from front cover. Place it in space provided at right. This automatically entitles you to receive four free books and a Cuddly Teddy Bear.

2. Send back this card and you'll get brand-new Silhouette Romance™ novels. These books have a cover price of $3.25 each, but they are yours to keep absolutely free.

3. There's no catch. You're under no obligation to buy anything. We charge nothing — ZERO — for your first shipment. And you don't have to make any minimum number of purchases — not even one!

4. The fact is thousands of readers enjoy receiving books by mail from the Silhouette Reader Service™ months before they're available in stores. They like the convenience of home delivery and they love our discount prices!

5. We hope that after receiving your free books you'll want to remain a subscriber. But the choice is yours — to continue or cancel, anytime at all! So why not take us up on our invitation, with no risk of any kind. You'll be glad you did!

6. Don't forget to detach your FREE BOOKMARK. And remember…just for validating your Editor's Free Gift Offer, we'll send you FIVE MORE gifts, *ABSOLUTELY FREE!*

P
FRI
S
F

YES! I have placed
in the space provided abo
books and a Cuddly Ted
no obligation to purchase
back and on the opposite

NAME

ADDRESS

CITY

Than

SILHOUETTE®

WITH OUR
COMPLIMENTS

THE EDITORS

THE SILHOUETTE READER SERVICE™: HERE'S HOW IT WORKS

Accepting free books places you under no obligation to buy anything. You may keep the books and gift and return the shipping statement marked "cancel". If you do not cancel, about a month later we will send you 6 additional novels, and bill you just $2.67 each plus 25¢ delivery per book and applicable sales tax, if any*. That's the complete price, and—compared to cover prices of $3.25 each—quite a bargain! You may cancel at any time, but if you choose to continue, every month we'll send you 6 more books, which you may either purchase at the discount price…or return to us and cancel your subscription.

*Terms and prices subject to change without notice. Sales tax applicable in N.Y.

had no intention of giving her heart away to a man who didn't want it.

For the rest of the meal, they said little except to exchange comments on the excellence of the food and pass those compliments on to Ann Jenson.

Nina had had a second glass of wine with the meal and was yawning by the time dessert was served.

"It would appear we're going to have to make this an early night," Alex observed.

"It's not the company," she assured him, finding herself wishing this evening could go on for a little longer. Immediately she chided herself. She was only asking for trouble. And as they drove back to his grandfather's place, she congratulated herself for not snapping up his offer. He'd made no romantic overtures and barely spoken since they'd left the table.

Studying the set line of his jaw, she said dryly, "Having second thoughts? I guess you didn't realize how tired a woman with three children could get by the end of a day."

Reaching over, he began to massage the back of her neck. "No. I'm not having second thoughts. I just figured you were too tired to make small talk. As for the implication that you would be too tired at the end of a day to give me the kind of time I want, if you accept my offer I intend to hire a governess to help with the children so that we can spend some quality time together."

His touch was having a destructive effect on her resolve. When he stopped to shift gears, she felt abandoned. *You barely know him,* she again reminded herself. For her children's sakes she had to be careful and go slowly. *And for my own sake, as well,* she added. She was very much an innocent where men were concerned.

Reaching his grandfather's house, Alex parked, then hurriedly exited the car. If she wanted romance he would give it to her. Nina had opened her own door and was climbing out when he reached her. In the next instant, he scooped her up into his arms. "You're much too exhausted to have to walk to your room," he said, in response to the surprise on her face.

"Really...this isn't necessary," she gasped out, her tiredness suddenly replaced by the kind of erotic thrill she hadn't experienced since Tom had been alive.

"Yes, it is. I want to prove to you what a kind and thoughtful husband I can be," he returned.

Being in his arms was awakening passion, and with it, again came the fear that this was all happening too fast. "What if my children are still up? They'll think I've been injured," she argued. "And what will Matilda and Helen think?"

"I suppose you do have your reputation to consider," he conceded. Reaching the door, he set her on her feet.

Nina breathed a shaky sigh of relief as she entered the house ahead of him. The desire he'd aroused still smoldered within her, but at least she'd escaped before the embers had become a fire.

Suddenly she was being scooped up and draped over Alex's shoulder like a bag of grain. "Put me down," she insisted, keeping her voice low.

"I cannot have you stumbling and falling on your way up the stairs. As tired as you are, the champagne and wine you had before and during dinner could easily cause you some unsteadiness."

"I am perfectly steady," she assured him.

"Hush and relax," he ordered.

A pair of legs in black, crisply creased pants appeared in her line of vision. Silently she groaned.

"Is Mrs. Lindstrom ill or injured, sir?" Charles inquired in his usual staid tones.

"You see. I told you what people would think," Nina hissed. Turning her head sideways so that she could meet Charles's gaze, she said curtly. "I am not ill or injured. Mr. Alex has, by some insane reasoning, decided that he should carry me to my room."

"She's exhausted. I didn't want her stumbling on the stairs," Alex said, nonplussed. Continuing past the butler, he added, "Good night, Charles."

"Good night, sir. Good night, Mrs. Lindstrom," Charles replied.

As the butler returned to wherever he'd come from, Nina scowled at Alex's back. "You've just destroyed my reputation!"

"This was the least romantic way I could think of for transporting you," he replied. It was not, however, the least erotic, he grumbled at himself, acutely aware of the cute shape of her buns right at his eye level. The urge to carry her into his room and see if he could make her forget Tom completely was close to overwhelming.

The embers he'd ignited earlier were flaming to life. Frantic to be freed before he guessed the effect he was having on her body, Nina said tersely, "A friend wouldn't embarrass another friend."

He heard the panic in her voice, and the worry that he had again moved too fast brought a frown to his face. Reaching the landing, he stood her up. "I just wanted to sweep you off your feet."

The fire he'd kindled within her was causing her to feel shaky. "I'm just not ready for that yet."

Reading the passion in her eyes, he smiled. "When you are, I'll be here." He cupped her face in his hands and his lips found hers.

She knew she should pull away, but she didn't want to.

Instead, the moist warmth of his mouth enticed her until she swayed against him, her body aching for his touch.

"Mom."

Nina jerked free and turned to find Elizabeth looking groggily up at her.

"I need a drink of water, and Grandma's in the kitchen with Matilda," the little girl said.

"I'll get you one," Nina replied, taking Elizabeth's hand and leading her back to her bedroom.

Elizabeth looked up at her mother thoughtfully. "Will you and Alex be getting married soon?"

"We haven't made any plans yet," Nina replied, noncommittally. Within, the fire he'd ignited raged, and she became more afraid than ever that she might let her hormones do her thinking for her—and live to regret it.

Watching them walking away, Alex smiled to himself. He knew Nina had been close to surrendering. She was ready to have a new man in her life, and he intended to be that man.

Nine

Nina rose early the next morning. Although William and Alex had informed the staff that they were to be available to her at all times, she'd been careful not to make too many demands on them. But she didn't want to face Alex this morning. He'd haunted her dreams all night, and she'd woken with him on her mind. Was her attraction to him a growing emotional attachment, or was she attracted to the security he could provide? The question tormented her. She didn't like to think she could be so mercenary. On the other hand, an emotional attachment could lead to pain. She needed time by herself to sort out her feelings and give the future some very practical thought.

Reaching the kitchen, she found Matilda sitting at the table drinking coffee and going over the household books. Rosemary was at the counter, busily combining ingredients in a large mixing bowl. To her relief, John was there, as well. His breakfast eaten, he'd pushed the dishes aside and was reading the morning paper.

"I was wondering if you'd mind taking me to the hospital right away?" she asked him.

He was instantly on his feet. "Yes, ma'am."

Rosemary turned with a worried, questioning expression on her face.

Concern spread over Matilda's features. "Is there a problem with your son?"

"No. I just want to be with him," Nina replied.

"You should have some breakfast," Rosemary scolded. "I've made some fresh scones. You can take a few along, and some jam and coffee, as well."

Before Nina could protest, Rosemary was organizing a basket of food.

A short while later, Nina sat beside Tommy's bed, the untouched basket of food on the floor beside her. He was still heavily sedated to keep him from moving around too much. Positioning her chair so that she could hold his small hand, she leaned back and closed her eyes and tried to conjure up Tom's image. Normally, especially when she was with one of her children, he came easily to her mind. But today it was Alex who appeared. She recalled him eating pizza with her children that first night in her apartment. He'd looked overwhelmed. Having observed him for several days now, she guessed that was a rare experience for him. He was a man who was used to being in control of any situation.

Now he was at ease with her children. But would he be a good father to them?

His very businesslike proposal of marriage replayed itself. It was followed by the memory of him carrying her to the house and then up the stairs. Just thinking about it caused the fires of desire to ignite. But was his playfulness merely a calculated act to break down her defenses? If she did marry him, would he take her and her children for granted...treat them like objects he'd purchased...never letting them touch his heart?

Silently she groaned. What she needed was some sort of sign, some sort of omen to guide her.

"John is waiting for you at the front door," Helen said firmly, entering the hospital room and approaching Nina.

Nina looked up in surprise.

"You've been spending too much time in this hospital. Your other children need you. And I could use the rest. I'll stay with Tommy. You go home," Helen ordered. Abruptly she turned to the private nurse. "Would you mind if I have a few words alone with my daughter-in-law before I shoo her out of here?"

The nurse smiled politely and rose. "I'll get some coffee. Let me know when you're finished."

Nina knew that look on Helen's face. It meant the woman had something very serious on her mind. "Is something wrong? Should I move you and the children out of William's house?"

"Nothing is wrong where the children or I am concerned." Helen pulled a chair over beside Nina's and seated herself. "Elizabeth told me that she saw you kissing Alex Bennett last night."

"He kissed me," Nina corrected her.

"Well, it's about time someone did. I know how deeply you loved my son. But you're a young woman. Neither Ray nor I want to see you living the rest of your life alone. Tom wouldn't have wanted that, either."

"I know," Nina replied.

Helen's jaw firmed. "And Alex Bennett would certainly be a prize catch."

"How can you be so sure?" Nina challenged.

"I've spent a lot of time with Matilda, and we've talked quite a bit. I trust her, and she says that Alex is as good a man as any woman would ever find. She says that he's got a good heart and that he's a man of his word."

Nina recalled the concern she'd seen on Alex's face while they'd waited for news of how Tommy's operation was going. Matilda was right. The man had a good heart. The problem was, he had no intention of ever letting her touch it. Needing someone to talk to, she said, "Both his father and his grandfather made bad choices of wives. He wants a marriage that is a business arrangement rather than an emotional commitment.''

Helen remained silent for a long moment, then said, ''I know this may sound crass, but you've had your great love. Perhaps a practical marriage is what you need now. I know I would rest easier at night knowing you and the children had the financial security Alex could provide. And I know you would make him a good wife. You've never short-changed anyone.''

''You could be right,'' Nina conceded.

Helen gave Nina's hand a squeeze. ''You do what you think is best for you and the children. I just wanted you to know that if you should want to marry Alex, you have my approval.''

A few minutes later, as she climbed into the back of the limousine, Nina wondered if she should think of her talk with Helen as the omen she was wishing for. She shook her head. ''Her counseling was merely that of a grand-mother wanting the best for her grandchildren,'' she con-cluded aloud.

Arriving back at the house, Nina went in search of her children. She found them by the fountain in the rose garden. Elizabeth had set Mary Beth and Sarah Jane, along with the new, so far unnamed doll Alex had bought her, on one of the white wrought-iron benches at the edge of the brick walkway surrounding the fountain.

Alex was lying on the grassy lawn between the beds of roses, and Pete was on his hands and knees nearby with an assortment of miniature cars he was driving through the grass.

Nina paused, hiding herself in a rose-covered archway before they saw her. As she watched, Pete drove his car up onto Alex's chest. Alex grinned and tickled the boy.

Pete laughed and Elizabeth looked their way.

"So, you're ticklish?" Alex said, his tone teasing Pete with the threat of another tickle.

Pete giggled as if he'd actually been touched. Then he eased up next to Alex as if inviting more playful contact. Taking his cue, Alex tickled him again. Pete giggled and tried to tickle Alex back. As Alex carefully roughhoused with the boy, Nina recalled Tom and Tommy playing this same way.

Out of the corner of her eye, she saw a movement and noticed Elizabeth was walking toward the males. "You're going to get all dirty just before lunch, and Matilda won't let you in the dining room," she warned.

"Then we'll have a picnic out here on the lawn," Alex replied, grabbing up Pete and sitting up with the boy. Reaching out, he took Elizabeth's hand in his. "Would you join us, m'lady?"

Elizabeth flushed with pleasure. "Shall I go inside and ask Matilda if it's okay?"

"Yes, do," Alex replied.

Nina was certain the warm smile on his face was genuine and that he was honestly enjoying her children's company. Was this the sign she'd hoped for? Or were her children merely a momentary diversion from work for Alex and would he bore of them after a while?

She again replayed his very businesslike proposal of marriage. Was that all she and her family were to him...objects to be purchased to satisfy his need for heirs? Or, in spite of his declaration that he intended to live his life his way, was his proposal still simply a desire to please his grandfather? Now that she knew his history, she could not discount that possibility.

She frowned at herself for looking for an easy answer. There was not going to be any omen to help her make her decision. She was going to have to make her choice strictly on her own instincts.

Seeing Elizabeth coming her way, she stepped out of her hiding place and said hello as if she'd just arrived. Elizabeth, her expression that of a person on a mission, quickly explained that she must find Matilda and hurried on.

By the time Nina looked back at Alex, she discovered that he'd set Pete back with the toy cars and was coming her way. "I hope you'll join us for our picnic," he said as he reached her.

She read the invitation in his eyes for a great deal more than a picnic, and a heated glow spread through her.

"I'm attempting to develop my parenting skills," he continued. "You can give me some pointers."

"You seem to be doing just fine on your own," she admitted, surprised by how easily her children had accepted him into their lives. But she could not help wondering if at least part of the reason he was spending time with them was simply to make a good impression on her.

Following lunch, Alex excused himself to do some work, but toward the end of the afternoon he again joined them and insisted on taking her and the children to an amusement park for the rest of the day.

Nina felt torn. Going to the amusement park would give her more opportunity to study Alex. But she hated leaving Tommy for the entire day. A call to Helen settled her dilemma.

"You go and have a good time," Helen ordered when Nina told her about Alex's invitation. "Tommy is resting peacefully and I'm enjoying having a day to just sit."

They stayed late into the evening, and by the time they returned home, Alex had to carry both children up to their rooms.

Walking behind him as he strode down the hall with one on each arm, Nina felt certain that his fondness for them was not an act or a short-lived interest. In their adjoining bedrooms, he helped Pete get into bed while she took care of Elizabeth. Then he left her so that she could have a private moment to tuck them in.

Exiting the rooms a few minutes later, Nina found him leaning against the wall across the hall, waiting for her.

"Well?" he asked.

"They're both already asleep," she replied.

"That wasn't what I was asking. You've been watching me all day as if you expect me to suddenly grow horns and a tail."

"I needed to satisfy myself that you're genuinely fond of my children."

Straightening, he cupped her face in his hands. "I am, and I'm genuinely fond of you, as well." To prove this, he found her mouth with his.

Fond of, but not in love with, she stipulated silently, determined to keep the truth firmly in the forefront of her mind. But being rational wasn't easy with his lips on hers.

Lifting his head away, he grinned down at her. "Admit it. You're fond of me, too."

"You can be very charming."

Desire flickered in the green depths of his eyes. "I'd like to charm the pants right off of you."

His hands had moved to her neck, and he was gently massaging its taut cords. Passion awoke within her again. It was followed by a surge of uncertainty. "I've never given in to pure lust, and that's all it would be between us."

"Lust can be very satisfying," he encouraged, nibbling on her earlobe.

"But how will I feel in the morning?" She could barely

think now. The fires of desire were threatening to consume her.

"You'll feel like a woman who has been sated," he promised, moving to the hollow of her neck.

Her body ached for his. But every fiber of her being rebelled against giving herself to a man when there was no emotional commitment, when lust was the pure driving force of their union. As his hands moved lower to draw her more intimately against him, she pushed away. "I can't."

Jealous rage coursed through Alex. "Tom again?" he asked icily as he freed her. *His ego was overreacting again,* he chided himself, but the bitter taste of rejection remained in his mouth.

"No. Me." She leaned against the wall for support. "I haven't felt this way since I was a teenager. I'm not a wanton person. It's difficult for me to throw caution to the wind."

Alex ordered himself to relax. "Then, marry me and you can feel comfortable about going to bed with me anytime the mood strikes us."

Yes, was on the tip of her tongue. But as her gaze traveled past him to the elegant furnishings in the hall, she bit it back. "None of this seems real," she said. "This house…your house…maids…butlers…you pursuing me. It's like a fantasy. I need to get back home, where I can think straight."

Maybe that would be a good idea, Alex thought. Her apartment would only serve to emphasize the advantages he could offer her. "The doctor has said we can move Tommy in two or three days. As soon as he gives the okay, I'll make the arrangements for him to go to Vanderbilt Memorial for the rest of his recuperation."

Nina nodded.

Tipping her face upward, Alex kissed her lightly. "I will convince you that marrying me is a wise choice."

As he walked away, Nina could still feel his touch, and the passion he'd ignited burned as hot as ever. Her inner voice called her a fool for not running after him and accepting his proposal. But as she pictured herself back in her real world, it was concern for him that held her back.

Alex was thinking only of heirs and his grandfather. But what about his friends? His social standing? What would they think of her? Would he find himself being excluded from their parties and whispered about behind his back?

"We both need a reality check before either of us pursues this marriage proposal any further," she muttered under her breath.

Ten

Two days later, Nina sank into the worn, overstuffed chair that had always been her favorite. Her apartment was empty except for herself. Elizabeth and Pete were with their grandparents. The two children and Helen had been driven back in the limousine.

Tommy had been transported by Medivac helicopter. Nina and Alex had followed in Alex's company's helicopter. Dr. Zycros, the neurologist who was to oversee Tommy's care, was waiting when they arrived. With him was Dr. Genkins, Dr. Karen Sloane and the private nurse Alex had hired. Dr. Sloane had been introduced to her as the resident who would be aiding the other doctors in monitoring Tommy's progress. Once the introductions had been completed, Dr. Zycros and Dr. Genkins dually examined Tommy with Dr. Sloane watching. Afterward, all had assured her that he was doing well. Still, she'd remained several hours by Tommy's bedside, convincing herself that he'd survived the trip from Denver to Grand Springs without any damage.

Alex had stayed for a while, then left to take care of some business matters that needed his attention.

It was after he'd gone that Dr. Sloane returned. After checking Tommy's vital signs, the woman had again assured Nina that Tommy was doing well.

"Dr. Sloane will keep a close eye on your son," the private nurse had told her after the doctor left. "She loves children, and she knows what you're going through. Her daughter was trapped in a cave by that mud slide...you know, the night of the big storm when most of the town lost its electricity.''

Nina had then remembered why Dr. Sloane's name had sounded familiar. The whole town had been holding its breath, praying for the child's rescue. Still, even knowing her son was getting the very best of care, Nina hadn't been able to leave his bedside.

Then, a short while ago, the need for some time alone had suddenly overwhelmed her. She'd left the hospital and come here. Her suitcase had been sitting in the middle of the living room floor when she arrived. The children's suitcases were at Helen's in case they needed to spend the night with their grandparents.

She'd carried her suitcase into her bedroom, but instead of unpacking, she'd left it there and come back into the living room. Now sitting in her chair, her feet propped on the coffee table, she looked around her. She'd expected to feel comfortable, relaxed, like a caterpillar snugly wrapped in its cocoon. Instead, she was restless and lonely. She pictured her children there with her. Along with them came Alex. Then the children were gone and only Alex remained. She missed him! She didn't want to, but she did.

"Well, he has been a pillar of strength for me during this ordeal." This admission forced her to face a truth she'd been avoiding. She hadn't wanted to lean on him, but he'd been there every time she needed support, and now she confessed that she'd begun to count on him. Her jaw firmed. Hadn't she learned her lesson yet? Her life was full of pillars who vanished overnight...her parents...her husband. "No more leaning," she ordered herself. She was home. Tommy was recovering. It was time for her to stand fully on her own two feet once again.

A knock sounded on the door. Any diversion to take Alex Bennett off her mind was welcome. Opening the door, she had to force a smile. Instead of the man merely being on her mind, he was on her doorstep with a huge bouquet of roses in one hand and a box of candy in the other. "I thought you had business to attend to," she said, moving aside to allow him to enter.

"I did and now it's done." He frowned at the false smile that did not reach her eyes. "Apparently I've done something to make myself unwelcome. Are you allergic to roses or chocolate or both?"

"No." Closing the door, she breathed a tired sigh. "It's not you. It's me." Leaning against the door, she met his gaze. "I came here to spend some time alone. But you refused to stay out of my mind."

Alex's frown turned to a smile. "I like that."

"Well, I don't. I realized I'd learned to lean on you, and I don't want to lean on anyone."

"Women," he muttered. For a moment he was silent, then said, "Standing totally alone can be very difficult. I know. I've done it. How about if you think of us as standing side by side? Sometimes I'll tilt in your direction and sometimes you can tilt in mine."

The image was tempting, but she forced herself to face reality. "I can understand why you're such a successful businessman. You paint an enticing picture, but you and I both know you'd never tilt in my direction. You're too firmly planted on your own two feet. As for me, I've leaned once too often on a pillar that fell. Thanks but no thanks."

Alex mentally cursed her stubbornness. In the next moment he was reminding himself that he wanted an independent woman. The most effective business arrangements were those where the parties involved developed no emotional ties, and people who leaned on each other were in danger of doing just that. "So be it. No leaning." He extended the flowers and candy toward her. "I still intend to court you and win you."

The purpose in his eyes told her that his mind was set. "I'm flattered by your attention, but I'm not convinced that I could ever really feel comfortable in your world," she said, accepting the gifts.

"I live in the same world as you," he countered, following her into the kitchen. "We breathe the same air. We stand under the same sky."

She scowled at him. "That's not what I mean."

He met her scowl with one of his own. "My friends will accept you. Those people who don't are snobs, and I've never paid any attention to them."

"You might find you have fewer friends than you think," she warned, finding a vase and filling it with water.

The phone rang, interrupting any further conversation. Fearful it was the hospital calling, Nina reached around him for the wall phone by the refrigerator.

"Nina," Gladys Cummings, the owner of a local catering service, said in a businesslike tone. "I wasn't certain if I should call. I know your son is ill, but I have a job for you. It's a week from Saturday. Nevil Rool is having a barbecue for a couple hundred of his closest friends."

"I could use the work," Nina replied, finding a pen and paper. "Where is it and when do you want me there?"

Alex watched her jotting down the details and frowned. Lifting the phone from her hand, he said, "I'm sorry, but Nina won't be available that day," and hung up before she could get the receiver away from him.

"What do you think you're doing?" she snapped. "That was my phone call, not yours. I don't intend to keep taking your money and I need that job." She reached for the phone to call Gladys back.

He blocked her with his body. "You cannot work at a party you will be attending."

Nina froze. "You can't be serious. The elite of the elite will be there."

"My invitation was at my home when I went by a little while ago. It said I could bring a guest. You're going to be that guest."

Nina backed away as if he was waving a weapon at her. "I don't think so. I've been exposed to bits and snips of those people's conversations. They talk about cars whose names I can't even pronounce, plays I've never seen and clothing designers as if they're on a first-name basis with them."

"I never thought I'd see you behaving cowardly," he admonished her.

"I'm not being cowardly. I'm being realistic. I wouldn't have a good time. You wouldn't have a good time. The only people who would enjoy themselves would be those taking snide shots behind our backs or maybe even to our faces."

"We're going. I'm going to prove to you that my friends are nice people and that snobs have no effect on me and shouldn't bother you, either."

"I'll have to wait on some of those people at other parties. That could be uncomfortable."

Closing the distance between them, Alex curled a hand behind her neck. "Not if I have my way with you." He'd wanted to kiss her ever since he'd entered the apartment, and it was taking a lot of effort not to act on that impulse.

Her legs weakened and she wanted to purr. "Stop that," she ordered, slipping free. She started to back away once again but, in the small kitchen, discovered she had gone as far as she could go. "I can't think."

"That's your whole problem. You think too much." He was a successful businessman because he knew when he had his opponent in a vulnerable state. So far he'd been treating Nina with kid gloves, backing off when he knew he had the advantage. But the time had come to stop backing off. Gently capturing her by the upper arms, he kissed her lightly on the lips, then began to feather kisses over her face. "From the first moment we met, there was a physical attraction. You know it and I know it."

He'd moved to the sensitive cords of her neck, and her blood was racing. "I've already admitted that there's a physical attraction."

"A very strong physical attraction." To prove his point, he pulled her against him and began to move his hands in a massaging motion over her back and then lower.

She felt his maleness, and the desire that had begun to smolder within her burst into flame. Her hands moved to his shoulders for support. Beneath the palms, the hard muscles of his body caused the fire to burn hotter. "Very strong." *Think!* she ordered herself. But that wasn't easy with every fiber of her being craving him.

"Marry me and we'll spend hours exploring that attraction," he cajoled. "It'll be fun."

Her breathing was becoming ragged, and she knew she was very near to agreeing to anything he asked. "But what happens when the lust dies?" she demanded, fighting to keep her thoughts rational.

He lifted his head and kissed her lips lightly. "I like you, Nina. By then, I'm sure we'll have become fast friends. Isn't that what really successful marriages migrate to? The couple becomes each other's best friend."

She forced herself to remember how different his lifestyle and his friends were from hers. "And what if it doesn't happen that way? What if you just get bored with me? Or what if I never feel comfortable in your social circle? What then?''

He returned to nuzzling her neck. ''Then we'll have enjoyed ourselves for a while and you'll have ensured your children's futures.''

She fought the urge to scream in frustration. A part of her wanted to give in to him while another part argued that she would only be inviting pain. ''You make it sound so simple.''

''It is.'' He kissed the hollow behind her ear. ''It's only when people allow their emotions to become involved that things get complicated.''

Nina was certain he was right, but she wasn't so sure she could keep her emotions from not getting involved.

Alex moved his body against hers enticingly. ''Let me prove to you just how much fun I can be,'' he coaxed, nibbling on her earlobe.

She pictured them going into the bedroom. Abruptly her body stiffened. Tom's picture was on the dresser. It would be as if he was watching. They'd be using the same bed she and Tom had used. She knew he wouldn't approve of her giving herself to a man she wasn't married to. And what if she and Alex never married? She pushed against him. ''No. Not yet. After the party, maybe. After I know if we really have a future together.''

Alex's hold on her tightened. Basic primitive needs had been aroused. He looked into her face, hoping to discover her passion was still strong in spite of her demand that they stop. What he saw was panic. If he took her now, he knew she'd never speak to him again. He drew a harsh, frustrated breath, then released her. ''All right. We'll wait until after the party.''

The hard set of his jaw told her that obeying her demand had not come easy for him. "Thank you."

He took another deep breath, willing his body to relax. "You're welcome." Inwardly, he cursed as his lust remained strong. Normally he had more control over himself. "But if I'm to keep my word, I'd better keep my distance," he said, stalking out of the kitchen.

"That," Nina murmured under her breath as he disappeared from her view, "would be a tremendous help."

Putting the flower in the vase, she noticed her hands were trembling. The passion he'd awakened still lingered. Was she being a fool not to just accept his proposal?

"And if I did and his social circle snubbed us, what then?" she asked herself through clenched teeth. "Then we'd both be miserable, and the marriage would be doomed from the start," she answered. She would wait until after the party to make any decision.

And maybe he was right. Maybe his friends wouldn't care who she was or where she'd come from. A truth caused her muscles to tense. She wanted to marry him.

"Well, I'm only human," she told the flowers in hushed tones. "And he does make a great Prince Charming."

In the living room, Alex cursed himself. He didn't like caring this much about winning a woman. They were unpredictable creatures, and Nina Lindstrom was proving to be the most unpredictable of all. He'd been certain he could buy her with the promise of security for her children.

Noah had been right about Nina. She was proving to be much more of a challenge than Alex had expected. He'd have to make certain she had a very good time at the Rools' barbecue.

In the meantime, he'd continue to court her in a gentlemanly fashion. He had planned to take her to dinner and then dancing. The dancing was out now. He only had so much control.

Instead, he'd take her, her children and her in-laws to dinner, and then, if she wanted to go back to the hospital, he'd go with her. "Keep her in sight but at a distance," he ordered himself, and headed back into the kitchen.

Eleven

Nina stood beside Tommy's bed. They had been back in Grand Springs for two days now, and, to her relief, he was growing stronger. He was frequently awake now and more alert when he was awake. His movements were still shaky, as if he hadn't totally regained control of all of his muscles, and his speech was slow, but Dr. Zycros, Dr. Genkins and Dr. Sloane had all told her Tommy was progressing as expected. At the moment, he was watching cartoons on television.

Her gaze left him and surveyed her surroundings. For a hospital room, it was unusually festive. Alex had seen to that. He'd sent two large balloon bouquets, and he'd brought Tommy several more toys. Glancing at her watch, she grimaced regretfully. "I've got to be going, sugar," she said, kissing him lightly on the cheek. "I've got a job this afternoon."

"Can I come home soon?" he asked.

"Soon," she promised, saying a prayer that this was so, then kissed him once more and left him under the watchful eye of his private nurse.

On the way down the hall, she paused at the window of the preemie nursery to look inside at Christopher, the baby who had been born and abandoned the night of the storm. Like her own son, he was growing stronger.

"Which one is yours?"

Nina glanced to her side to see a man of obvious native

American heritage standing there. Unlike many native Americans, his thick black hair was not long but cut in a semiconservative style, off his ears but hanging to his collar in the back. He was dressed in tailored slacks and a button-down shirt. His manner was polite and his smile pleasantly friendly. "My child is in a room down the hall. I just stopped to peek in at the babies for a moment."

He took a small recorder out of his pocket. "I'm Rio Redtree. I work for the *Herald*. We're doing a follow-up story on Baby Christopher."

"Have the police found the mother?" she asked, knowing she'd missed a lot of news while she was out of town.

"No."

Nina turned back to look again at the small, helpless child in the incubator. "I could never walk away from a child I bore. But I suppose there could be extenuating circumstances in Christopher's mother's case. Maybe she thought she was doing what was best for him. I hope so. I'd hate to think we've become so callous a society that we can turn away from our young and leave them to fend for themselves."

"We won't know why she did it until the police find her. And even then we may never know the truth. It's been my experience that some women do what they want without feeling any need to give an explanation for their actions."

Nina caught the hard edge in his voice, and for a moment had the impression he wasn't talking only about Baby Christopher's mother. "I suppose." The tiny life in the incubator began to cry, pulling her attention back to him. "He's so fragile," she said, watching the nurse who came to see to his needs. "What will happen to him if the mother isn't found?"

"He won't lack for a good home. The hospital administrator has received several requests from people wanting to adopt him.''

Nina smiled. "I'm glad."

Rio's manner became businesslike. "For the record..." He snapped on the recorder. "What would you tell the mother if you could speak to her?"

"I'd tell her that she has a beautiful baby boy, and that if she gave him up because she was thinking of his welfare, then she has my sympathy because I know that couldn't have been an easy choice. If she gave him up because she was too callous to care, then she still has my sympathy because someone with that cold a heart must be very unhappy."

"And your name?" Rio asked.

"Nina," she replied, choosing to remain anonymous by not giving her last name. Suddenly realizing how long she'd delayed, she added hurriedly, "I've got to get going. I'm due at a job."

"Thanks," he called out to her departing back.

Entering the elevator she turned to see him, standing ramrod straight, his mouth set in a grim line. He struck her as a man with a lot on his mind. Then the doors closed and the reporter was forgotten as she willed the machine to move swiftly.

Nina turned in at the delivery entrance of the Efrons' estate and parked in the back by the kitchen. The function at which she was waitressing was a charity tea to raise money for the children's wing of the hospital. She knew that many of the women attending would also be at the barbecue, and a part of her had been hesitant about accepting this job. But she had to work, and right now these temporary jobs were all that were available.

"I was worried. You're late," Gladys said as Nina entered the kitchen.

"I'm sorry. I stopped by the hospital to see Tommy," she apologized, tying on the ruffled white apron over her black slacks and white blouse.

"It's no spilled milk. Everything's on schedule. I've got Iris and Henry setting the tables. You can arrange the sandwiches while I work with the desserts," Gladys instructed.

Nina quickly washed her hands, then joined her employer.

"That man who said you couldn't work the Rool barbecue," Gladys said as she worked deftly, "he wouldn't have been Alex Bennett, would he?"

An uneasiness curled through Nina. She'd been so involved with Tommy, she hadn't thought about the gossips finding out about her and Alex. "How did you guess?"

Gladys paused to give her an indulgent glance. "Guess? That was no guess. I did a private dinner party the other night. The hostess's daughter volunteers as a Candy Striper at the hospital, and she mentioned that she'd noticed Alex Bennett taking a strong interest in your son Tommy and in you. She knew Alex from the country club and recognized you from the diner. It seems she and her friends used to stop in there after school."

Silently, Nina groaned.

"So?" Gladys prodded. "What's going on? How'd you manage to land such a great catch?"

"It's kind of complicated," Nina hedged. "And he's not landed."

Gladys's expression became stern. "Don't you let him take advantage of you just because he has money. Some of these wealthy people think they can buy anyone they choose and then discard them when they get bored."

Nina wondered what Gladys would think if she knew

how close she'd come to describing Alex's attitude. The description wasn't exactly correct. She knew him well enough to feel certain he didn't discard people with a backward wave of his hand. But he did think he could purchase them. "I won't," she promised.

Gladys nodded, then fell silent as the Efrons' maid entered and began to help.

Nina noticed the maid give her a quick appraisal and wondered if the news of her and Alex had reached every quarter. *No use worrying,* she told herself, and concentrated on arranging the sandwiches.

But a little later, as she wandered among the arriving guests, offering glasses of champagne, she chided herself for being so naive not to realize that Alex's movements would not go unnoticed. A tight circle had gathered in one corner of the garden. She'd offered them refreshments and was walking away when she heard her and Alex's names mentioned in hushed tones.

Her shoulders stiffened. So what if people knew. It wasn't against the law for him to be courting her.

Determined to ignore any remarks made behind her back, she refilled her tray and again began to circulate among the guests.

A tall, slender woman with exotically beautiful features snapped her fingers. "Over here." She waved Nina in her direction. "I'm dying of thirst."

Smiling politely, Nina made her way to the woman. But as she drew nearer, her smile began to feel plastic. There was a malicious gleam in the dark eyes following her progress.

"You're Nina Lindstrom, aren't you," the woman said, lifting a glass of champagne from the tray while her gaze raked over Nina in critical appraisal.

Nina's shoulders squared. "Yes."

The gleam in the woman's eyes became stronger. "I suppose Alex has to be forgiven for slumming once in a while," she said in a voice loud enough to carry for several feet.

Nina flushed scarlet.

A redhead standing in a nearby group glanced over her shoulder. "Sour grapes don't become you, sister dear. Just because he wouldn't give you the time of day doesn't give you the right to go around insulting others."

The exotic-looking woman's gaze turned hostile as it shifted to the redhead. "It's obvious Alex prefers subservient women who will answer to his every beck and call, Jocelyn, darling. An independent woman with a mind of her own intimidates him."

"Or maybe he simply prefers a woman who doesn't behave like a spoiled brat and show her claws every time she doesn't get her way," the redhead retorted.

"Veronica. Jocelyn. This is a charitable gathering, not a catfight," a distinguished, gray-haired woman admonished, approaching with a reproving frown on her face. "If the two of you don't start limiting your barb-throwing to your father's house, people are going to have to start flipping coins to determine which of you gets invited to their parties, since you cannot behave when you are both present."

Both women abruptly smiled.

"You're such a wonderful peacemaker, Clara," the exotic beauty cooed, giving the woman a hug.

"And so right," the redhead agreed, also giving her a hug. "We both apologize if we've caused any harm to your lovely party."

"I'm sure no harm has been done," Clara Efron replied, clearly satisfied that the calm had been restored.

The conversations across the lawn had ceased; now they began again. As Nina continued serving, she noticed that when she approached a group, they were talking about dress designers or the golf tournament coming up at the country club. She knew from having worked these kinds of functions before that those were signs of quickly changed topics of conversations. Many times she'd been a witness to groups gossiping about a particular person, then noticed that person close by or actually approaching them, and the group quickly changed the subject to something innocuous.

Or maybe I'm being too sensitive, she argued. Her chin held stiff with dignity, she continued to serve. But the feeling of being an insect under a microscope grew stronger. Her nerves were growing frayed when something that felt almost like a current of electricity ran through the gathering. Eyes that had been glancing covertly her way suddenly went to the back veranda as a new arrival garnered everyone's attention.

"It's Eve. She came," a woman near Nina said in lowered tones.

"I understand she's trying to meet all of her mother's obligations," her friend replied.

"She looks drained, poor thing," the woman who had identified Eve commented.

"Well, how would you feel if your mother had been murdered?" the third woman making up the trio asked dryly.

"And just when she'd finally returned to town after staying away for six years," the original speaker noted.

"Talk about peculiar happenings," the second woman muttered. "If you ask me, that storm we had the night Olivia was killed wasn't just weather patterns. There were angry spirits at work."

The other women turned back and scowled at her patronizingly. "You've gotten much too involved with that psychic stuff," the third woman admonished.

"Well you have to agree that a lot of peculiar things happened. Randi Howell disappeared from her wedding, leaving the groom standing at the altar," the second woman defended herself.

"Cold feet, nothing more," the third woman stated. "I heard from someone I consider a very reliable source that it was her mother who wanted the marriage more than Randi."

"I've heard those kinds of rumblings myself," the first woman confirmed.

"Still, it was the night of the storm that she fled and poor Olivia was murdered," the second woman argued. "And then there have been those rumors about that Hanson woman suddenly being able to predict things."

The other two cast each other a glance that said they weren't certain their friend was operating with all her faculties functioning properly. Obviously deciding to turn their conversation back to more solid ground, the third woman asked in hushed tones, "Have you heard anything about any suspects?"

"None," both of her companions responded in unison.

Nina moved away, offering champagne to the next group, glad that she was no longer the main object of gossip.

A couple of hours later, Nina breathed a sigh of relief. The tea was over and the guests were leaving. After Eve Stuart's arrival, she hadn't been aware of any further interest in herself. Still, she'd remained tense, as if waiting for the second shoe to fall. It hadn't. *I became instant old news,* she told herself, carrying a trayload of used dishes into the kitchen.

Maybe not totally old news, she corrected, coming to a halt in the doorway. Gladys was at the far end of the center counter. Clara Efron was facing her with her back toward Nina.

"I know that Ms. Lindstrom is an excellent worker and you value her highly," Clara was saying, "but you might want to consider not using her when you're catering functions in Alex Bennett's social circle. It would save her embarrassment and the host and hostess a few white hairs from worrying about trouble breaking out. I was only joking about flipping a coin to decide which of the Charleston sisters would be invited. We can't eliminate our own for the sake of a waitress."

Nina moved forward, letting the door bang loudly behind her to announce her entrance.

Clara looked over her shoulder, flushed slightly, then turned back to Gladys. "You and your staff did a lovely job today," she said, then left.

"You heard?" Gladys asked as soon as she and Nina were alone.

Nina nodded.

"Well, don't you worry. I'm sure I'll have jobs for you. Besides, you need something steady. Maybe someone will buy the diner soon."

In spite of Gladys's encouraging tone, Nina could not shake the curl of uneasiness weaving its way through her. She recalled the mention of Jessica Hanson and her supposedly newly found ability. So far, Jessica's prediction about Nina's future was not proving to be accurate.

Her jaw firmed. She'd find work and make certain that prediction did come true.

Alex's frown deepened as he listened to the woman on the other end of the line.

"I'm fairly certain Nina overheard what I said to Gladys,

and I didn't want you hearing a version that would make you angry with me," Clara Efron finished.

The implication that Nina would come to him and try to cause trouble for Clara grated on his nerves. "Nina isn't the kind of woman who would lie about an incident to gain an advantage over another person," he said curtly. "In fact, I doubt she'll even mention the incident to me."

"I didn't mean to imply that she was a troublemaker," Clara apologized quickly. Her voice took on a quality of self-righteousness. "And my advice to Gladys was for Nina's sake as well. It couldn't have been comfortable for her. You know how cutting Veronica can be."

"Yes." Alex was not a man who normally resorted to physical violence, but the urge to strangle the exotic beauty was powerful.

"And I feel I really should warn you," Clara continued. "This business with you and Ms. Lindstrom has a lot of noses out of joint. You are, after all, one of our most sought-after bachelors."

Time to play a little hardball, he decided. Vern Efron and several others had approached him about joining them in a business venture to build a resort a few miles out of town. They needed the kind of capital he could provide. "I'm planning to bring Mrs. Lindstrom to Nevil's barbecue. I hope I can count on you and your husband being gracious toward her. She will be nervous, and knowing that you accept her into our social circle will ease her mind a great deal and will make up for any hurt you may have caused her today. Your kindness to her would mean a great deal to me." A hard edge in his voice warned her that he would not be pleased if she did not obey this request. And just in case she was not aware of her husband's business dealings, he added, "You could pass this along to your husband, as well."

"Yes, of course," Clara said quickly.

He heard the underlying panic in her voice and knew she'd gotten the message. Vern, he was certain, would inform the others, who would see that their wives behaved.

"But I really feel my warning to Gladys should not be retracted," Clara said, her voice holding a plea for understanding. "If you want us to accept Nina socially, we can't have her serving us at one party and being a guest at another. That would be extremely uncomfortable for people."

"I understand," Alex assured her. "And I agree that you do have a point." Hanging up, he frowned thoughtfully. Maybe Clara's warning to Gladys wasn't such a bad thing. If Nina couldn't find enough work to support herself and her children, she might feel more inclined to accept his proposal. His frown turned to a self-mocking sneer. He was thinking like the villain in an old silent movie. But his motives weren't all self-serving, he argued in his defense. He could and would give Nina and her children a much better future than they could achieve any other way.

Twelve

Nina sat slumped in her favorite chair, her legs stretched out in front of her, her feet propped on her coffee table. It was Saturday. *The* Saturday. Elizabeth and Pete were at their grandparents and would be staying there all night. She'd spent the morning and half the afternoon at the hospital with Tommy. He was doing well, and she told herself she should be elated. Instead, she was worried and depressed.

Since the Efrons' tea party a week ago, Gladys hadn't called her for any jobs. One of the other catering services whose customers were more middle class had hired her for a bridal shower. But intermittent jobs were not going to pay the bills. During the past two days, she had, for the third time, made the rounds of every place in town that hired waitresses. Several had said they might have part-time jobs opening soon, but those didn't include benefits. However, they would help pay the bills until something permanent came along, she told herself, trying to find a bright side.

And she wasn't in dire straits yet, she added. Alex had paid her rent for the next two months. He'd also deposited money in her checking account to cover food and other necessities. An uneasiness caused her back muscles to tighten. She hated accepting his charity. He didn't think of it that way. He'd reminded her several times that part of the bargain they'd struck was that he would provide living expenses for her until she found a job. But he was spending a small fortune on Tommy and she didn't feel right about accepting more. As far as she was concerned, any monies spent on her, Elizabeth and Pete were loans that she fully intended to pay back.

Unless she married him.

This thought caused a current of excitement. Lust wasn't a good reason to marry the man, she admonished herself. And marrying for her children's sakes didn't feel right. *In the past and in some countries today, marriages are arranged for the benefit of both parties or the benefit of the families of both parties,* she argued. Still, her uneasiness increased as memories of the Efrons' tea party came back to haunt her.

Although she hadn't mentioned the overheard conversation between Gladys and Mrs. Efron, she'd told Alex about her encounter with the woman named Veronica. She'd wanted him to have fair warning about what might happen at the barbecue if he insisted on taking her.

Alex had known immediately whom she was talking about. "Veronica is only tolerated because her father is so wealthy. No one takes her seriously," he'd assured her.

Nina wasn't convinced.

Today will be a lesson in reality for one of us, she mused. This thought caused the muscles in her back to knot painfully.

Grudgingly, she admitted that it wasn't not being able to find a job that had her so worried and depressed. She'd never been afraid of hard work. She could hold down two jobs, three if she had to, until something permanent came along. And they didn't have to be waitressing jobs. She would clean houses. That was good, honest work, as well. It was the barbecue hovering over her that was causing her distress. She didn't want to be a source of embarrassment for Alex.

Trying to find some small grain of encouragement, she reminded herself that, luckily, she had the right kind of clothes to wear. Tom had loved to go out dancing to country and western music. Because of that she had a couple of pairs of nice western-cut boots and a couple of denim outfits that would be acceptable even in Alex's social circle.

She glanced at her watch. It was time to start getting ready.

A couple of hours later, as Alex led her around to the back patio of the Rools' estate, her nerves were near the breaking point.

"Alex, you're looking fit," a blond woman in her midforties greeted them loudly. "And who is your lovely date?"

"Afternoon, Rita," Alex replied. "This is Nina Lindstrom. Nina, this is Rita Rool." Silently he congratulated himself for his little talk with Clara. Nevil Rool was another of the group of businessmen who wanted his financial support, and clearly that held a great deal of sway with his wife.

"How lovely of you to come." Rita spoke in elevated tones, letting those standing nearby know she was pleased to have Nina present.

Nina smiled and thanked her, but she wasn't fooled. The woman was much too effusive. "What did you blackmail her with?" she asked in a hushed voice as she and Alex left their hostess and headed across the lawn.

Deciding that playing innocent would be best, he cocked a questioning eyebrow in her direction. "I told you, not everyone is a snob."

"I know not everyone is a snob, but I've worked at

enough of these functions to know that Mrs. Rool likes people with money or pedigree, preferably both. If you're lacking in those categories, she's generally cool.''

Realizing he was going to have to tell her something of the truth, Alex said, ''Her husband wants me to join him in a business deal. Obviously, she wants to please me.''

Clara Efron approached and extended her hand to Nina. ''I'm so glad to see you here,'' she said.

Nina saw the nervous glance the woman cast toward Alex, clearly asking if she'd behaved in a manner that would win back his good graces. ''Thank you. It's nice to see you, too,'' Nina replied.

''That was real sincere,'' Nina noted cynically as she and Alex continued toward the bar at the far end of the lawn.

''Come along. I see an old friend.'' He hooked his arm through hers, and began guiding her in a wide arc past the Jackson sisters. He knew that the two elderly spinsters, like spiders waiting for fresh prey, were preparing to give her a thorough inspection. In the past, he'd attempted to intimidate them into leaving him alone. His efforts had proved futile. He'd made big, burly men cower, but these two pink-cheeked women refused to be thwarted. They weren't snobs. However, they could be very inquisitive and blunt.

Nina saw the tall, slender May Jackson with the short, plump June Jackson following in her wake, making their way on an intercept course. ''We're not going to be able to avoid them all evening,'' she said, letting Alex know she knew what he was up to. ''I've seen them at work on other occasions. Nothing deters them.''

Groaning silently, Alex stopped and turned to the sisters. ''Good evening, ladies.''

''For a moment there, we thought you might have been trying to maneuver yourself away from us,'' May noted.

''That would be an act of futility,'' Alex returned dryly.

"If you're implying that we're nosy, you're right," June replied. "We don't make any bones about it. Someone has to keep track of what's really going on. Otherwise we'd all be mired in false gossip."

"You do, in fact, owe us your gratitude," May announced. "There was talk that Mrs. Lindstrom's youngest child was your bastard. However, we did some checking and discovered that her children seem to have all been sired by her late husband, and that you and she have only recently become acquainted."

"My late husband is most definitely the father of my children," Nina assured them tersely.

May smiled brightly. "And that is exactly what we have informed everyone."

"However, you can't blame people for talking," June interjected. She leveled her gaze on Alex. "You did suddenly appear and begin paying all of her eldest son's medical bills. If he'd looked the least bit like you, I don't believe we could have stopped the rumors."

"Alex has always had a strong philanthropic bent," Noah Howell said, joining the group. "I mentioned Nina's son to him. The boy needed delicate, expensive surgery."

Realizing that Dr. Howell, as well as several others standing nearby, had overheard the sisters, a flush of embarrassment began to build from Nina's neck upward. Although grateful to the doctor for coming to their rescue, she cynically wondered if he wanted Alex to donate to a new wing of the hospital.

"Yes, of course." May giggled happily. "I see it all now. The knight in shining armor riding to the rescue on his white charger with checkbook in hand." Her mouth formed a musing pout. "Better still…the tycoon and the waitress. What a wonderful Cinderella story."

Her sister gave her a dry look. "You and your fairy

tales." She cast her glance on Nina. "I wish you luck, my dear. Just remember that 'happily ever after' only happens in books. In the real world, there is no such thing as smooth sailing."

"You're such a spoilsport!" May complained.

"And you're such a romantic!" June snapped back.

"Better to be an optimist than a pessimist," May returned. "I'll have less wrinkles and live years longer."

"You're the one who's always saying I'm too mean to die," her sister reminded her.

May cast her a disparaging look. "I need a drink. Bourbon neat," she announced, and headed to the bar.

"A nice Scotch would taste good," June said, accompanying her.

As they left, Alex breathed a sigh of relief and turned to Noah. "Thanks, pal. Those two scare me."

The grin that passed between the two men told Nina that her cynical thoughts had been wrong. These two were close friends.

"No problem. Besides, it wasn't a total lie. I did tell you about Nina's son being tested," Noah replied.

Nina looked at Dr. Howell questioningly. "You told Alex about Tommy? Why?"

Noah's gaze shifted to Nina. "He came looking for a dark-haired, pretty woman named Nina. Since you were the only person I knew who matched his description, I told him where to find you. Apparently you were the one he was looking for."

"Yes, she was," Alex replied.

Realizing that she had remained on Alex's mind following the night of the storm caused a rush of pleasure. Curtly, Nina reminded herself of June Jackson's warning not to believe in fairytale endings. It was probably his ego. No doubt he wasn't used to women running away from him.

"Where is Amanda, your very lovely second half?" Alex changed the subject, afraid Noah might cause Nina more embarrassment by revealing that he knew of the reason Alex had sought her out.

"She had an emergency. She's supposed to join me here as soon as she's finished."

Nina noticed a woman a few feet away give her companion a hard nudge. She looked in the direction the woman was looking and saw that Hal Stuart had arrived.

Alex and Noah both followed her line of vision.

"Has Randi contacted Hal?" Alex asked, drawing their attention back to each other.

"No." Noah frowned worriedly. "As far as I know, that one short phone call I received has been the only contact from her."

Alex again glanced toward Hal Stuart. "How's he holding up? It must be difficult to have had his fiancée leave him at the altar and his mother murdered, both in the same night."

"He seems to be handling it all right. He's a little edgy but in control," Noah replied. "As acting mayor in his mother's place, he's been kept busy. And with the murder investigation going on, I don't think he's had a lot of time to dwell on my sister getting cold feet and running out on him." Noah's beeper suddenly sounded. Looking at the number, he said, "It's the hospital," and hurried off to find a phone.

Nina had continued to covertly watch Hal. "I know this isn't nice to say, especially with Hal going through all he's been going through, but Dr. Howell's sister was probably smart to have second thoughts."

Alex looked at her questioningly. "You sound as if you know something I don't."

Nina shrugged. "I don't really know Hal Stuart. Tom

did, though. They were both in the same class, three years ahead of me. Hal was president of their class and very popular with nearly everyone, except Tom. Tom never liked him. He said he didn't trust him. He said Hal would sell his own mother for a pot of gold." She suddenly flushed. "I shouldn't have said that. Tom never had any specific reason for disliking Hal. It was just a personality clash kind of thing. I'm sure Hal didn't have anything to do with his mother's death. I've seen them together. I'd swear he honestly cared about her."

Alex was frowning thoughtfully. "But if Hal can be bought, that makes the people who are trying to renew the leases for the strip mining prime suspects. Olivia was prepared to fight them tooth and nail. Now Hal will have her vote. If they can buy his allegiance, that's probably all the leverage they need."

"I suppose that is a possibility," Nina conceded. She shook her head. "It's still hard to believe she was murdered. She was a good woman. She did so much for this town. Even her opponents admired her."

Alex abruptly frowned at himself. He hadn't brought Nina here to discuss murder and mayhem. He wanted her in his arms. "The band is playing a slow melody. Would you like to dance?" Without waiting for a response, he guided her toward the wooden platform that had been placed on the lawn for a dance floor.

As they began to move to the slow melody, a possessiveness nearly overpowered him. *Such intense desire where a woman is concerned will only lead to trouble,* he warned himself. Still, he pressed his hand more firmly against her back and drew her closer.

Nina breathed in a heady whiff of his after-shave. All of her senses were awake. His hand holding hers...his hand on her back...wherever their bodies touched, the contact

was enticing her to melt against him fully. The thought of
her thighs entangled with his played through her mind and
her blood began to race. *You've got to control these wanton
fantasies,* she admonished herself.

Trying to guide her mind in other directions, she covertly
studied the other dancers, only to discover many were
watching her and Alex. Some were being discreet. Others
were open about their interest. Most seemed merely curious. But a few showed subtle signs of disapproval.

Giving in to a desire too great to deny, she leaned her
head against his chin. Being in his arms felt so right. If he
loved her, she wouldn't care what anyone thought. But he
didn't love her, she reminded herself curtly. She'd closed
her eyes. Now she opened them to catch a glimpse of the
critically raised eyebrows of the woman who was part of
the couple next to them and she stiffened.

He'd been surprised and pleased when she'd relaxed in
his arms. When her body tensed, he looked to see what had
caused the reaction and saw the critical look being cast her
way. Dire warning showed in his eyes as his gaze made
contact with the woman who was scrutinizing them in the
unfriendly manner. She cowered and quickly averted her
attention, but the damage was done. Silently he cursed as
Nina remained stiff in his arms.

"She's just angry because she had plans for me to marry
her daughter," he whispered in Nina's ear.

His warm breath teased her senses, and the thought that
she had succeeded where others had failed buoyed her spirits. *But succeeded at what?* her inner voice asked, refusing
to ignore reality. The woman's daughter would probably
have slapped him in the face and stalked away if he'd made
the same proposal to her as he had to Nina.

Leaving the dance floor, Alex guided her toward a group
he knew would be friendly. Some were friends. Others were

people with a vested interest in pleasing him. He was aware of Nina's suspicions as they were greeted warmly. It took a while, but finally, to his relief, she began to relax.

"Now that Olivia isn't around to fight the strip mining, are you going to invest a little something in it?" one of the men asked Alex when his wife finally ended her tirade about a current movie she'd thought was supposed to be a comedy but had turned out to be merely an exercise in bad taste as far as she was concerned.

"No." Recalling the conversation he and Nina had had a little earlier, he asked, "Does that question mean that you assume Hal will not continue his mother's fight?"

"Hal has a more fiscal bent than Olivia," the man replied, confirming Nina's assessment.

"Or maybe he's just had the fight knocked out of him," one of the other women suggested. The subject of their discussion was talking with a group on the far side of the lawn. Sympathy showed in the woman's eyes as she looked his way. "He has certainly been more subdued since his mother's death."

"*Nervous* would describe it better," one of the men corrected her with a scowl. "Maybe he knows why Olivia was killed and is afraid whoever did her in might come after him."

Clearly not one of Hal's supporters, Nina observed. She also realized that the woman who had shown sympathy toward Hal was the man's date, and she guessed that jealousy rather than any real truth was behind his remark.

"You'd be on edge, too, if your mother had been murdered and your fiancée had dumped you at the altar," the woman retorted.

"Maybe Randi felt she couldn't ignore all the rumors about Hal's womanizing," another female in the group said, looking pointedly at the woman who had been defending the new mayor.

A flush began on the defender's neck, working its way upward. "I need a drink," she said, and stalked off.

Her companion watched her go. "She only came," he said through clenched teeth, as if finally admitting a distasteful truth to himself, "because she was hoping to catch Stuart's eye again now that he is unattached. I should have guessed."

"I don't know what she sees in the man," the second woman soothed.

"Some women like weak-willed charmers. They bring out the mothering instincts," a third woman said with a shake of her head in the direction of the defender's departing back.

"And some men don't know when they should leave trouble alone," the defender's companion grumbled under his breath, the remark clearly addressed to himself as he watched her approach the bar. In the next instant, he bid the others a quick goodbye and headed in her direction.

"Kendal has it bad," the first woman remarked with a sad shake of her head.

Nina looked up to see Alex watching his departing friend with a dry look in his eyes. She could almost hear him silently vowing that he would never allow a woman to get that kind of hold on him.

Excusing herself a few minutes later, she went inside to use the rest room. On her way back outside, Gladys Cummings found her and drew her aside.

"I want to apologize for not calling you for jobs," the caterer said. "But it has been made clear to me by more than one of my clients that either you work at these parties or you're a guest, but you cannot be switching back and forth." A plea for understanding showed on the woman's face. "And I can understand how they feel. It's an uncomfortable situation."

Losing the work bothered Nina, but she admitted that Gladys and the people who hired her had a point. Associating herself with Alex Bennett was going to cause a few financial problems, but it was too late to worry about that now. Besides, she added a few minutes later as she left the house and saw him waiting by a pillar at the edge of the patio, she refused to regret having known him. Just looking at him gave her pleasure.

Pausing for a moment to enjoy the sight of him, hushed whispers, clearly meant not to reach her ears, were carried on a light summer breeze. "A widow with three children. I could understand if she was wealthy."

"It's either lust or love."

"Either way, he'll live to regret it. She's really rather common and only has a high school education. He needs a sophisticated wife, someone more his level."

Nina wanted to be angry, but the same thoughts had been plaguing her.

Thirteen

It was nearly midnight when Nina and Alex left the party. Sitting back in the smooth leather bucket seat of his Porsche, Nina found herself fantasizing about going home with him.

Alex was trying to concentrate on the road but couldn't. He'd been very patient. He'd courted her with flowers and candy. He'd spent evenings with her and her children when all he'd wanted to do was to get her alone. And patience hadn't gotten him anywhere. It was time to be more aggressive. He laid his hand on her knee, then slowly ran it up to about midway on her thigh. There he stopped and waited for a reaction.

Nina considered removing his hand. She knew that to leave it would be an invitation to more intimate advances. But his touch was stirring an excitement too delicious to stop. Could it do any harm, just once, to throw caution to the wind?

Noting that she had made no move to stop him, Alex moved his hand to the inside of her thigh and then upward.

A tremor of delight ran through Nina, and she allowed her legs to part and give him access. He stopped his ascent at the very top of her thigh. His hold was firm...possessive. She found herself regretting that the fabric of her jeans was between his touch and her. When he released her to downshift, she felt deserted.

Stopped at a red light, Alex looked at her. Neither had spoken since he'd begun his intimate exploration.

Nervous and uncertain what to say or do, Nina wetted her dry lips and tried to think of something clever.

"My place?" Alex asked curtly, breaking the silence.

Her throat now as dry as her lips, Nina could only nod.

He gave her thigh a squeeze.

Panic swept through her. What was she doing? They were moving again, and his hand had again returned to its intimate position, stirring the fires of passion within her. *I'm doing what I want to do,* she answered herself, and the moment of panic passed. She trusted Alex. The realization of how fully she trusted him stunned her. Sitting back, she closed her eyes and allowed the erotic pleasure he was creating to fill her senses.

"I hope you're just resting in preparation for an active night and not already bored," he said. Mentally he frowned at himself. He wasn't usually this insecure where women were concerned.

"I'm not bored."

He heard the gruff edge in her voice and smiled to himself. This night was turning out well. He'd been worried when they'd left the barbecue. There had been moments during the affair when he'd noticed that "I'd rather be anywhere but here" look in her eyes. Or maybe she was simply wishing that she was alone with him. That thought he liked. And he definitely liked the feel of her beneath his hand. He was already aroused, and he ordered his body to relax. It didn't obey.

If he moved too fast he could lose her, he warned himself, and this time his body cooperated. But just how long it would cooperate, he didn't know. They were only halfway to his home, and already he was causing a strain on his control by mentally undressing her. *Concentrate on the traffic, man!* he commanded. Again forced to release her to shift gears, he considered not returning his hand to the seductive feel of her body. But he was, after all, only human, he mused as he sought the intimacy she was so freely offering.

When they turned onto the private drive leading to his home, a fresh nervousness swept through Nina. The house was familiar to her because Alex had brought her and the children up here for a picnic dinner a couple of days ago. She'd known then that he'd wanted her to see what he could offer. But it hadn't been his home that held her attention then and it wasn't his home that held her attention now. She was constantly aware of Alex...the man who had given her the courage to believe that Tommy would recover fully and who had kept her from fleeing the barbecue when she was certain there were people there who wanted her gone.

"We're home." Alex breathed a mental sigh of relief as he parked and switched off the engine.

Home. She liked the sound of that. But as she climbed out of the car and walked toward the massive piece of architecture that fitted so well into its wooded environment, she wondered if she could ever really belong here. Alex slipped an arm around her waist, and the feeling of being enveloped in a warm blanket spread through her. *Don't think about tomorrow,* she told herself. For once she would live for the moment.

"Would you like some wine?" he offered, opening the door and allowing her to enter ahead of him.

"No wine," she replied, wanting nothing to interfere with her senses.

"No wine." He liked the fact that she didn't need any alcohol to bolster her courage. Drawing her into his arms, he sought her lips.

His possessive mouth brought every fiber of her being to life. When he left her lips to seek the hollow behind her ear, she wrapped her arms more tightly around his neck so that she could bring her body into even closer contact.

"Our clothes are much too restrictive," he muttered.

"Much," she agreed.

Scooping her up into his arms, he carried her into the bedroom. Setting her on her feet facing the bed, he seated himself on the bed and spread his legs so that she stood between them. "Take off your vest," he requested.

Nina quickly complied.

"And now the blouse."

She expected to be at least a little embarrassed. Instead, watching him watching her unbutton the buttons, she saw the arousal building in his eyes, and a womanly power began to weave its way through her. "What next?" she asked, tossing the clothing aside.

"The bra." He was having a hard time keeping his hands off of her, but he wasn't certain of his control and knew he would move too fast if he touched her.

Nina obeyed.

Alex could resist no longer. His hands on her waist, he pulled her closer and tasted the hardened nipples. He was at full arousal. Normally he had more command over his body. *I've been waiting a long time for this,* he reminded himself. She trembled beneath his lips as he began a sensuous exploration of her exposed flesh. Looking up, he saw the passion in her eyes. He would not have to move too slowly.

Nina gasped with delight as his hand sought the snap of her jeans, then worked the zipper down. When he kissed her stomach, the fires within blazed.

Alex slipped her jeans down over her hips, leaving her bikini panties for later. Her exposed curves were even more enticing than he'd imagined. Rising, he lifted her onto the bed.

He pulled off her boots and then her jeans. Next, with him nibbling along her leg as he slid them down and then off, came her panties. Her arousal was now so intense she was afraid she would explode before he could join her. Squirming away from him, she shifted into a kneeling position. Sitting back on her haunches, she said, "You are vastly overdressed."

For a moment, Alex had been afraid she'd suddenly changed her mind. Relief that she hadn't washed over him, and he began to remove his clothing.

Unable to take her eyes off of him, Nina worked the bedspread back by touch. The sheets felt crisp and cool beneath her, inviting a tryst.

Discarding his clothing, Alex watched her as she wiggled the covers from beneath her. He was aware of her gaze, but it was the movement of her hips and the way her legs parted as she eased the bedspread and then the sheets past her that came close to his undoing. It took every ounce of command not to pounce on her like a lion claiming his prey.

Nina expected to feel at least a little nervous when he was finally fully unclothed, and she did. He was intimidating but in a fascinating, erotic way. Knowing that neither of them could wait much longer, she lay back and looked up at him with a seductive expression that invited him to take possession.

Accepting the invitation, he sought her velvetness. Masculine pleasure surged through him. There had been no resistance and the fit was perfect. *She was his woman now!*

Nina had forgotten how whole the union between a man and woman could make her feel.

As their bodies began to move in rhythmic unison, she

ran her hands over his hair-roughened chest. His possession grew more fierce, letting her know that he found her touch stimulating. She raked her nails gently over the path her palms had traveled and felt a tremor run through him. The thought that she'd found a way to increase his satisfaction brought a surge of triumph.

Alex had wanted this tryst to last much longer, but everything about her felt too good.

Nina knew he was climaxing. Her own breathing grew more ragged as her body came into unison with his. Now the two of them were moving as one to a spiraling height. Reaching the summit together, they clung to each other, gasping for breath, their bodies still so stimulated they refused to relax even when they should have been sated.

Rolling onto his back, Alex carried her with him.

Lying on top of him, Nina kissed his neck then nuzzled her face into it. "That was incredible," she murmured against his skin.

"Very," he agreed. She started to slip off of him, but his hands moved to her hips and he held her there. "I like you right where you are."

She smiled at the order in his voice and relaxed, letting her body mold into his.

Alex was not used to remaining so stimulated. He should be relaxed and ready for a short nap. Instead, he began to slowly massage her back, then worked his way lower to her hips and her thighs.

Nina felt his maleness hardening again, and the need for him began to grow within her once again. She began to nibble on his shoulder, then worked her kisses up his neck and to his mouth.

A low growl of one claiming his own issued from deep within Alex as he once again took possession of her.

Nina levered herself upward and felt him grow even

more fully. Again a womanly triumph washed through her and she began to move in a slow rhythm, wanting this time to last longer than the first.

For a long while, Nina had been lying quietly watching Alex sleep. Now she shifted her gaze to the windowed wall on the far side of the room. The sun was beginning to peek over the crest of the mountains. For as far as the eye could see there was only wilderness. It was as if she and he were in a world all their own. For several minutes more, she lay very still, savoring this moment in time.

Finally, she returned her full attention to Alex. They'd had a very active night. But she didn't feel tired. Nor did she regret her actions. Her gaze traveled slowly over him, drinking in every detail of him. When she left here today, she would have only memories to keep her company.

Alex woke feeling comfortable and relaxed. Opening his eyes and seeing Nina, he smiled softly. "Good morning."

"Good morning," she replied.

He read the worried look on her face. Well, he knew how to get rid of that. "It's time to set a date. We'll make it as soon as possible. You belong here in my bed."

"I can't marry you." She knew she was making the right decision. Still, saying those words hurt like a sharp knife driven into her heart.

Anger flooded through Alex. "I suppose you woke up this morning thinking you'd betrayed Tom." He levered himself on an elbow, his gaze boring into her. "Tom's dead, and it's time you realized that."

"It's not Tom."

"Why, then?" The cynicism in his voice told her that he didn't believe her.

She looked into the cool, guarded green depths of his

eyes. "Because I've fallen in love with you. I tried not to. But this morning when I woke up, I realized I had."

Confusion replaced his anger. "Then, I don't understand why you won't marry me."

The tiny spark of hope she'd been harboring that he would confess that he felt the same about her died. "Because I would wake every morning hoping I'd broken down the barriers you've built around your heart. And I'd spend each day fearing that it would be our last together. That you'd get tired of having me around or that someone else would touch your heart and succeed where I'd failed."

"That won't happen. My word is as strong as any emotional bond."

"I know you're a man of your word. I trust you implicitly. I wouldn't be here if I didn't. But a marriage bound by duty isn't enough for me. Maybe I'm being too naive and old-fashioned, but I want a husband who loves me."

He didn't want to lose her, but he would not risk suffering the fate of his father or his grandfather. Both had been used and betrayed by the women they loved. He would not fall into that emotional trap. His gaze hardened. "You're asking too much."

Hot tears of regret burned in her eyes. "I know. Would you take me home now?"

He nodded and rose.

Neither spoke as they dressed and he drove her home. It was not an angry silence, but one of two people caught in an awkward moment and uncertain what to say to each other.

As he pulled up to the curb in front of her apartment building, she studied the hard line of his jaw. "I want to thank you for everything you've done for me and my family."

"You're welcome," he replied, reaching for the latch of his door.

"No." The word blurted out in a rush of panic. Her tears were too near the surface. She needed to get away from him as quickly as possible. "There is no need for you to see me to my door," she continued in a more controlled voice.

He considered insisting on seeing her safely inside, then decided against it. A clean break would be best. "Whatever you want."

She quickly slid out of the car and walked away without looking back.

Inside her apartment, Nina leaned against the door and allowed the streams of salty water to flow freely down her cheeks. "That was one of the hardest things I've ever done," she said, looking toward the chair that had been Tom's favorite and speaking to it as if he was sitting there.

She tried to conjure up his image to give herself strength. It refused to appear. The apartment was cold and empty.

Driving home, Alex glowered at himself. Maybe he should have lied and told her that he loved her. But those words carried too much weight. Saying them could possibly crack the shield he was determined to maintain.

"And then one day, I'd discover that all along she was still in love with her former husband and I'd been nothing more than a surrogate mate," he growled acidly.

No. Only fools fell in love and he was no fool.

A couple of hours later, Alex sat in the office in his home on the mountain. When he'd returned from dropping off Nina, he'd taken a shower and then thrown himself into his work. But in the middle of an E-mail message to his secretary in Denver, Nina and her children had come back to haunt him.

Staring out at the panoramic mountain landscape in front of him, he scowled darkly. He'd created employment problems for her that would not go away simply because he was no longer seeing her. And even if Gladys did start hiring her again, there would be awkward moments he wanted to spare her.

"Besides, she needs full-time employment with a schedule that gives her time to spend with her children," he muttered. A solution occurred to him. Quickly finishing the E-mail message to his secretary, he then turned his mind to solving Nina's employment problem. He already had the hospital sending him all of Tommy's bills. Once he had the boy's mother set up with a good job, then he could get on with his life.

Suddenly he was recalling how good she'd felt in his arms. Regret pierced deeply and his scowl darkened even more. "She would have made the perfect wife if she'd been willing to be more practical," he grumbled.

Nina sat slumped in her chair. After returning from Alex's house, she'd showered, then gone to see Tommy for a while. After that, she stopped by her in-laws' place for dinner. Helen, she could tell, was disappointed to learn that she'd broken up with Alex.

"Don't worry. I'll find a job soon," she'd assured her.

After returning to her apartment with Elizabeth and Pete, she'd played with them until it was their bedtime. Then, she'd spent a long time going through the Help Wanted section of the newspaper. There were plenty of part-time jobs she qualified for.

"I'll just work at two or three of those until something better comes along," she said, setting the paper aside. Closing her eyes, she leaned back in her chair. Immediately Alex's image filled her mind. All day, she'd been fighting thinking about him. Now she gave up the struggle and admitted that she missed him.

Both Elizabeth and Pete had missed him, too. They'd asked about him several times. She'd been unable to bring herself to tell them that he would no longer be coming around to see them. Instead, she'd chosen to ease them into his absence by telling them that he had to spend more time working.

She wanted to think of him as coldhearted. But she knew that wasn't fair. He just wasn't in love with her. She told herself not to take it personally. The man refused to fall in love with any woman. Still, the hurt lingered.

A knock on the door gave her a start. It sounded like Alex's knock. *A knock is a knock,* she told herself. Hoping it was Alex was nothing more than wishful thinking. He wouldn't be crossing her threshold again.

Opening the door, she stood frozen. She'd been wrong.

"May I come in?" Without giving her the opportunity to reply, he brushed past her.

Closing the door, she turned to face him. Had he decided to risk his heart? The seed of hope that had again formed died as she read the cool, businesslike expression on his face. He'd come with a purpose, but it wasn't to relinquish his heart. Silently she ridiculed herself and vowed never to let herself hope again.

"I realize I've placed you in a difficult position for finding a job," he said crisply. "I will not leave you and your children in a worse situation than the one I found you in."

Her shoulders straightened with pride. She would take nothing more from him. "We're not your private charity. I took care of my family before you came along and I can take care of them when you're gone."

He ignored this declaration. "I'm in the process of buying the Grand Springs Diner. I'll need a manager and I'm hiring you. You'll have a salary fitting your position and full benefits."

Certain he was buying off his conscience for having slept with her, a bitter taste entered her mouth. "You don't owe me or my children anything. And I think that the less we have to do with each other, the better."

"You're letting pride rule good judgment," he growled. "You have to consider your children. You want to provide a good life for them, don't you?"

"Of course," she snapped. "But I'm not a charity case."

"I don't think of you as one. The diner is a good business investment for me. However, I don't know the ins and outs of the restaurant business and you do. I'll expect you to make a profit."

Again the words to order him out were on the tip of her tongue, but she bit them back. He was offering her an opportunity she would never have again. With hard work, she was certain she could make the diner as profitable as it had been. Maybe even more so. Then she could repay him and give her children a decent life. "All right."

Relief spread through Alex. "I'll set up an account that will allow you to renovate the place as extensively as you wish. And I don't want you cutting corners. I've had a tour. There's a lot of water damage. In addition to redoing the floors, you will probably have to replace all of the drywall to get rid of that musty odor. Also, I want all the kitchen appliances replaced, as well. Some of them were too damaged by the lightning to make it worthwhile to repair them. What's left of the rest is too old and outdated. We'll end up spending more on repairmen over the next couple of years than it will take to replace them. When the place is ready to open, we'll arrange a major publicity campaign to get it off to a good start.''

She didn't relish the idea of working with him, but she refused to let him know how greatly he affected her. ''Fine.''

''Alex?''

Alex turned to see Pete standing at the end of the hall rubbing sleep out of his eyes. A couple of times today, he'd found himself missing the children. He told himself it was a sign that it was time to have a few of his own. Tomorrow, he'd begin seriously looking for a practical mate. Grudgingly, he admitted that finding someone as perfectly suited to his needs as Nina would be difficult. And he'd grown fond of her children... very fond. He would have enjoyed being a father to them. But he wouldn't pay Nina's price.

''You should be in bed,'' Nina said, the words coming more sharply than she'd intended.

Pete blinked and looked at her worriedly.

''I just don't want you getting overly tired,'' she added in more soothing tones.

Pete stretched his hand out toward Alex. ''Will you tuck me in?''

No matter what happened, he'd make sure Nina's children got an education and a good start in life, Alex vowed. ''Sure,'' he said, striding to the boy. Tucking Pete in would be good practice for when he had children of his own.

Nina followed a little behind as Alex accompanied Pete back to his room. From the doorway, she saw him lift her son into bed, cover him, then give his hair a playful tousle.

''Good night, little guy,'' Alex said.

''Good night, Alex,'' Pete replied, and with a smile, closed his eyes and drifted off to sleep.

''I told the children that you were going to have to spend less time with them and more time at work,'' she informed him when they were both alone again in the living room. "They've become attached to you, and I didn't want to just tell them that you wouldn't be coming around anymore. But the less you come around, the better it will be. I don't want them to become attached to someone who sees them as objects to be purchased and then discarded."

Alex scowled. "I don't think of them that way."

Mentally she kicked herself for having made such a bitter accusation. She was convinced that he really did like her children. He just didn't love her and that was still a raw nerve. "I'm sorry. That was unfair. But it would be best if you stayed away. I don't want them to begin to think they can rely on you to always be here. Once you have children of your own, you won't have time for them."

"I don't turn my back on friends, and I consider both you and your children friends. I'll always have time for them, and I'll always be available if you or they need me."

Nina breathed a frustrated sigh. "It's me," she confessed tersely. "I need time to get over the way I feel about you, time to learn to think of you as only a friend. For my sake, I'd appreciate it if you'd stay away for a while."

"You could reconsider and marry me," he suggested.

"No," she said firmly.

Driving away a few minutes later, Alex told himself her refusal was for the best. An emotional involvement, even one-sided and to his advantage, had never been in his plans. He'd always feel guilty about not being able to give her what she wanted. He did have to admit to a hollow feeling inside. That, he assured himself, would be cured when he had a family of his own.

Fourteen

Monday morning, Alex was sitting in Noah's office, in the same chair he'd used the day he'd come looking for Nina.

"This is twice in less than a month that you've come to me in search of a woman," Noah said with dry amusement.

Alex wasn't in a joking mood. He'd spent a restless night debating his approach to producing heirs. It would be nice for his children to have a mother like Nina, but how would he find a woman like her who would agree to the arrangement he wanted? The answer was always that he couldn't. In the end, he'd decided to return to his original plan. "I trust your judgment. I've seen news reports about women who are willing to have children for childless couples. I'm looking for someone like that. I figured you could ask around among your colleagues and find out if they know anyone they would recommend. I want someone who is intelligent, kind, pleasant-looking, with an agreeable personality, no history of hereditary problems and, preferably, someone who already has produced healthy children."

Noah's amusement turned to a thoughtful frown. "It's a shame things didn't work out between you and Nina Lindstrom. From what I've seen and heard, she's excellent mother material."

"She's a romantic. We'd have made each other miserable."

"You didn't look all that miserable at the barbecue."

"Physically, we found each other appealing. But she insists on an emotional commitment."

"And you're still determined not to fall in love." Noah's expression became brotherly. "From what you've told me about your family history, I'd say that Nina Lindstrom is a whole different breed of woman from your grandmother and your mother. She could be worth taking the risk for."

"I'll let you and the rest of the male population wallow in the murky mire of romance," Alex replied. "All I want is an heir."

"Raising a child on your own isn't easy," Noah cautioned.

"My grandfather raised me and did just fine. Besides, I thought single parenthood was the current trend."

Noah's gaze hardened. "Children aren't fads. Parenthood is a big responsibility."

"I've never thought of children as fads, and I've always lived up to my responsibilities," Alex reminded him curtly. "Are you going to help me or not?"

"If you're determined to go through with this, then I'll see what I can find out," Noah conceded. "But if I were you, I'd reconsider courting Nina Lindstrom."

"Nina Lindstrom is out of the picture," Alex said firmly.

Noah regarded him in silence for a long moment, then shrugged as if to say he realized that arguing would do no good. "I think there are a couple of agencies that specialize in finding surrogate mothers. I'll start asking around about them today. And will give you their contact number once I find it."

Alex nodded with satisfaction. Rising, he held out his hand to his friend. "Thanks."

"Don't thank me yet," Noah cautioned. "I'm not sure this is a good idea."

"I know what I'm doing," Alex assured him.

Leaving Noah's office, Alex felt confident about the course of action he'd chosen. There would be no games of the heart for him. As he headed for the exit, he suddenly changed direction. As long as he was here, he would stop by and see Tommy. Nina had asked him not to hover over her and her children, but that didn't mean he had to avoid them completely. Besides, he wanted to make certain the boy's recovery was still coming along on schedule.

He entered the room to find the private nurse helping Tommy with his physical therapy.

"Alex." Tommy greeted him with a grin.

Alex grinned back. The boy's smile always brought a rush of pleasure. He would miss that. *I'll have a child of my own soon*, he reminded himself. "Looks like you're getting back into great shape fast," he said, approaching the bed.

"Very fast," the nurse replied. "The doctors are extremely pleased. He may be able to go home sooner than they first predicted."

"I don't want them sending him home before he's entirely ready," Alex ordered protectively.

"They won't," she assured him.

Tommy gave Alex a disgruntled look. "I want to go home."

"You will," Alex replied, hating to have caused the boy to be angry with him. "You just keep up those exercises and do what the nurses and doctors tell you."

"Do I have a choice?" the boy grumbled under his breath.

Alex raised an eyebrow in surprise. Tommy had sounded so adult. Children were a constant source of amazement, he mused.

The nurse's mouth formed an exaggerated pout. "I thought we were having fun."

"I guess so," Tommy admitted.

Relieved to see the boy's good humor restored, Alex glanced at his watch. He was running late now. "I'll leave you two to continue," he said.

Walking to his car, he found himself regretting that he would not be a part of Tommy's homecoming celebration. He should never have allowed his relationship with Nina and her children to become more than business, he admonished himself. However, today he would take steps to assure their futures, then he could get back to living his own life.

It was late afternoon, and Nina was with Tommy when a knock sounded on the door of the hospital room, followed by the entrance of a tall, white-haired man, dressed in a three-piece suit. "I'm Bill Ophemhier, Alex Bennett's lawyer," he introduced himself as he entered. "And from the description he gave me, you must be Nina Lindstrom."

Nina rose to accept the man's handshake.

The lawyer smiled at Tommy. "I'm glad to hear you're doing so well, young man." His voice became apologetic. "I hope you won't mind if I take your mother away from you for a short time."

Wondering why Alex had sent a lawyer, Nina accompanied the man to the cafeteria. Once there, he guided her to a table in an unoccupied corner of the room. Setting his briefcase on the table, he opened it and took out a set of keys. "It will take a week or so for all the paperwork and inspections needed before the actual sale of the diner can be completed," he said, putting the keys on the table in front of her. "However, the Olsens have agreed to allow you free access to the place beforehand so that you can begin your plans for the renovations."

Nina picked up the familiar-looking key ring. "Alex Bennett is definitely a man of action."

"Definitely," the lawyer agreed. Extracting a manila envelope, he placed it in front of her, as well. "An account has been set up at the bank. If the funds are insufficient, you're to let Alex know. One of his accountants will be coming from Denver to explain how to keep the necessary records for tax purposes and how to set up employee records and payroll. I've made reservations for him at the Squaw Creek Lodge. He's expecting you to meet him there at noon tomorrow. If that's inconvenient, his name and number are on the front of the envelope. You can call and change the appointment. Also, if you need the names of reliable contractors, please feel free to give me a call and I'll do what I can to help you locate them."

"I know some people I can trust," Nina replied, fighting back a sudden feeling of being overwhelmed.

The lawyer rose, smiled and extended his hand. "Good luck."

"Thank you." She amazed herself by how confident she sounded accepting the handshake. As she watched him walk away, her hands tightened around the keys and her jaw firmed. She could and would made the diner a success.

From Tommy's hospital room, she called Helen and told her mother-in-law she would be a little late picking up the children. Then, staying only a few more minutes with Tommy, she left and headed directly for the diner. As she unlocked the front door and entered, it was like returning home. "A home in need of some repair," she muttered, switching on the lights for a better view.

The interior smelled dank, and she recalled the wet walls and the inch or so of water that had still been on the floor when she'd come by the day after the storm.

The lightning that had damaged some of the kitchen ap-

pliances had also split the old oak beside the diner. Half of
the tree had fallen toward the diner, landing on the roof
above the kitchen. It had knocked a hole in the roof and
let the rain in. The water pipe beneath the kitchen sink had
been leaking and Pa Olsen hadn't gotten around to replacing it. The impact caused the already faulty fitting to break,
and more water had poured in. A neighbor had seen the
tree fall and called the Olsens, but by the time they got to
the diner a small lake had built inside. They'd turned off
the water and opened the doors to let the water run out but
there was still the hole in the roof allowing the rain to
continue to pour in. They couldn't do anything about that
until the storm had passed.

Going into the kitchen, Nina looked upward. The Olsens
had had the roof patched, but the ceiling was still in need
of repair. Clearly they'd chosen to spend as little as possible
toward mending the place. "At least there was no major
structural damage," she murmured.

Looking under the sink, she saw that they'd also had the
broken pipe fixed. She made a mental note to have a
plumber check all of the pipes and fittings and to have an
electrician come in and recheck the wiring.

She'd expected to be nervous and scared. The place
looked a shambles, and making it into a paying proposition
was going to take some doing. Instead, she found herself
excited by the challenge.

Driving to her in-laws' home, her enthusiasm grew. During dinner she, Helen and Ray discussed possible contractors. Since all three had lived in town their entire lives,
they knew several and, of those, which were reliable and
which were not. Helen suggested she contact the interior
designer who had helped renovate the Old Elm Bed and
Breakfast, and they all agreed a bit of professional help in
that direction would be wise.

Anxious to get started as quickly as possible, she placed calls from her in-laws' home to the contractors they'd decided she should get estimates from and left messages on their answering machines.

A couple had already called back by the time she and the children arrived home. Returning their calls, she set up appointments for the next day to meet with them at the diner.

"Mr. Alex Bennett is going to get his money's worth from me," she declared as she showered and prepared for bed.

A few minutes later, when she crawled in between her sheets, Alex continued to linger in her mind. She remembered his lovemaking, and her body ached for more. Scowling at herself, she brought the image of the diner into her mind. Immediately, plans for renovating it erased all else. "Burying oneself in one's work isn't such a bad thing," she mused. "It can keep a person from dwelling on paths that will only lead to trouble."

However, the ploy wasn't entirely successful, she admitted as she drifted to sleep. In a shadowy corner of the diner she'd conjured in her mind, she could see Alex leaning against the wall watching her. He was in a tuxedo, just as he had been that first night they met. He looked out of place amid the rubble. "And he is out of place," she murmured. He didn't belong in her world and she didn't belong in his. Still, as sleep enveloped her, he moved toward her, and she found herself in his arms, swaying to a slow melody.

A knock sounded on Alex's front door, bringing his pacing to an abrupt halt. He glanced at his watch. The dial told him that it was a little past midnight. "It's about time," he muttered under his breath, striding to the door and opening it.

"Jarvis P. Farley, at your service," the short, slightly plump, white-haired man standing on his threshold said, extending a hand. His smile was open and friendly, and his face, in spite of a few wrinkles, had a cherubic quality.

"Thanks for coming." Alex accepted the handshake, then motioned the man inside. He'd expected someone who looked more hardened. Jarvis P. Farley had a naive quality that made Alex wonder if he'd made a mistake. Then he noticed the man's eyes. They were darting around, taking in all the details of the house.

"Nice place you have here," Jarvis noted with enthusiastic admiration.

Alex knew when he was being flattered. *The man is good!* he conceded, realizing that Mr. Farley's seeming naive was merely a facade to put others at ease or to make them think they were smarter than he was and cause them to be less careful about what they said to him. "Would you like a drink?" he offered as they entered his study and he motioned for his visitor to be seated.

"A beer would be nice," Jarvis replied.

Alex opened the refrigerator in the bar and pulled one out.

"Most people think private detectives lead an exciting life. That's not true. I don't often get flown in private helicopters and have late-model Mercedes waiting at the airstrip for my use so that I can attend late-night meetings in secluded mountain estates," the man said while Alex poured the beer, then handed him the glass.

"I appreciate you coming." Alex seated himself behind his desk. "You've been highly recommended."

Jarvis dropped his naive facade and studied his companion narrowly. "I'll be honest, Mr. Bennett, I don't do much fieldwork anymore. I let my operatives do it. They're young and energetic. But because your grandfather is an old friend and he asked me to do this for you, I figured I'd come listen to what you wanted." He grinned sheepishly. "Besides, the money was exceptionally good."

This was the man he'd thought he'd hired, Alex noted with approval. From the scrutiny he was getting, he guessed not much escaped Jarvis P. Farley. "The job I'm asking you to take on isn't strenuous or dangerous."

"Then why so much money?"

"Because it does require discretion."

Jarvis took a sip of the beer and leaned back in his chair. "So what's the job?"

"There's a woman, Nina Lindstrom. I want you to keep an eye on her."

"The name sounds familiar."

"My grandfather hired you to do a background check on her."

Jarvis nodded. "Ah, yes. One of my men handled it. I recall glancing at the file. A widow with three children. Right?"

"That's her," Alex confirmed.

"Do you have a photograph? I don't recall there being one with the file."

"No. She's in her early thirties, black hair, hazel eyes, pretty. I'll tell you where to find her."

"And why am I keeping an eye on her? As I recall, she turned out squeaky clean. Did my man miss something that has come back to bite you?"

"No. I'm in the process of purchasing a diner, and I've hired her to manage it. The place is a mess right now, and she's in charge of the renovations. Although I've been assured by her former employers that she has a good business head on her shoulders, I'm aware that her experience is limited. I want you to make certain she isn't duped by unscrupulous contractors or distributors or that any of them try to take advantage of her in any way because she's a woman."

"Seems to me you could do that, being as you're the boss," Jarvis said, regarding him thoughtfully.

"I've promised I won't hover over her."

For a long moment Jarvis regarded him in silence, then asked bluntly, "Is the diner job payback for services rendered?"

Alex bristled at the insinuation in the man's voice that he'd purchased Nina's intimacy. In the next instant he was mentally chiding himself for overreacting. *Wasn't he the one who was always claiming that any woman could be bought?* In calmer tones, he said, "Mrs. Lindstrom did me a favor. A purely platonic favor. I want to pay her back by making certain that she and her family have a financially sound future. But she's proud. She wants to make it on her own."

"And you want me around to let you know if she gets into trouble and needs help she's too proud to ask for," Jarvis elaborated.

"Exactly." Alex lifted a sheet of paper from his desk and extended it to the detective. "This list should get you set up. The apartment complex at the top is near the diner. You can rent a place there. I've checked and they have a couple available. Rent all the furnishings you need to be comfortable."

"This little surveillance job is going to cost you a bundle," Jarvis observed, continuing to study Alex closely. "That must have been some favor the woman did for you."

Alex's gaze turned icy. "That's between her and me."

Jarvis met Alex's glare with equal coolness. "I'm not prying out of idle curiosity. I've survived because I've learned the hard way to get to know as much about a situation as I can beforehand. Not knowing all the facts can be as stupid as wandering blind through a minefield.''

"The favor had to do with a family matter," Alex said, his tone warning the man not to ask any more questions. "I can guarantee it will not endanger you in any way. Are you going to take the job or not?"

Jarvis's expression relaxed. "It's too cushy to turn down. Besides, some of my operatives are beginning to think I'm getting soft. It's time to prove to them that the old man can still work in the field."

Alex picked up a check he'd written earlier and extended it toward the man. "This should get you started."

Jarvis read the figure and nodded with approval.

Alex rose and extended his hand. "Thanks," he said with dismissal, adding, "I'll expect you to let me know when you've made contact."

"I'll keep in touch," Jarvis replied, pocketing the check, then accepting the parting handshake.

Fifteen

Nina stood in the gutted kitchen of the diner. It was almost two weeks since Alex had offered her the job of renovating and running the place. He'd steamrollered the sale through. But she'd expected that and already had the new appliances, shelving and linoleum on order. She'd also had a crew lined up to begin working as soon as the sale was complete. Because restocking and organizing the kitchen would be her biggest job, she'd ordered them to concentrate on it first and worry about the rest of the place when the kitchen was finished.

Yesterday the workmen completed moving out all of the old appliances and ripping out the water-damaged walls. To her relief, the skeletal structures were as solid as she'd been told.

The plumber was already on the job, replacing worn fittings, and an electrician would be coming in today to install a new box and more updated wiring. To anyone else, the place would have looked even more a shambles than it had a week ago, but to her it was progress.

Her gaze shifted to the floor. The linoleum had been in need of replacing before the flooding. They'd be stripping that out today. She stomped her foot to test the subflooring. It sounded solid. The inspector had assured Alex that it was in good shape, but until she saw it for herself, she would remain uneasy.

A knock on the front door startled her. It was too early

for the workmen. Besides, they would have just come right in. Striding through the dining area, she opened the door to discover a round-faced, white-haired man with a friendly smile.

"Guess you're not quite ready to open for business," he said in a jovial voice.

"Not quite," she replied.

Concern showed on his face. "Saw them taking out all the kitchen equipment. Hope you're not going to turn this place into a dress shop or something like that. I just moved into an apartment around the block and I don't like to cook. I was hoping you were going to reopen the diner."

"I am," she replied, happy to know that she had at least one customer anxious to be served.

He peered around her at the room beyond. "Looks like you've undertaken quite a project."

"Looks like I have," she agreed, the fear of failure she was keeping locked away suddenly escaping and causing a rush of anxiety.

"I'm sure you'll do a terrific job," the man said with confidence.

His smile rebuilt her courage. "I'm certainly going to try."

"The name's Jarvis, Jarvis Farley." Jarvis extended his hand. "I'll be looking forward to being your first customer."

"It's a pleasure to meet you, Mr. Farley," Nina said, accepting the handshake. "I'm Nina Lindstrom."

"It's a pleasure to meet you, Nina, and you must call me Jarvis. Mr. Farley makes me feel ancient." He gave her a friendly wink, then glanced over his shoulder at the truck that had just arrived. "Looks like I'd better get going and let you get to business."

Pleasant man, Nina thought as she watched him walk away. Then he was forgotten as the workmen approached.

Alex drove home from his midmorning meeting, deep in thought. The agency Noah had recommended had found a woman who was willing to produce a child under the conditions stipulated. She was married with a healthy child of her own and had provided similar childbearing services to two other couples who had not been able to produce offspring. She was tall, pretty, blond with blue eyes, intelligent, health-conscious and had a good character. He'd been impressed. But...

The frown on his face deepened. His plan for heirs didn't feel as right as it had before. Memories of Nina and the love and support she gave her children haunted him. Curtly he reminded himself that he'd done just fine without a mother, but a nagging uneasiness persisted.

Matilda's image came into his mind. When he'd needed a woman's soft touch and warm sympathy, she'd provided it. He recalled a time when he was around six years old. His grandfather had become impatient with him because he hadn't been able to rebuild one of the toy oil rigs properly. Matilda had come out onto the patio, admonished William Bennett sternly, then knelt beside Alex, given him a hug and told him that she was sure he would get the knack of it if his grandfather would stop hovering over him. Her confidence and warm understanding had calmed him and made him feel good about himself once again. An hour later, he'd put the rig together like an expert.

Of course, Matilda's warm side wasn't the only side he'd seen. She hadn't been sparing when it came to telling him when he was wrong or behaving childishly. But that side had also taught him some very valuable lessons. The truth was, he would have missed a great deal if she hadn't been in his life, and he didn't want to think about what growing up without her would have been like.

He drew a terse breath.

So maybe a woman's touch was important in the rearing of a child. He'd simply have to find another Matilda. The frown on his face deepened. That wouldn't be easy.

Impatience etched itself into his features as he drove by the diner. Why did Nina Lindstrom have to be so...so *female* about choosing a mate. Why couldn't she be more practical, like a male, and realize that they would have made a great team. Both would have benefited and enjoyed themselves in the process.

Stopped at the corner stop sign, he saw her in his rearview mirror as she came out the front door and stood studying the exterior. The remembered feel of her caused arousal.

"Water under the bridge," he growled at himself, and stepped on the accelerator.

Nina watched the Porsche out of the corner of her eye. She'd been aware when Alex had driven past earlier that morning and wondered how many times he'd driven by when she hadn't noticed him. Anger bubbled within her. He'd promised not to be continually watching over her shoulder.

Going inside, she dialed the number of his mobile phone. When he answered, she said tersely, "I thought we had a deal. I thought you trusted me."

Alex mentally kicked himself for giving in to the impulse to drive by the diner yet another time today. "I do trust you."

With everything but his heart, she thought bitterly, then chided herself for still caring so much. She'd known the rules when she'd entered the game. "Then, why do you keep driving by the diner?'' she demanded. ''I know it can't possibly be on your route to every appointment.''

''I was just curious about your progress.''

His cool, businesslike tones caused a burst of angry frustration, forcing her to realize that again she'd let herself hope that he was having trouble staying away from her. *The only trouble he's having is trusting me to be competent enough to handle the diner on my own,* she mocked herself. ''I'll fax you a daily progress report,'' she snapped.

''That won't be necessary.'' Reminding himself that Jarvis Farley was watching over her and that he had a company to run and didn't need the distraction of her and the diner continually occupying his thoughts, he added, ''I'm leaving for Denver tomorrow. Computer hookups are fine, but I don't want them to forget my face at corporate headquarters. If you need me, you have my number there.''

She told herself she was relieved to know he was going. But a void deep inside called her a liar. Anger at her continued weakness for the man increased. ''Have a good trip,'' she said coolly, and hung up.

Alex dropped his phone into its cradle. The dismissal in her voice made him feel as if he'd been cut out of her heart with an icy knife. *No emotional involvement. That was what he wanted,* he reminded himself, and stepped on the accelerator.

Nina glared at the phone. She hated the way Alex could rattle her so easily.

''Trouble?'' a male voice asked.

She looked up into the ruggedly handsome face of Walt Obert. It was his construction company she'd contracted to do the work on the diner. Tall, muscular, with dark eyes and black hair, she knew he was used to women admiring him. But he showed no signs of egotism. Instead, there was a boyish charm about him, and the concern in his eyes warmed her. "Just a boss who promised to be invisible but is having trouble keeping his word."

He frowned in puzzlement. "I thought you were the boss."

"I'm in charge of getting this place operational and running the business, but I'm not the owner."

"Does youse want me ta punch him in the nose for youse?" he asked in a mock gangster voice.

Nina smiled at his attempt at humor. "No. He's leaving town."

"Good, 'cause I'd hate to lose this job. I don't often get to work for such a pretty boss." Masculine appreciation showed on his face. "You, in those jeans, can really light up a guy's day."

Nina flushed under his playful leer. She knew his reputation as a womanizer. Helen had sternly warned her not to let his sweet talk go to her head. Still, he made her feel desirable and she liked that. "We'd better get back to work. I want this place ready to open on schedule."

"Yes, ma'am." He gave her a sharp salute, then, whistling a jolly tune, returned to his crew in the kitchen.

A few minutes later, Penelope Galleger, the interior designer Helen had suggested, showed up.

They were going over some sketches the middle-aged divorcée had made when Walt strode through the room and out the front door. "If I were ten years younger, I'd take a stab at settling that man down," Penelope said, a glow of feminine admiration in her eyes.

"Three women have already tried," Nina returned, recalling Helen's motherly delivered history of the man's lusty past. "His third marriage lasted less than six months. His wife found him fooling around with her sister."

"Well, she shouldn't have let the sister move in with

them. Walt's a hunk. The sister probably made a play for him, and he is, after all, only human."

Nina frowned. "I prefer a man with more commitment."

"They're not so easy to come by these days," Penelope complained. "Besides, I like my independence. All I want is a little fling in the hay once in a while to satisfy my more primitive cravings, then I'm happy to be on my own again."

Nina had to admit that since the night spent with Alex, she was missing male companionship in her bed. But a fling in the hay wasn't her style. "To each his own," she said, and returned the conversation to the sketches.

The ringing of the phone interrupted them. It was the doctor with the news she'd been waiting to hear. Tommy was to be released the next day.

Cutting her meeting with Penelope short, she drove to her in-laws'. Helen was sitting on the front porch, rocking and sipping a lemonade.

"You're looking rested," Nina said with approval as she mounted the porch and took a seat in a nearby chair.

"Since you started earning that nice salary and enrolled Elizabeth and Pete in Janice Blare's day care, I've had plenty of time to do nothing," Helen replied. "I miss them," she added.

"You still pick them up every day and bring them here and feed both them and me dinner," Nina reminded her.

"Well, you've got a lot to do getting that diner fixed up. I'm merely doing my part."

Nina took Helen's hand in hers. "You've done more than your part since Tom died, and you'll never know how truly grateful I am to you. I don't know what I would have done without you."

"We're family," Helen said simply, and gave Nina's hand a squeeze.

"And speaking of family—" Nina's smile widened "—Tommy is coming home tomorrow."

"That's wonderful." Helen beamed, then suddenly frowned. "But you can't put him in Janice's day care. I know she runs a fine place, but he'll have to be careful for a while, won't he? He shouldn't be involved in any rough-housing, and children his age do get to playing rough and running around more than they should sometimes in this heat."

"I'm planning to hire Polly Bridges to watch over him at my apartment," Nina replied. "She's baby-sat for my children before, and she's a responsible girl."

Helen's mouth formed a stern line. "Polly's nice. I'll grant you that. And for a teenager, she's more responsible than most, but you'll do no such thing. Tommy is going to come here and stay with me when you're working."

"But you've already done so much," Nina protested, feeling guilty about imposing yet again.

"I won't have any peace of mind worrying about him getting himself hurt. You and I both know how quick he can be to get into trouble." Helen's expression remained firm. "He's coming here."

Nina gave the woman a hug as tears of gratitude welled in her eyes. She'd spent a lot of time convincing herself that Polly would do a good job, but knowing Helen was watching over him sent a wave of relief through her. "I'm so lucky to have married into this family."

"We feel lucky to have you," Helen replied, returning the hug.

Straightening, Nina met her mother-in-law's gaze levelly. "But I insist on paying you. I can afford it now. Alex is paying me very well."

Helen frowned. "I won't accept money for an act of love."

"You could put it away for a special vacation or to buy one of those big-screen televisions you're always looking at," Nina insisted.

"No."

Silently Nina vowed that she would set the money aside on her own, and would one day give them a vacation or the television set as a gift. Aloud, she said, "I feel guilty about burdening you with a child when I've just managed to free you."

"It's not a burden."

"I owe you so much."

"It's a mutual debt," Helen assured her. "I don't know how I would have been able to handle Tom's death if I hadn't had you and the children."

Nina gave her another hug.

"And now," Helen said, as they moved apart, "we need to plan a welcome-home party. I'll bake his favorite cake and make fried chicken."

Nina nodded. "He'll like that."

Helen's jaw firmed. "I know you told me that you and Alex have decided to keep your relationship strictly on a business basis, but I feel that we should invite him."

Nina wasn't ready to spend an evening in Alex's company. "What he did for Tommy was part of a business arrangement we'd made. Tommy's homecoming should be confined to a family affair."

Helen became more determined. "I watched that man with the children, and it's my opinion that he cares about Tommy, Elizabeth and Pete beyond any business deal."

"Maybe. Maybe not." Nina expressed the doubt that had been nagging at the back of her mind. In spite of the evidence to the contrary, Alex had walked away too easily for someone who really cared. Honest emotions couldn't be turned off and on like a spigot. Admittedly, she'd caught him hovering over her, but that could be explained by guilt and an overly developed sense of responsibility.

"Well, I'm going to ask. He's paying for Tommy's hospital bills and should be invited to the party," Helen declared.

Nina knew her mother-in-law well. "I know you were hoping that Alex and I would marry, then you would never have to worry about the future of your grandchildren. But if you think that we broke up over some silly lover's quarrel that can be mended if we're forced to face each other and talk, you're mistaken."

Motherly concern spread over Helen's face. "If it's Tom's memory that's keeping the two of you apart, then you're behaving foolishly. Tom would have wanted you to get on with your life."

"Tom's memory had nothing to do with Alex and me breaking up."

Helen didn't look convinced. "Well, I don't understand what did, then. I saw the way you looked at him. And he obviously cares for you. You and I both know he only bought that diner and made you manager to insure your future. A man doesn't do that for a woman he doesn't care for."

"I fell in love with him, but he didn't fall in love with me," Nina said stiffly. "As for the diner, he's a man with a strong sense of responsibility. We're his good deed for society."

"If you say so," Helen replied without conviction.

"I know so," Nina declared.

"I still think I should invite him," Helen persisted. "He went through the operation with you, he's seen that Tommy had the very best of care, and he showered the boy with gifts to make his stay in the hospital tolerable."

Nina breathed a sigh of resignation. Just because he

hadn't fallen in love with her didn't make it fair for her to react so harshly to him. "You're right. He did more than was necessary to live up to his part of the bargain. Inviting him would be the polite thing to do."

Helen smiled triumphantly and went inside. A few minutes later she returned. Her smile was gone, and there was a look of disillusionment on her face. "He can't make it. He's leaving for Denver to take care of some business that can't wait."

So I was right about his true feelings toward all of us, Nina mused dryly.

"I guess we were, like you said, his good deed for society," Helen muttered grimly.

Nina was tempted to say "I told you so," but the words refused to issue. Her victory felt hollow. Instead, she gave Helen's hand a squeeze and forced a smile. "We should never look a gift horse in the mouth. Alex Bennett is providing the means for me to make a good life for myself and my children. We should be grateful he came along."

Helen's expression brightened. "Yes, we should."

"And now," Nina said, pushing herself to her feet, "I'm going to go visit Tommy and tell him the good news."

Pulling into the hospital parking lot, she recognized Alex's car. She guessed he was there to visit Noah Howell. Although there was a parking space near the Porsche, she chose one several rows away. She knew it was cowardly, but she didn't want to take the chance of encountering him when she was leaving.

At the door of Tommy's room, she came to an abrupt halt. From inside she heard a male voice...Alex's voice. Opening the door a crack, she saw him standing beside the bed, his back to her.

"I have to leave town for a while," he was saying. "I

want you to keep up your therapy even after you leave the hospital. Promise?"

"Promise," Tommy replied. "Will you be back soon?"

Nina heard the plea in her son's voice and again was forced to admit how much her children had come to truly care for the man.

"I'm not sure," Alex replied. The apology and regret in his voice told her she'd been wrong to think he only thought of her and her children as a good deed. He was simply staying away at her request.

My children don't need a father figure who's a cynic about love and marriage, she told herself, quelling a rush of guilt.

Hearing Alex say goodbye, she hurried down the corridor to the ladies' room and stepped inside so that he wouldn't see her. She waited a couple of minutes, then peeked out and saw him enter the elevator.

Returning to Tommy's room, she knew she was going to have to tell Helen that Alex had stopped by to say goodbye to Tommy. It was only fair that her mother-in-law know the man wasn't as cold as he'd appeared. But she'd make it equally clear that Alex Bennett was no longer a part of their private lives.

Sixteen

Nina stood in the completely refurbished kitchen of the diner. It was just three weeks since the renovations had officially begun. The new appliances had been installed that afternoon, and she was feeling a deep sense of accomplishment. There was still work to be done in the dining room and bathrooms, but while that was being accomplished she would test the equipment, and when the workmen were finished with the dust-producing repairs, she'd begin restocking the shelves with dishes and glasses.

"Looks good" a male voice noted from behind her.

She turned to see Walt, smiling at his handiwork, a pizza box in one hand and a brown paper bag in the other.

She smiled back. "Yes, it does." She nodded toward the food. "I thought you were finished for the day."

"I am, but I heard you telling Helen to go ahead and eat without you. I guessed you'd stick around here after everyone left, inspecting your new equipment." He held the box and bag up toward her. "So I got some pizza and beer. I don't want my pretty boss lady fainting from hunger."

He was a handsome charmer, Nina thought, noting the long dimple in his left cheek that gave his face a mischievous, boyish flavor. "Thanks, but I'd better be going. I need to pick up my children soon so I can have a little time with them before they go to bed."

"All work and no play makes Nina a dull girl," Walt admonished, setting the pizza and beer on the center counter. "Come on. Just stay long enough to eat with me. I hate eating alone."

Nina felt herself weakening. He made her feel feminine and desirable. *Women are a game to him,* she reminded herself curtly. "I really need to be going."

He cocked an eyebrow in a playful manner. "I could get the impression you're afraid to be alone with me."

"Maybe I am," she admitted.

He moved toward her. "I like the sound of that."

She held a hand up, silently warning him to come no closer. "You collect women like trophies, and I don't intend to be one of your conquests."

"Maybe I just haven't met the one who can tame me."

Nina read the glimmer in his eyes, challenging her to try to be that one. It was enticing. "You're good...very good," she said with admiration. "But I don't believe there's a woman who can tie you down forever."

"You could be selling yourself short," he warned, again taking a step toward her.

"It's a wise woman who knows when the wolf is knocking at her door," she returned, taking a step back and again holding up her hand to warn him to come no closer.

He stopped and laughed. "I like you, Nina Lindstrom. You're not afraid to speak your mind. If you'd just mellow a little, we could make some beautiful music together."

"We don't move to the same tunes."

"I could teach you a few new steps," he coaxed.

Nina couldn't help smiling at his persistence.

"Come on." He held his hand out toward her. "I'll hum. You follow my lead."

Nina was tempted. Surprise at her reaction puzzled her. Walt and men like him had never appealed to her before. It was a rebound response, she realized abruptly. In spite of her attempt not to think about Alex, deep inside, his refusal to love her had been gnawing away at her. "I'll just keep moving to the beat of my own drummer."

"You have one hell of a stubborn streak," Walt complained with a quirky grimace.

"Hello." A male voice called out from the dining area. Nina looked through the serving window to see Jarvis Farley. She wasn't surprised. His doctor, he'd informed her during their second encounter, had told him he should take a long walk at least twice a day. The diner was on his usual route, and he came by both morning and evenings. Sometimes he paused to talk. Other times, when he saw she was busy, he'd just wave and go on.

"I was out for my evening stroll and saw the lights still on. Thought I'd stop by and see how the job is progressing," he said, entering the kitchen and looking around. "Looks like this place is really taking shape." He grinned at Nina. "Must be getting pretty close to that first meal."

Nina had liked Jarvis Farley from the first. Now she liked him even more. He'd shown up at the perfect moment to save her from Walt's continued advances. "I've been promised the renovations will be completed within three more weeks. I've got food on order, the ad campaign mapped out and two cooks hired. Tomorrow I start interviewing waitresses and getting this kitchen wiped down. I'm planning to open on September 15."

"Wonderful!" Jarvis proclaimed.

Nina slipped an arm through the older man's arm. "But before I officially open, I want to have a practice opening. I'm going to have my children and in-laws here and I'll invite the workmen and their families. And I'd like you to be one of my guests."

Jarvis beamed. "I'd love to."

"And now you can walk me to my car," she said. "It's been a long day."

His gaze quickly darted from her to Walt, then back to her. He patted her hand in a fatherly fashion. "Yes, of course."

As they started toward the door, she looked back at Walt. "Will you lock up on your way out?"

"Yes, ma'am, boss lady," he replied good-naturedly. A hint of triumph in his voice suggested he saw her departure as a flight from an encounter she felt she was losing.

"I have the distinct impression I interrupted something," Jarvis said in lowered tones when they were outside.

Nina heard the concern in his voice. "Walt's a flirt...a persistent flirt...but harmless."

"Well, you take care. A wolf in sheep's clothing is still a wolf," Jarvis cautioned, opening the door for her.

She rewarded this observation with a friendly smile. "I'll keep that in mind."

Alex Bennett paced the floor of the study in his Denver home. Jarvis had just made his nightly call, and Alex wasn't pleased with the report. When Nina had hired Walt Obert to do the reconstruction on the diner, Jarvis had checked the man out. Obert was an honest contractor and did above-average work. But the report had added that he was a womanizer. And now it appeared that he had his sights on Nina.

"She can take care of herself," Alex growled under his breath, but he couldn't get the image of her lying beside him in bed out of his mind.

He paced more briskly. He'd known several Walt Oberts. Where women were concerned, they loved a challenge and would do anything to win. Nina's resistance would be like waving a red flag in front of a charging bull.

Alex's breathing became ragged as he recalled making love to her. He'd reawakened desire in her...shown her what she was missing. It would be his fault if she succumbed to Obert's persistence. Suddenly he was picturing her with Obert, and his stomach churned with disgust. The man would never think of her as more than a plaything. He wasn't good enough for her.

"If she does give in to him, she'll live to regret it." His jaw hardened. "A man should protect his investment, and any involvement between her and Obert could affect the diner."

Picking up the phone, he punched in Obert's number.

The next evening, Nina walked the length of the newly refurbished counter in the dining area, inspecting it with a critical eye. Climbing up onto one of the new stools, she swiveled around, testing the seat's comfort and mobility. Both met with her approval.

The smile on her face turned to a thoughtful frown as she recalled her various encounters with Walt during the day. He'd been polite but cool. This abrupt change in attitude made her uneasy.

So maybe he found someone else to pursue, she reasoned. But if that was the case, she would expect him to simply behave in a friendly manner without any flirting. *Or maybe he just got up on the wrong side of the bed.* She drummed her fingers on the counter as her frown darkened. Whatever the cause, she didn't like this new tension that was in the air.

Hearing the door of the diner open, she twisted around to see the object of her musings enter. His frown matched hers, and there was purpose in his eyes. She saw him glance around and realized he was making certain they were alone.

Stopping a few feet from her, he said curtly, "Why didn't you tell me that you and Alex Bennett had something going on?"

The accusation startled her. "We don't have anything going on."

"Then, how come I got a call from him last night warning me to stay away from you?" he demanded.

Nina stared at him. "You got a call from Alex?"

"He *suggested* that I keep my mind on the job or the next time he or any of his friends needed a contractor around here, my name would not come up."

Anger bubbled inside of Nina. Alex had no right to determine who she associated with. "I'm really sorry. Apparently he's developed a big-brother complex where I'm concerned."

"I was just doing a little harmless flirting. There was no reason for you to go running to your bossman to get me to lay off."

"I didn't go running to Alex."

He cocked an eyebrow in a disbelieving manner. "Then, how'd he find out?"

"I don't know." A roundish, pink-cheeked face suddenly entered her mind. "But I have a suspicion." She extended her hand toward him. "I apologize for any trouble you've had because of me. I promise you, there won't be any more, and your business will not suffer because of me."

He regarded her hand dubiously. "I'm not so sure that any contact with you is safe. Bennett was pretty blunt."

"I can handle Alex Bennett," she assured him.

He took a step back. "Just the same, I think I'll do as he suggested and keep my distance. See you tomorrow, boss lady."

As the door swung closed behind him, she swiveled the stool around and looked into the kitchen through the long serving window. "You can come out now, Mr. Farley."

Jarvis's round body appeared in the doorway. "How did you know I was there?"

"I didn't, at least, not for sure. But I figured that if you were the one Alex had spying on me, then you'd be nearby."

He leaned against the doorjamb and studied her thoughtfully. "I saw Obert come in and he looked angry. According to my file on him, he's the nonviolent type, but you can never be sure about that kind of thing. I figured I should be close by in case you needed help."

She allowed the anger she was holding under control to show. "You tell Alex Bennett that I don't need a babysitter. If he doesn't trust me to be able to handle this job on my own then he can find a new manager!" Slipping off the stool, she stalked toward the door.

Farley moved swiftly to block her exit. "He trusts you to know what you're doing as far as getting this place into shape and running it is concerned. But he's been in the business world all his life. He knows it's a boys' club. He just wanted me around to make certain you weren't taken advantage of. You can't fault him for trying to protect his investment."

"You have a point," she conceded grimly. "But he has no right to interfere in my private life."

"So he's being a little overly protective. You're a nice lady. He just didn't want to see you make a mistake you'd regret."

Did Alex think he'd enticed her to become so wanton, she'd be willing to jump into bed with any man? This was an insulting thought and her anger intensified. "You tell Alex Bennett to stay out of my private life."

"I suppose that includes walking orders for me." Farley grimaced with regret. "Too bad. I was enjoying this assignment and looking forward to that free meal."

In spite of her fury toward Alex, Nina found herself smiling crookedly at Jarvis's woeful expression. "Walt Obert isn't the only charmer," she said, her voice softening. "Besides, if I insist Alex take you off my tail, he'll probably hire someone else to replace you."

"Most likely," Jarvis agreed.

"So you might as well stick around for the free meal." At least this way, she'd know all the players in the game, Nina reasoned. Besides, she liked Jarvis.

He smiled brightly and offered her his arm. "May I walk you to your car?"

"Just give me a minute to lock up," she said, heading into the kitchen. Passing the phone, she paused momentarily, considering calling Alex and giving him a piece of her mind. In the next instant, she shrugged off the impulse. What was done was done, and she was sure Jarvis would give him her message about not interfering any further in her private affairs. But even as she talked herself out of making the call, she knew she was just making excuses. The real reason she wasn't going to phone him was because she didn't want to speak to him. She still cared too much and was afraid of what she might say.

Nina waited until after dinner, when she and Helen were alone in the kitchen doing the dishes, before she told her mother-in-law about Alex's call to Walt.

"Well, I'm glad he did it," Helen said. "Ray has been worried to death about you and Walt. He knew Walt would make a move on you, and it's been all I could do to keep him from having a talk with the man. It's not that we don't like Walt, but three failed marriages, and all of them failures because he was chasing other women, doesn't speak well for his sense of commitment."

Nina frowned. "I don't understand why everyone seems

to think I'm such a pushover. I know about Walt, and I know it would be foolish to take him seriously."

"I know that, but Ray feels protective toward you. And you have to admit that Walt is a charming hunk of a man. Come on, admit it. You're not dead. Weren't you just a little bit tempted?"

"Tempted, yes," Nina conceded. "But not foolish enough to let it go beyond that." She finished drying the dish she was holding, then asked, "Aren't you a little curious about how Alex found out Walt was making a play for me?"

Helen's expression became defensive. "It wasn't from Ray or me. We tell you to your face how we feel. We never go behind your back."

"I know."

Helen paused to regard her with interest. "How did he find out?"

"Jarvis Farley."

"That nice man who's taken such an interest in the diner?"

"He's a private detective hired by Alex to make sure poor little me wasn't hoodwinked by some unscrupulous contractor or distributor."

Helen suddenly looked worried. "I realize you think Alex has gone too far, but I wouldn't do anything rash if I were you. You've got the kids to think about. An opportunity like the one he's given you doesn't come along every day. Besides, he was protecting you as much as his investment."

"I'm not going to do anything rash."

Helen studied her narrowly. "I expected you to be furious."

"I was for a while." Nina drew a terse breath. "But I'm

tired of fighting Alex, and I'm even more tired of fighting the way I feel about him.''

''Just how do you feel about him?''

''I'm crazy about him.''

''So what are you going to do?''

''I'll let you know tomorrow,'' Nina replied with a finality that said she didn't want to discuss this topic any further.

For a moment, Helen regarded her in silence, clearly considering pursuing this subject further. Then, with motherly acquiescence, she said, ''Tomorrow.''

Alex stared at the phone. Ever since Farley had reported on his encounter with Nina, like someone waiting for a second shoe to fall, he'd been waiting for her to call. Farley had said she was angry at first but had calmed down. Alex didn't believe that for a moment. He was certain she was simply hiding her feelings. His gaze traveled from the phone to the clock on the mantel.

''But I could be wrong,'' he muttered, noting the lateness of the hour. ''Maybe she's decided to be practical about this and accept my interference as a gesture of a concerned friend.''

The ringing of the phone split the air, and he tensed. ''Or maybe not. Maybe she was just waiting until she had the children in bed so she could give me a piece of her mind in private.'' Lifting the receiver, he said, ''Hello.''

''Hello, Alex,'' Nina replied from the other end. She'd thought it would take her a while to build up her courage to make this call, but as soon as she was sure the children were asleep, she'd punched in his number.

His uneasiness increased. She sounded calm, like a woman who'd made a firm decision. He should have warned Obert not to mention his call to anyone. ''Look, before you say anything, I want to apologize. I realize I've overstepped my bounds, but I was thinking of your future and that of your children. The world is full of people who will try to take advantage of you."

"I'm not angry anymore." Although, she admitted, she was enjoying his nervousness. He deserved to squirm a little.

"I'm glad to hear that." Her continued calm was making him more uneasy by the moment.

Nina's hand squeezed around the arm of her chair as she fought to keep the tension out of her voice. She didn't want him to guess how much this call meant to her. "I was wondering how your search for a breeder for your children is coming?" That had sounded a little too caustic, she chided herself.

"Slowly," he replied, surprised by the question. A sudden thought occurred to him. "Are you pregnant?" He found himself exceptionally pleased by this possibility.

"No."

"Too bad," he said with regret. "I still feel you'd be the perfect choice to bear my children."

In spite of the fact that this was what she'd wanted to hear, doubts suddenly assailed her. *A person has to take a chance once in a while,* she reminded herself for the umpteenth time. Still fighting to keep her voice level, she gripped the arm of the chair until her knuckles were white. "I'm glad to hear that, because I've decided to accept your proposal of marriage, if it's still open."

Alex wondered if he was hearing things. "It's still open."

"Then, you can set the date." Suddenly dizzy, she realized she'd been holding her breath and forced herself to breathe once again.

"Do you want a small wedding or a large one?" he asked, still wondering if this was real or his imagination.

"Small. Just family."

Wanting to clinch this deal before she could change her mind, he said, "How about as soon as we can get a license?"

"Fine." Her jaw tensed. "I do have a couple of stipulations. The first is that we live in Grand Springs. When you proposed, you said that was possible."

"It is and we will."

"And I will continue to manage the diner."

Alex hadn't expected this. "I thought you would prefer to stay at home with the children."

"I would," she admitted. "But Tom's death taught me a very hard lesson. If this marriage doesn't work out, I want to be able to support myself and my children without your charity."

Alex told himself to accept her decision to marry him without any further discussion. Instead, he heard himself asking, "What made you change your mind about marrying me?"

"I changed my mind because you're right. I am the very best choice of a wife for you," she replied, and hung up. Her hands were shaking. She'd followed her heart on an uncertain course. "I don't expect the path to be smooth," she murmured under her breath. "I just hope it doesn't lead me to a briar patch."

Alex stared at the receiver still in his hand. Triumph surged through him. He'd won!

Seventeen

Two days later Nina stood beside Alex in the living room of his home in Grand Springs, exchanging wedding vows.

Helen, Ray, William Bennett and Matilda were seated to one side. Elizabeth, Tommy and Pete stood by their mother. Alex had requested that. He'd said he wanted the children to know they were as much a part of this marriage as their mother.

Gladys was catering the affair, providing an elegant dinner to follow the ceremony. As Nina had started to the living room to join Alex and the children waiting for her with the minister, the caterer had come out of the kitchen and given her a hug. "It's just like a fairy tale...Cinderella and Prince Charming," Gladys had said with a wide grin.

Not exactly like the fairy tale, Nina thought as Alex slipped the ring on her finger. Doubt about the wisdom of her decision came back to plague her. Prince Charming had been madly in love with Cinderella.

But as June Jackson had pointed out, the "happily ever after" without any bumps in the road only happens in fairy tales. Just because two people start out their marriage madly in love doesn't insure its survival, either, she countered, slipping a gold band on his finger.

"I now pronounce you man and wife." The minister smiled at Alex. "You may kiss your bride."

William Bennett began to applaud loudly.

Nina saw Matilda give him a "behave yourself" glance.

Then all other thoughts were forgotten as Alex drew her into his arms. His kiss ignited the fires of passion. She and Alex had as much of a chance of forming a solid, long-lasting union as any other couple, she again told herself.

The kiss ended, and, holding on to that thought, she turned to face their guests.

"I wish you the best of luck," Matilda declared, rising and heading over to give Nina a hug. Releasing her, the housekeeper turned to Alex, and her expression became stern. "I hope you realize the prize you've won."

"I do," Alex assured her.

Nina hid the sudden jab of pain at being reminded that in his eyes she was just that…a prize like the stuffed lion at a carnival. *Too late to turn back now,* she chided herself, and pushed the hurt aside.

"Good choice, boy," William said, clasping Alex's hand. Then, beaming at Nina, he hugged her, too. "Welcome to the family." Next, he turned his attention to the children. "And welcome to you, as well," he said.

Ray had approached Alex. "I'm trusting you to do right by Nina. She's more of a daughter to me than a daughter-in-law."

"I'll take good care of her," Alex promised, extending his hand.

Ray accepted the handshake, his expression that of one man accepting another's word. Then he moved to Nina and he gave her a hug. "If this doesn't work out, you know you have a home with us," he whispered in her ear.

Tears welled in Nina's eyes. He hadn't said much about her marriage to Alex, and she'd been afraid he was angry with her…that he thought she was betraying Tom. Now she realized that he was simply worried about her. "Thank you."

Helen was the last. "Welcome into our family," she

said, giving Alex a hug. Then, turning to Nina, she embraced her tightly. "You made the right decision."

I wish I could be that positive, Nina thought as the photographer moved forward and began to arrange them for a formal photo. *Forever is never guaranteed,* she again reminded herself. She would live for the moment and not worry about tomorrow.

Several hours later, Nina and Alex stood on the front porch waving goodbye to their guests as well as her children. Helen and Ray had insisted on taking their grandchildren home with them so that Nina and Alex could have uninterrupted privacy during their first night of marriage.

Today was the beginning, but tomorrow the real changes would come, Nina mused. The movers would be bringing her things here. And Helen would be officially on Alex's payroll. He had informed her that he intended to hire a nanny for the children or she could allow herself to be compensated for being their daytime caregiver. He'd been persuasive, encouraging Helen to accept his offer of employment. In the end, she'd relented.

"You were very generous to Helen," Nina said as the last of the cars disappeared from view. "Thank you."

He shrugged. "The children love her and she loves them. Who better to watch over them when they aren't in school and you're working."

Going inside, they found Ann Jenson waiting for them. Alex had brought her and her husband here to help with getting Nina and her children settled and to see to their needs until he could find another couple to take their place. Then they would be returning to his house in Denver.

A suite of rooms off the kitchen had been included in the design of this house in the event Alex ever decided he wanted live-in help. Ann and Jed were being comfortably housed there.

Recalling him mentioning that Roberta Nyes would also continue to come on a weekly basis to help with the heavy cleaning, Nina was again struck by how much marrying Alex was going to change her life. No longer would she have to worry about housekeeping, laundry and cooking as part of her daily routine. *Relax! Enjoy your good fortune,* she ordered herself.

"I've put the leftovers in the refrigerator," Ann said. "Jed and I will be spending the night in town, but we'll be back in time to fix breakfast."

"Thank you," Alex replied with dismissal.

Ann's gaze turned to Nina. Interest flickered in her eyes. "Congratulations."

Nina sensed no hostility from the other woman, but it was obvious that the housekeeper was wondering how a poor widow with three children could get so lucky as to snag Alex Bennett. Thoughts Nina had been avoiding all day rushed in on her...thoughts about those in this town who would be wondering the same thing—only their attitudes would be hostile. She imagined the remarks Veronica Charleston was making at the moment, and her stomach knotted. "Thank you," she said, unable to keep a stiffness out of her voice.

Abruptly Ann flushed. Apology flashed in her eyes, then her expression became one of polite deference and she quickly turned to Alex. "Congratulations to you both," she added, and hurried away.

Alex drew Nina into his embrace. "Our marriage is bound to spark some curiosity," he said, letting her know he'd seen the look Ann had cast her way. He kissed the tip of her nose. "But we won't let that bother us."

In his arms, her doubts faded. Every fiber of her being told her that she was where she belonged. "No, we won't."

Smiling lecherously, he scooped her up into his arms. "And we won't waste any of this privacy."

All was forgotten but him. "I should hope not."

In the bedroom, he began to undress her. "I've been a very patient man during the past two days, but it hasn't been easy."

"It hasn't been easy for me, either," she confessed, working the buttons of his shirt open.

He kissed her neck, then trailed kisses along the line of her shoulder. "You taste good," he murmured against her skin.

"And you feel good," she replied, running her hands over his now bare chest. Being with him was even more exciting than she'd remembered. And stimulating. Very stimulating. She unfastened his belt and pulled it free. Next came his slacks as she concentrated on undressing him as quickly as possible.

Her obvious impatience increased Alex's arousal. When she'd finished her task, he gladly moved swiftly to help her out of the rest of her clothes.

Every brush of his hand fanned the flames within her until she burned with a desire so intense she could barely breathe. "I want you now," she groaned. "Now, please."

"Now it is," he replied, and claimed her.

Nina lay propped on an elbow, smiling down at Alex's face. Her stomach growled and she grimaced. "I'm starving," she announced, kissing him lightly, then wriggling out of the crook of his arm and off the bed.

"A bit of nourishment to give us renewed energy sounds like a good idea," he replied with an exaggerated leer, and rose as well.

Both took only the time to pull on robes before heading for the kitchen. Once there, Nina began to pull out the leftovers. She'd barely been able to eat after the ceremony. Now she dove into them, nibbling as she spread them out on the counter.

Alex glanced up from his task of opening a bottle of champagne and grinned. "I like a woman with a strong appetite."

Nina grinned back at the double entendre in his voice and shoved another piece of cold chicken into her mouth.

The cork popped and he poured them two glasses. "To us," he toasted.

"To us." She searched his face for any sign of love. What she saw was triumph. *I should be flattered to be such a prize,* she told herself, but deep inside was a stirring of disappointment. *You knew the bargain you struck,* she reminded herself and turned her attention to the food.

Alex sat on a stool by the counter and watched her as she reheated the vegetables in the microwave. Having her there pleased him more than he ever thought anything could. "I missed you and the children," he confessed. "I guess I got used to having all the activity."

She glanced at him. He seemed genuinely surprised by how much he'd missed having them around. "We can liven up a place."

"I've got men coming tomorrow to begin cutting trees and clearing some acreage. I want to have a helicopter pad up here so that I don't have to drive to the air field. That will also give us easy access off the mountain during the winter. And I'm going to have a swimming pool put in and tennis courts built. I want the children to be happy here."

"I'm sure they will be," she replied, recalling how excited they'd been to have Alex back in their lives.

"I was also thinking that since I'm going to be wrapping

up my current project in a couple of days, you could postpone the opening of the diner for a short while and we can all go to Disney World or Disneyland. You and the kids can choose.''

Nina abruptly froze in mid-motion and frowned. A swimming pool. Tennis courts. *And* a trip to Disneyland or Disney World! She turned to face him. ''You don't have to buy the children's affection. They like you and they missed you, too. There wasn't a day that didn't go by when one of them didn't ask about you or mention you.''

Silently admitting that he was pleased by the knowledge that the children had missed him, Alex gave her a look that mocked her accusation. ''I promised you that I'd do my best by your family. I'm simply trying to live up to my part of the bargain.''

Nina's stomach knotted. In spite of the fact that she knew he considered their union more of a business deal than a real marriage, it still hurt to have him remind her so bluntly. *When you agreed to this marriage, you knew it would be on his terms,* she chided herself curtly. ''You don't have to spoil my children to live up to your part of the bargain.''

''I consider them my children, as well, and I have no intention of spoiling them.''

She cast him a disbelieving scowl.

''Well, maybe a little,'' he confessed. He grinned sheepishly, hoping to wipe the scowl from her face.

''A little? You call swimming pools, tennis courts and trips a 'little bit' of spoiling?''

''I was thinking as much about us as about them,'' he said, defending himself. ''The swimming pool and tennis courts are for exercise. All children need to get a lot of exercise.'' He leered playfully and raised his eyebrows up and down in Groucho Marx fashion. ''The more they exercise, the tireder they get, and the tireder they get, the better they sleep at night so their parents are not disturbed.''

She'd never seen this boyishly charming side of him so openly displayed. "I suppose you do have a point," she admitted, finding it hard to stay perturbed with him.

"And the trip to the amusement park is as much for me as for the children. I haven't taken a vacation in ages." His playful leer turned into an expression of exaggerated lecherousness. "People keep warning me that all work and no play isn't good for me."

She couldn't stop herself from smiling. *Enjoy what you have,* she told herself. "They're right, and I wouldn't want to be accused of keeping you from playing."

Mentally, he breathed a sigh of relief that her good humor had returned. "I'm glad to hear that, because I've got a couple of games in mind for after we eat."

Embers of desire again sparked to life. "I thought you might," she said, handing him a plate, then beginning to dish food onto hers.

As they left the kitchen, their hunger sated, he guided her into his study, instead of going directly back to the bedroom. "I have a wedding gift for you." He lifted a prettily wrapped, long, flat box off the top of his desk and handed it to her.

"I thought we'd agreed that we wouldn't exchange gifts," she said, feeling guilty for not having one to give in return.

"It was important to me that you have this one."

She read the purpose in his eyes and wondered what was going on. Opening the box, she found a folded legal document. Unfolding it, she frowned uneasily. It was the deed to the diner.

"I promised you security for marrying me," he said. "I

wanted you to know that I fully intend to live up to that obligation.''

Her jaw trembled. She felt like a piece of merchandise. "I didn't marry you for your money."

Silently he cursed. He hadn't meant to make her unhappy. "I know you didn't. But I also know that you're uncertain this marriage will last. You shouldn't be. I'm a man who lives up to his commitments, and I've committed myself to you and your children. However, since you have your doubts, I don't want you worrying about your future. You're fond of the diner. I thought it would be a good gift. In fact, I thought you would be excited. I know how much you've enjoyed getting the place fixed up."

Silently, she scolded herself for letting what he considered an act of thoughtfulness cause her hurt. "I just didn't expect this," she said shakily. "It's very generous."

"I enjoy being generous to you." His voice became coaxing as he trailed a finger along the curve of her earlobe. "Besides, I do have an ulterior motive."

She looked up at him, hoping he would say something about having fallen in love with her and wanting her to have anything her heart desired.

"I thought that if you owned the place you wouldn't be so insistent about being the full-time manager. As owner, you could hire someone for that job and have more time to spend at home," he elaborated.

A sharp jab of disappointment pierced her. It was followed by anger. He was attempting to manipulate her. "I don't take bribes." She shoved the deed at him. "I married you on your terms, but I will not allow you to rule my life."

He cursed himself for having revived her ire. This wasn't going as he'd planned. She was taking everything the wrong way, but then she was a woman and women were never predictable. "It's not a bribe. There are no strings attached. If you want to manage the diner on your own, I'll accept that."

Nina glared at the deed in her hand. Because she'd hoped for more than he was willing to give, she'd overreacted again. For the umpteenth time she reminded herself of the terms she'd agreed to when she accepted his proposal. Taking a calming breath, she said quietly, "In that case, thank you for the gift."

Alex drew a relieved breath. He hadn't wanted to be locked out of their bedroom on their wedding night. "You're welcome." Taking the deed, he laid it on the desk, then captured her hands in his. "I only wanted to please you."

She read the sincerity in his eyes and forced a smile. "I know you did."

He kissed her hands and then her lips. "Pleasing you makes me happy," he said against her skin.

Desire rekindled within her. "And you do please me," she admitted huskily.

Hearing the lust in her voice, he decided it was time to return to the one activity he knew would not make her angry with him. Straightening, he grinned mischievously, then hoisted her over his shoulder. "And now it's time to burn off some of those calories."

Her first husband had married her for love, her second for practical reasons. Both were men of commitment, making either motive as binding as the other. So it should make no difference that Alex would never open his heart to her, she reasoned while he carried her down the hall. Yet even as her body burned for his, she could not entirely rid herself of the nagging worry that she might find her decision too difficult to live with.

Eighteen

"Well, Elizabeth, you are now officially moved in," Nina announced. It was Tuesday, three days since the wedding. Nina had spent the morning in town at the diner. At noon, she'd returned home to have lunch with Alex, Helen and the children, then remained to help Helen and the children complete the unpacking. Rising from her kneeling position, she picked up the empty carton.

Elizabeth whirled around, her arms outstretched. "I love it. There's so much room."

Nina smiled at her daughter's enthusiasm. "We should check on your brothers and your grandmother and see if they need any help."

"Mrs. Bennett."

Nina looked toward the door to see Ann.

"You have a caller," the housekeeper said with polite deference, clearly still trying to make up for her less-than-discreet behavior the evening of the wedding. "A Miss Veronica Charleston."

Veronica Charleston. The name sent a chill through Nina. What was that woman doing here? Had she decided that since Nina and Alex had married, she should make peace? That didn't seem like Veronica's style. Still, Alex was a wealthy man and one that most people did not like to cross. She forced a smile. "You run along and help your grandmother," she directed Elizabeth, then followed Ann down the stairs.

In the hall mirror, she caught a glimpse of herself. Dressed in shorts, a T-shirt and sneakers, with her hair tied back by a bandanna, she looked more like the help than the mistress of this house.

Entering the living room, she found her visitor waiting. And as she'd suspected, Veronica looked as if she'd stepped out of one of the casual fashion pages in *Vogue*. She was dressed elegantly in a designer slacks outfit with Italian sandals that showed off her perfectly pedicured toenails.

"You look…" Veronica paused as if searching for something polite to say. "As if you've been busy," she finished with an exaggerated smile.

"I have." Self-consciously, Nina wiped at a smudge of dirt on the leg of her shorts. "I wasn't expecting company."

"I won't keep you long," Veronica promised. "But I just couldn't let your wedding go by without a gift." She lifted a large square package from the coffee table and extended it toward Nina.

Nina noticed that the woman's smile did not reach her eyes. Instead, they held a cynical glimmer. Her forced smile felt even more plastic. Not knowing what else to do, she accepted the box. "Alex and I thank you."

"Actually, it's for you." Veronica lowered her voice in a conspiratorial whisper. "I have a friend at the hospital. She told me about Alex's interview with a woman who produces babies for those who can't do it on their own. It was easy to conclude that he was getting desperate for an heir but didn't want a wife who would shackle him. The next thing I know, he's marrying you. I had to ask myself why." Malicious amusement spread over the woman's face. "And then the answer came to me. He chose you for his breeder and decided he'd marry you for the duration of the pregnancy so that he wouldn't have to explain a motherless child to his friends and family.''

Nina's stomach knotted. She wished she could deny the woman's words, but there was too much truth in them. ''Get out of my house.'' She shoved the woman's gift back toward her.

Veronica's smile deepened. ''So I am right.'' Her gaze shifted to the gift. ''Keep it. It's a replica of the Breeders' Cup awarded at the Kentucky Derby.''

''Get out and take this with you,'' Nina repeated.

Refusing to take the gift back, Veronica moved gracefully toward the door. Before reaching it, she paused and turned back. ''I hope he's paying you well. Of course, putting up with your three brats should earn him a discount. And he is a hunk. Bedding him shouldn't be such a strain.'' She laughed lightly. ''I'll show myself out.''

Alone in the living room, Nina stood frozen, bile rising in her throat. She knew Veronica would share her theory with anyone who would listen.

''Are you all right, Mrs. Bennett? You look pale.''

Realizing Ann had entered, Nina tried to force a smile. Her muscles refused. A stiff ''Yes, I'm fine'' was all she could manage to say.

''I'm sorry. I thought the woman was a friend coming to wish you well,'' Ann apologized.

Nina looked more closely at the housekeeper. When Ann averted her gaze, she knew the woman had overheard all that Veronica had said and believed it. Embarrassment flowed through her. She realized this was only the beginning, and the threat of nausea increased. Setting the still-wrapped gift on the coffee table, she left the room.

The walls of the house felt as if they were closing in on her. Facing Alex's friends and acquaintances had been difficult before. Now it would be humiliating. She'd made a horrible mistake! Tears trickled down her cheeks. Not wanting anyone to see her crying, she brushed them away as she went out the front door and kept going.

The lumbermen Alex had sold his trees to were harvesting them. Coming to a halt a short distance from where the loggers worked, she stood watching with unseeing eyes, her mind occupied with her misery. They felled a huge tree, and the sound caused her body to flinch, but her mind barely noticed. Her children, Alex, any children she and Alex might have, Helen and Ray would all end up sharing the embarrassment she'd created with this marriage. She should have considered the consequences of someone discovering the truth behind Alex's motives.

An ominous rattling reached her brain. She looked down to see a timber rattler only inches away, coiled, ready to strike. "This seems to be my day for snakes in the grass," she muttered dryly, so absorbed in her misery that she was momentarily oblivious of the danger. Then the snake coiled tighter and the rattling increased. Fear swept through her.

"Don't move," a man's voice cautioned.

She looked up to see a couple of the lumbermen approaching. One was carrying a shovel and the other an ax.

"Mommy," Tommy shouted in a panic.

Out of the corner of her eye she saw him and Pete on the back sundeck of the house. Thank goodness she'd told them that if they wanted to watch the lumbermen, they had to do it from there, she thought. Then she realized that Tommy was moving toward the stairs, clearly intending to come to her aid, and Pete was following. "No. Stay where you are!" she shouted.

Her shout was the signal the snake was waiting for. It struck, biting her in the calf. Before it could strike again, the workmen had killed it, but the damage had been done.

She looked down at the two fang marks in her leg, then up at the men.

"Mommy!" Tommy shouted again in panic.

"Get your stepdad," the bigger of the loggers ordered him.

Immediately both Tommy and Pete headed into the house.

The logger returned his attention to Nina. "Just take a couple of deep breaths and stay calm. The slower your heart rate, the slower the venom moves through your system."

That's easy for him to say, Nina thought, feeling her heart pounding in her chest. But knowing he was right, she tried to obey.

"We'll get you to the hospital in plenty of time," the second man said encouragingly. "That antivenin the docs have works great. Just last year my brother-in-law got bitten. Arm swelled up like a balloon...."

"She doesn't need to hear the details," the bigger man snapped, shutting up his companion.

The smaller man flushed and clamped his mouth shut.

"What's going on!" Alex yelled, coming out of the house on the run with Helen and Ann following close behind.

"Rattler got her," the bigger logger said.

Seeing the children following the adults, Nina called out to Helen. "Make the children stay on the porch."

Immediately, Helen stopped and turned back to take charge of her grandchildren.

Reaching Nina, Alex knelt beside her leg. "We have to get the poison out."

"No. The docs say not to waste time trying that if you're this close to help," the smaller logger said. "Just get her to the hospital as soon as possible."

"She needs to stay calm and keep the leg lower than her

heart," the bigger logger instructed as Alex scooped Nina up in his arms and headed to his car.

"Call the hospital and tell them I'm on my way!" Alex ordered Ann. "Then call Dr. Noah Howell and tell him what's happened and ask him to meet me in the emergency room."

"Mommy?" Tommy called out from the porch.

Alex glanced toward him to see all three children watching with stricken looks on their faces. "She's going to be just fine," he called back to them.

Nina saw trust replace her children's fear. Looking up at the hard set of Alex's jaw, the thought that if anyone could defy death it was Alex Bennett played through her mind.

"Tell the hospital it was a timber rattler," the bigger logger yelled both to Ann and Alex. "You want to make sure she gets the right stuff."

"It hurts," Nina said as Alex buckled her in her seat and then positioned the back as upright as possible. "I thought it was supposed to go numb."

He looked down at where the snake had bitten her. The area around the fang marks was already swelling. Fear, more intense than any he'd ever felt, raced through him. Determination etched itself into his features. "I'll get you to help."

Behind his resolve, she heard an edge in his voice she'd never heard before. He was afraid. "I know you will," she said, more to calm him than herself, then realized that the words she'd spoken were the truth. She had complete faith in him.

Alex stepped on the gas and took off down the drive. Fighting the panic building within, he concentrated on the road. It was hard to keep himself from accelerating to top speed, but there were too many dangerous curves to allow that. Still, he drove down the mountain at a record pace.

Using the sight of him to help quell her fear, Nina kept her gaze locked on him as they rounded bends at breakneck speed.

She was concentrating so hard on thinking only of Alex, the ringing of the car phone startled her.

Not wanting his concentration to be broken, she grabbed the receiver.

"Nina, this is Noah Howell." The man on the other end identified himself. "How are you feeling?"

"Like I'm in a rocket ship," she replied.

"Tell Alex to take it easy. I'm in an ambulance heading your way." He told her the route they were taking, then hung up.

She relayed the message.

Alex nodded but did not slow down.

As they reached the bottom of the mountain, she heard a siren ahead of them, then saw the ambulance. It pulled off onto the shoulder. Alex did a U-turn and pulled up behind it.

The back door of the ambulance opened and Noah Howell alighted. As he strode to the car, she saw the attendants behind him getting the stretcher out.

Alex was at her door, opening it. She eased herself out and he lifted her into his arms. Noah frowned at her leg, then nodded with confidence. "We'll have you as good as new in no time."

"I'm counting on that," Alex growled, carrying her to the stretcher and placing her on it.

In the next instant she was being lifted into the ambulance. While one attendant secured the stretcher, the other raised the headrest.

"I'm coming along," Alex said, his voice holding no compromise.

Noah ignored him, concentrating on Nina. "I'm going

to put in an IV and then give you some antivenin. It's great stuff for what ails you.''

She forced a smile. ''Thanks.'' Trying not to think about the needle, she looked out the still-open back door at Alex. He was pale. She'd never seen him pale.

''Is she going to be all right, Noah?'' he demanded when the IV was in.

''She's going to be just fine,'' Noah assured him, filling a needle with antivenin.

''I can't lose her,'' Alex said.

The intensity of the emotion in his voice shook Nina.

''Sounds like a man in love,'' Noah commented.

Nina smiled, the needles and the snake bite forgotten for the moment. ''Yes, he does.''

Alex said nothing, grimly continuing to watch Noah work.

Once he finished administering the antivenin, Noah turned to the attendant waiting outside the ambulance. ''Time for transport.''

Alex climbed inside. ''You can drive my car,'' he ordered the attendant who was inside with Noah. ''I'm riding with my wife.''

The man looked to the doctor.

Noah met Alex's gaze levelly. ''You'll have to follow us. There's a slim chance she might have an allergic reaction to the antivenin. If she does, I need an experienced set of hands nearby.''

Alex's jaw tensed until it was painful as he attempted to control a fresh rush of fear. ''I'm counting on you, Noah,'' he said.

Noah nodded, then returned his attention to Nina.

Watching the ambulance doors being closed, Alex experienced a frustration more intense than any he'd ever experienced before. He wanted to be by Nina's side. If she did have a reaction, he wanted to be able to will his strength into her.

Climbing into his car, he pulled out behind the ambulance. Until this moment, he'd refused to admit how much she meant to him. Now he confessed that the thought of life without her was too painful to consider.

Nina lay in the ambulance. The IV, the concern on the doctor's face, the pain in her leg...none of these things bothered her. All she could think about was Alex. He hadn't actually admitted it, but she knew he loved her. Veronica and her gossip-mongering no longer mattered. As long as Alex loved her, Nina knew she could face anything.

In the early morning hours of the day after she arrived home following the snake bite, Nina woke from a restless sleep. At the hospital, Alex had been insistent about her getting the best care. Since she'd returned home, he'd been overly attentive. But there was a stiffness in his manner toward her that made her uneasy. And when they'd retired for the night, he'd barely touched her.

She turned to discover his side of the bed was empty. He was standing at the window looking out at the night, his posture rigid. She could feel the tension in the air like static electricity. Swallowing back the fear that had been tormenting her, she said, "We need to talk. Something is obviously wrong."

He turned to her. "Nothing is wrong. But I have been doing some serious thinking. I've decided there's really no reason for you to have to go through another pregnancy. You've already got three kids and I'm satisfied to have your children as my heirs."

She felt as if she'd been punched in the stomach. The suspicion she hadn't wanted to face was a reality. Frustration bubbled to the surface. "I was right. You're so afraid of loving me, you're trying to shut me out of your life. I suppose you'll be suggesting separate bedrooms next.''

He scowled. ''No, I won't. And, I'm not trying to shut you out of my life. I'm trying to keep you in it.''

She frowned in confusion. ''You're not making any sense.''

Returning to the bed, he sat down beside her and cupped her face in his hands. ''That snake bite made me realize how much you mean to me. I *have* fallen in love with you…madly, passionately in love with you. And I will not put your life in danger again.''

The gruff tenderness in his voice, brought joy. ''I had wonderful pregnancies,'' she assured him. ''I'll admit the labor part was a bit rough but having your baby will not put me in danger.''

''No one can be certain of that.'' He kissed her tenderly. ''I don't want to take the risk.''

''But I want to have your child…to feel *your* baby growing inside me and know that it was conceived in love.''

For a long moment he studied her determined features, then breathed a resigned sigh. ''I'm going to lose this battle too, aren't I?''

''I hope so.'' Reaching up, she circled her arms around his neck. ''Now, stop worrying and kiss me.''

''I hope we aren't going to stop there,'' he said huskily.

''No,'' she assured him. ''We won't stop there.''

Chalk another correct prediction up to Jessica Hanson, Nina thought, as Alex joined her in the bed.

* * * * *

continues with

FATHER AND CHILD REUNION

by Christine Flynn
available in December

Here's an exciting preview...+

Father and Child Reunion

June 6

It was an awful, impossible dream. Any minute, Eve Stuart was sure she would wake up in her own bed and the horror would be over. She leaned her forehead against the window, too numb to notice the sunlight dancing off the puddles left by yesterday's storm. She'd come to attend her brother's wedding and to spend the weekend with her mom. Instead, the wedding had been called off, massive mud slides had thrown the town into utter chaos, and she had just spent the morning on a park bench across from Vanderbilt Memorial.

Her mother had collapsed on Friday night. A heart attack, Dr. Jennings had told her. But that was impossible. Her mother had never had anything more serious than a cold. Now she was dead.

"Are you sad, Mommy?"

Eve wiped her cheek with the back of her hand, sank into the maple rocking chair behind her and opened her arms. Leave it to a child to reduce a myriad of emotions to their simplest term. "Yes, I am," she whispered when Molly climbed into her lap. "I need to tell you something, honey. About Grandma Olivia. Do you remember yesterday when I told you they had taken Grandma to the hospital in the ambulance because she was very sick?"

Molly gave a sober nod.

"Well, the doctors did everything they could to make

her better...but they couldn't." Eve swallowed past the knot in her throat. "She died."

A frown swept Molly's delicate features. "Angela Abramson had a fish that died." Innocent blue eyes turned troubled. "Did they flush Grandma down the toilet?"

"Oh, no, honey," Eve assured her, hugging her close. "It's different with people than it is with fish. The part of her that we can see is still at the hospital. But the part of her that made her the person we knew...her spirit...is in heaven. Heaven is where the angels are, Molly. You remember me reading to you about angels, don't you?"

Eve felt Molly nod and curl closer. "Mommy?"

"What honey?"

"Is your daddy an angel, too?"

Eve's father had died so long ago that she had no mental image of him at all. "I suppose he is."

"So Grandma won't be lonesome up there?"

"No, honey. She won't be lonesome."

"Mommy? How come I don't have a daddy?"

"You do have a daddy," Eve replied, numbness buffering the jolt she might have otherwise felt at the question. "Everyone does. Some of us just don't live with them."

"Oh." Molly wriggled in tighter. "We live with just us, huh?"

"Just us," she repeated, and was grateful that Molly didn't press further. Rio Redtree was the last person on earth Eve wanted to think about. It had been six years since Eve had seen him. Six years that seemed like a lifetime. Only her mother had known that he was the father of her child.

And Rio didn't even know Molly existed.

July 15

Eve stopped in the doorway of her mom's bedroom, packing boxes in hand. She wouldn't think about what she had to do. She'd just do it. The resolution made, she dropped the boxes and opened the doors of a tall cherry armoire. She didn't want to be here. She wanted to be home in Santa Barbara. Back in her sunny apartment with the tulips she and Molly had planted. Back at work, arguing about whether or not she could handle major accounts on her own. Back in the familiar world of shuttling Molly to day care and tumbling class on Saturday.

What did she know about filing for probate and liquidating assets and whatever else the attorney had said she needed to do? She knew how to design interiors that were functional and appealing. She knew "Barney" and how to make cupcakes with smiley faces. What she didn't know was what she was supposed to do with all the things her mother had loved. But taking care of her mother's belongings was part of the reason she'd come back.

Shortly after the funeral, Eve had returned to Santa Barbara to finish what design projects she could, then begged for a leave of absence from her job. Though she'd been gone from Grand Springs for more than a month, she still couldn't believe what the police had told her. Her mother hadn't just had a heart attack. She'd been murdered.

"A lethal injection of potassium" was how the detective had so calmly described it.

The refined, two-tone chime of the doorbell cut off any consideration she might have given that disturbing development. As shaky as she was feeling, she could only handle one problem at a time, anyway. The doorbell sounded again, and for one totally indulgent moment, Eve considered not answering. Only the thought that Molly might be returning early from St. Veronica's summer day camp had her shoving her fingers through her hair and heading for the stairs.

It wasn't Molly. By the time Eve reached the bottom step of the wide, carved oak staircase, she could see a shape visible through the beveled glass on the front door. It was definitely adult. Big adult.

As she headed across the wide foyer, her caller could see her approaching through the door's window. And she could see him.

Tall, broad-shouldered, dark. The impressions registered a millisecond before her heart bumped her ribs and her steps faltered to a stop.

Rio.

Her heart jerked again, her thoughts scrambling. She'd known she'd have to see him. She knew, too, that she had to tell him about Molly before he found out about her on his own. But Eve had no idea how to do that. Or what he would say when she did.

A thread of panic tangled with the other emotions knotting her stomach. She might have known she'd see him. But she'd never thought he'd come here....

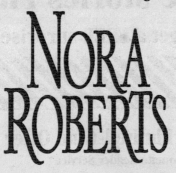

Take 4 bestselling love stories FREE

Plus get a FREE surprise gift!

Special Limited-time Offer

Mail to Silhouette Reader Service™

3010 Walden Avenue
P.O. Box 1867
Buffalo, N.Y. 14240-1867

YES! Please send me 4 free Silhouette Special Edition® novels and my free surprise gift. Then send me 6 brand-new novels every month, which I will receive months before they appear in bookstores. Bill me at the low price of $3.34 each plus 25¢ delivery and applicable sales tax, if any.* That's the complete price and a savings of over 10% off the cover prices—quite a bargain! I understand that accepting the books and gift places me under no obligation ever to buy any books. I can always return a shipment and cancel at any time. Even if I never buy another book from Silhouette, the 4 free books and the surprise gift are mine to keep forever.

235 BPA A3UV

Name	(PLEASE PRINT)	
Address	Apt. No.	
City	State	Zip

This offer is limited to one order per household and not valid to present Silhouette Special Edition® subscribers. *Terms and prices are subject to change without notice. Sales tax applicable in N.Y.

USPED-696   ©1990 Harlequin Enterprises Limited

Return to the Towers!

In March
New York Times bestselling author

NORA ROBERTS

brings us to the Calhouns' fabulous
Maine coast mansion and reveals the
tragic secrets hidden there for generations.

For all his degrees, Professor Max Quartermain has a
lot to learn about love—and luscious Lilah Calhoun is
just the woman to teach him. Ex-cop Holt Bradford is
as prickly as a thornbush—until Suzanna Calhoun's
special touch makes love blossom in his heart.
And all of them are caught in the race to solve
the generations-old mystery of a priceless
lost necklace…and a timeless love.

Lilah and Suzanna
THE
Calhoun Women

A special 2-in-1 edition containing
FOR THE LOVE OF LILAH and
SUZANNA'S SURRENDER

Available at your favorite retail outlet.

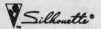

**When tomorrow is uncertain,
the only sure thing is love...**

36 HOURS

If you missed any 36 Hours titles, then order now and
discover how, for the residents of Grand Springs, Colorado,
the storm-induced blackout was just the *beginning!*

WELCOME TO *Love Inspired* ™

A brand-new series of contemporary inspirational love stories.

Join men and women as they learn valuable lessons about facing the challenges of today's world and about life, love and faith.

Look for:

Promises
by Roger Elwood

A Will and a Wedding
by Lois Richer

An Old-Fashioned Love
by Arlene James

Available in retail outlets
in October 1997.

LIFT YOUR SPIRITS AND GLADDEN YOUR HEART with *Love Inspired* ™!

Steeple
Hill™

LI1197

Share in the joy of yuletide romance with brand-new
stories by two of the genre's most beloved writers

DIANA PALMER

and

JOAN JOHNSTON

in

LONE STAR
CHRISTMAS

Diana Palmer and Joan Johnston share their favorite
Christmas anecdotes and personal stories in this
special hardbound edition.

Diana Palmer delivers an irresistible spin-off of her
LONG, TALL TEXANS series and Joan Johnston crafts an
unforgettable new chapter to **HAWK'S WAY** in this wonderful
keepsake edition celebrating the holiday season. So
perfect for gift giving, you'll want one for yourself...and
one to give to a special friend!

Available in November at your favorite retail outlet!

Only from

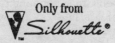

Silhouette®